T0129414

1 DOWN: DEATH BY HOMICIDE

Quinn Carr wishes her life could be more like a crossword puzzle: neat, orderly, and perfectly arranged. At least her passion for puzzles, flair for words—and mild case of OCD—have landed her a gig creating crosswords for the local paper. But if she ever hopes to move out of her parents' house, she can't give up her day job as a waitress. She needs the tips. But when a customer ends up dead at her table—face down in biscuits and gravy— Quinn needs to get a clue to find whodunit . . .

6 LETTERS, STARTS WITH "M"

It turns out that solving a murder is a lot harder than a creating a crossword. Quinn has plenty of suspects—up, down, and across. One of them is her boss, the owner of the diner who shares a culinary past with the victim. Two of them are ex-wives, her boss's and the victim's. A third complication is the Chief of Police who refuses to allow much investigation, preferring the pretense that their town has no crime. To solve this mystery, Quinn has to think outside the boxes—before the killer gets the last word . . .

Visit us at www.kensingtonbooks.com

Books by Becky Clark

Puzzling Ink

Published by Kensington Publishing Corporation

Puzzling Ink

Becky Clark

LYRICAL UNDERGROUND
Kensington Publishing Corp.
www.kensingtonbooks.com

LYRICAL UNDERGROUND BOOKS are published by
Kensington Publishing Corp.
119 West 40th Street
New York, NY 10018

All Kensington titles, imprints, and distributed lines are available at special quantity discounts for bulk purchases for sales promotion, premiums, fund-raising, educational, or institutional use.

Special book excerpts or customized printings can also be created to fit specific needs. For details, write or phone the office of the Kensington Sales Manager: Kensington Publishing Corp., 119 West 40th Street, New York, NY 10018. Attn. Sales Department. Phone: 1-800-221-2647.

Lyrical Underground and Lyrical Underground logo Reg. US Pat. & TM Off.

First Electronic Edition: November 2020
ISBN-13: 978-1-5161-1063-6 (ebook)
ISBN-10: 1-5161-1063-3 (ebook)

First Print Edition: November 2020
ISBN-13: 978-1-5161-1066-7
ISBN-10: 1-5161-1066-8

Printed in the United States of America

Hey, Dad ... this one's for you.
I did it in ink.

Chapter 1

The perfection of a pristine crossword puzzle grid always made Quinn Carr's pleasure center buzz. Like being touched by the hands of a lover, but better. Not that she'd felt that in a while, but she had a vague memory. The puzzle was orderly. Symmetrical. No chaos. No mess. No negotiation. Only one correct answer.

A puzzle grid never looked at you funny when you agonized over some marketing sociopath who couldn't understand that "pepper, black" was worlds apart from "black pepper."

Crossword puzzles never judged you. Unlike the people who thought they knew all about you simply because you were in your thirties, had to move home with your parents, and needed—*needed*—to alphabetize their spices before you could continue creating the crossword puzzle for the local *Chestnut Station Chronicle*.

Quinn placed the turmeric next to the sesame seeds, not at all happy with the varying sizes of containers. Christmas was six months away. Maybe a new spice rack with matching jars would be a good present for her mom. *But would that make her worry I was slipping? I could say it wasn't about me at all. Just trying to bring out her inner Julia Child.*

Georgeanne, Quinn's mom, definitely needed to get in touch with her inner Julia Child. Or Betty Crocker. Or even that Gorton's fisherman. Anyone who could help with her culinary endeavors.

As if on cue, Georgeanne shoved a cupcake with white frosting toward Quinn's face.

"Taste this. I'm experimenting with cumin."

"Gross." Quinn twisted away from the distinctively intense chili flavoring, returning to her laptop at the kitchen table.

Georgeanne glanced at her phone and laughed, clearly in the middle of a text conversation with someone, maybe one of her piano students.

Georgeanne's dimples deepened as they did whenever she smiled, which was pretty much constantly. Quinn loved those dimples despite the fact they were not symmetrical. It was quite obvious that her mother's cheeks didn't match. When Quinn was young, she'd gently tilt Georgeanne's head so the dimples would cross the same imaginary line bisecting her face. As she got older she learned she could simply tilt her own head if she wanted symmetry in her mother. Quinn had read once that the attractiveness of a face was in direct proportion to how symmetrical it was, but she had scoffed. Everything about her mother was appealing. Except maybe when she shoved a cumin cupcake in your face.

Quinn's dad, Dan, intercepted the cupcake intended for Quinn and took a big bite. He accepted the culinary abomination with the good cheer of someone who hadn't been subjected to it for thirty-some years. Quinn admired her dad's skill at diplomacy. Was it possible he actually liked his wife's cooking? The world would never know.

"Hm." He chewed thoughtfully, frowning slightly. "The cumin is interesting, but what kind of frosting is that?"

Georgeanne beamed. "That white frosting is miso"—she pointed to the others— "the red is smoked paprika, and the blue is just food coloring I added to a can of cream of mushroom soup."

"You've done it again, Georgie." Dan polished off the cupcake, then gave Quinn a kiss on the top of her head. "Solving a crossword or making one?"

"Making one."

"What's the theme?"

"Over. Like overshadow, overactive, overcharge, overexpose."

Georgeanne cocked her head. "Not Fourth of July?"

"That ran in the last edition. You overlooked it."

"Don't overreact. Aren't you going to be late for work?"

"Overexcited to get me out of here?"

"Trying to overcome my separation anxiety from my favorite child."

"Only child, but point well-taken. Jake's not opening the diner until after the parade. Nobody will be in before that." Quinn gestured toward the cupcakes. "I can help carry those to your booth if you want."

"I'm overwhelmed with joy for the offer." Georgeanne dipped a rubber scraper into the bowl of red frosting. "I need to finish these first, though."

Quinn marveled at her mother's ability to do so many things at once: Mix, taste, and adjust the flavors of three different kinds of frosting and create a huge pot of Dan's oatmeal, all while texting someone.

Same with Dan. Running his own independent insurance agency meant he had to understand and keep up-to-date on multiple companies' policies and all the different lines of insurance, like homeowners, auto, health, and liability, and even obscure ones like bed bug and kidnapping coverage. He also had to juggle, and often soothe, the varied personalities of his employees, clients, attorneys, and insurance company contacts.

It was a superpower lost on Quinn, who maintained the right way to do anything was from beginning to end. Dan often came home from the office talking about all the fires he'd had to put out over the course of the day. If Quinn was in charge, the agency would have burned down—hopefully only metaphorically—many times over.

If she were in Georgeanne's shoes, she would have made the cupcakes yesterday so they'd be cool enough to frost today. Then she would have made the white frosting and frosted one-third of the cupcakes. Then made the red and frosted the second third. Then the blue. Of course, she'd also have used only food coloring and not miso, paprika, and mushroom soup, but that was an entirely different can of worms.

It was beyond Quinn how her parents could shift activities and trains of thought in such a nimble manner. She watched with increasing alarm one day while Georgeanne parked the vacuum in the center of the living room—with less than half of it cleaned—to go take a load of laundry from the dryer. But did she then fold it? No. She left it on the couch while she washed the pots that had been soaking in the sink. And she didn't even dry them before returning to fold the laundry. Quinn had needed to leave the house in case Georgeanne decided to weave cloth for new drapes, or draft a screenplay, or climb Machu Picchu before finishing with the vacuuming.

She realized later that a good daughter would have vacuumed the rest of the room, but that's not what she had been focused on.

"Eat some breakfast, Dan," Georgeanne said. "I already made your oatmeal."

Dan and Quinn exchanged a smile behind Georgeanne's back. For the 8,000 years they'd been married, Georgeanne had been making Dan oatmeal for breakfast. In the beginning it was normal oatmeal, like most people ate. But over the years, Georgeanne increasingly expressed her creativity through her cooking. These days, Dan's oatmeal was virtually unrecognizable, buried under layers of dried and fresh fruit, nuts, seeds, roasted chickpeas, basil, and tarragon. The pièce de résistance, however, was the artfully arranged spoonful of dill pickle relish on top. This flourish was added after Georgeanne heard a Japanese chef extol the virtues of "eating with your eyes," something Quinn desperately wanted to learn, if it meant she needn't use her mouth.

Quinn had never once seen her father refuse to eat something Georgeanne prepared, or even grimace in the slightest. Quinn tried to emulate him as much as possible because Georgeanne was the sweetest, kindest, best mother on the planet, but more often than she wanted, a wrinkled nose and a "gross" escaped her lips. Luckily, Georgeanne was the sweetest, kindest, best mother on the planet, and such comments slid right off her like she was coated in Teflon.

Dan scooped a spoon into his hearty bowl of oatmeal and offered it to Quinn.

"No thanks, Dad. I already ate." Since Quinn had boomeranged back home a few weeks back, she'd learned to set an early alarm, drag herself out of bed, and force herself to eat a few bites of cereal before Georgeanne padded into the kitchen to begin her culinary calamities. Now that she had to be at the diner before seven, she had an excuse and it wasn't even awkward anymore. It also served to hide from her mother how little appetite she had these days. No need to encourage that kind of scrutiny.

Dan finished his oatmeal just as Quinn put the finishing touches on the remaining clues for the puzzle.

"Knock, knock." Rico Lopez stuck his head in the back door.

"Rico, you're just in time for oatmeal." Georgeanne opened the cupboard for another bowl.

"Sorry, Mrs. Carr. I can't. I'm on duty."

"Hence the uniform." Quinn smiled. Rico dodged that bullet.

Georgeanne detached the top from a blue frosted cupcake. "Well, just a taste of this, then. I'd like your opinion."

Everyone knew Rico couldn't tell a lie. It was his albatross. When Quinn and Rico were kids, if Georgeanne suspected that Quinn was fudging the truth, all she had to do was ask Rico. If he attempted even the tiniest of fibs, he'd wrinkle and twitch his nose like a bunny sniffing ammonia. "Has Quinn been smoking? Did she ditch chemistry on Thursday? When are report cards coming out?"

Being best friends with Rico was like being perpetually hooked up to a lie detector. She learned early on to keep Rico out of the really important loops, especially ones where direct questions might be asked of him.

Rico broke off a small bit of the cupcake. He swallowed fast, a trick he'd learned from Quinn. Fewer taste buds got assaulted. "It's...something I've never had before."

Truth won again.

Dan held out his hand for the rest of Rico's cupcake. "Why do you have a fish in a bag, Officer?" Quinn asked. "Is this some sort of fishy perp walk?"

"Oh." Rico held the clear plastic bag aloft and peered in. "I helped Abe set up his booth at the festival and he paid me in goldfish. It's a gift for you to say thank you for helping me with that bicycle theft case. Who knew crossword puzzles were a crime-fighting tool?"

"Oh, please. It was kismet. The clue *transportation with a kickstand* was BICYCLE, *waiter outside a seafood restaurant* was ALLEYCAT, and *class with a flexible schedule* was YOGA. So, when I was doing the crossword waiting for yoga to start and saw that kid getting sushi when he should have been in school, well, all the puzzle pieces dropped into place and it just made sense that he was the bike thief. Just a matter of doing the *New York Times* crossword at the right time in the right place."

Bemused, Rico handed the bag to Quinn. "Regardless, your skill at working crossword puzzles saved my butt. I never would have figured it out if you hadn't pointed everything out to me."

Quinn had been doing crosswords for as long as she could remember, but had kept from Rico that she created them as well. She was nerdy enough in high school; she didn't need him broadcasting things she wanted to keep secret. It was one secret she'd continued to keep from him. She closed her laptop so he wouldn't see her crossword-creating software. Quinn accepted the goldfish from him.

"Thanks. I'll name it"—she held the bag up and studied it from all angles—"him...Fang."

"You can tell the sex of a goldfish?"

"Of course. Can't everyone?" Dan caught Quinn's eye and winked at her.

"Remember not to overfeed it...him. The directions are very clear." Rico pulled a small jar of fish food from his pants pocket, handing it to Quinn.

"Remember who you're talking to, dude. Clear, explicit instructions are my nirvana." Quinn unscrewed the lid and took a whiff of the briny flakes, immediately wishing she hadn't.

"Don't joke about that, Quinn," Georgeanne said. "It's not funny."

"Yes it is, Mom, but it's fine."

Quinn knew her parents were worried about her, so she tried to change the subject. "I'm fine. You're fine. Dad's fine. Fang is obviously fine. And Rico would be fine too, if you'd quit feeding him cumin cakes with miso frosting."

"Ignoring problems doesn't make them go away, Quinn. You've got to move on. I wish you'd call that therapist." Georgeanne turned back to the stove. Quinn assumed it was to hide the sadness in her eyes. As fantastic as Quinn was at hiding her emotions, Georgeanne was hopeless.

"Rico, can't you get her to call?"

"I don't think so, Mrs. Carr, but—"

Quinn interrupted Rico. "I am moving on, Mom. In fact, I'm going to move on and get ready to go to the festival with you." Quinn collected up her computer and returned it to her bedroom, making a point of not glancing at the therapist's business card tacked to the kitchen corkboard.

Wasn't it enough she was taking her meds like a good little girl? *I'm not ashamed of being who I am and neither should anyone else. Despite everything that happened, I don't need therapy. I just need a fresh start with this new job at the diner so I can save some money, move out, and be normal.*

She sat at the end of her twin bed, pulled on some socks, and laced up her waitressing shoes, a pair of well-loved sneakers. She sighed at her reflection in the mirror before gathering up her shoulder-length hair, giving it a twist, and clamping it into a messy bun. It was all she could accomplish in the grooming department most days. At least she was washing it again. Progress, eh?

She grabbed her purse and returned to the kitchen in time to see her dad and Rico carefully coaxing Fang into a large Pyrex mixing bowl. They watched him explore his new home.

Quinn read the instructions on the fish food, keeping it a good distance from her nose, and tapped a few flakes into the bowl. Fang inhaled a few, letting the rest drift to the bottom of the bowl. Quinn prepared to shake more flakes to replace the fallen ones, but Dan held out his hand for the jar.

Rico tapped the glass to get Fang's attention. Fang did not give in to his demands.

After Dan put away the jar, he nudged Quinn, dropping two pills into her hand.

"Thanks, Dad," she said quietly. She tossed the capsule toward the back of her throat, then swallowed it down with a gulp of water. The pill she placed on her tongue, the acrid taste intense and bitter.

"You guys going to the festival? It's going to be a scorcher today." Rico picked up his duty cap, organizing it over his tight curls, the bane of his existence. In middle school Quinn had to squelch rumors that he got regular perms at the beauty salon. It only took one whispered threat to expose perpetrator Molly Campbell's secret shame, a padded bra. The rumors stopped immediately.

They organized themselves to walk the few blocks to the festival while Georgeanne put the finishing touches on the boxes of bake sale items, which consisted of toothpick tent poles in each cupcake to support a canopy of protective plastic wrap.

Every so often they passed a statue of a chestnut, even though Chestnut Station, Colorado—out on the plains—was named after a person from Merry Olde England and not the tree. In fact, there was not a chestnut tree to be found in Chestnut Station, but long ago, some artsy type began sculpting chestnuts, large and small, and planting them around town, often in the dead of night. One particularly productive summer saw more than thirty chestnut statues installed at intersections throughout town; quite remarkable, since there were only about twice that many streets. In the years since, many more had materialized depicting raw chestnuts, shelled chestnuts, chestnuts fuzzy from the tree, and, of course, roasting on an open fire. Made of wood, metal, clay. Large, medium, and small. Loud and proud, hidden and demure. Earth tones and neon. You name it, there was one like it somewhere in town.

Quinn and Rico passed several of these chestnut statues decorated for Independence Day, one sporting a Lady Liberty crown, one with an American flag print bikini top tied around it at a jaunty angle, and Quinn's favorite, one wearing sunglasses and a beer hat. She stopped to adjust the glasses.

As they strolled through the residential area of Chestnut Station, they collected neighbors heading to Square Park. Georgeanne and Dan fell in step with friends and dropped behind Quinn and Rico. It wasn't technically the festival parade, but it might as well have been. Problem was, with a town so small, there's no one to watch the parade since practically everyone was in it.

Quinn and Rico crossed Parliament Avenue into the park.

"As a kid, it used to bug me so much that this was called Square Park," Quinn said. "It's not anywhere near square. In fact, if one of those enormous chestnuts was planted at the corner by the fountain, you'd have a fairly anatomical depiction of the side view of a brown bear."

"Not Kodiak or grizzly?"

"Nope. Definitely brown. And if you turn the map forty-five degrees, it looks suspiciously like the Facebook logo."

"Why suspicious?" Rico asked.

"Because what would Facebook gain by branding Chestnut Station? It's like crop circles. Completely baffling."

"You know it's actually called Town Square Park," Rico said.

"Well, I know that now."

"Hey, Quinn, hey, Rico. Like our booth?" The publisher/editor/typesetter/ sometime reporter of the *Chestnut Station Chronicle*, Vera Greenberg, gave a Vanna White sweep of her arm.

Rico wrinkled his nose. "Can't say I'm wild about it. Think you missed your mark this year."

Vera rolled her eyes at Quinn. "When will I learn?"

Quinn jabbed Rico in the ribs while pulling him away. "What is wrong with you?"

"What? She asked!"

Quinn sighed. "Rico, we talked about this. She wanted you to say something nice. Not truthful."

"Then she should've—"

"Have you been practicing like I told you?"

"I'm not going to practice fibbing, Quinn."

"There's no hope for you. You need to learn how to fib. You can hurt people's feelings that way. Like yesterday when you said I was too skinny."

"That hurt your feelings? But it's true!"

"Be that as it may. If you really felt it necessary to comment on my weight, why couldn't you just have said, *It seems like your jeans are fitting better?*"

"I don't know." And he didn't.

They found the Music Teachers Association booth and set down their boxes of cupcakes. Georgeanne and Dan followed soon after.

Dan saw Abe the handyman two booths over. "You have everything under control, Georgie? I want to go talk to Abe."

"Off you go!" Georgeanne shooed him away. She motioned to Quinn and Rico to pick up the boxes while she fluffed and smoothed a musical motif tablecloth. Georgeanne began placing her cupcakes randomly on the table.

As soon as Georgeanne turned away to chat with the orchestra director at the school, Quinn carefully chose a red frosted one, then a white, then a blue, repeating the pattern after offsetting the first cupcake in the row, creating a multicolored parallelogram centered on the table. The cupcakes marched like little soldiers along a line of the treble clef staff.

Rico thought he'd figured out the pattern and tried to help. Quinn simply held out her hand until he returned the cupcake to it.

"I guess I better get to the station," he said.

"Anything interesting going on at the police department these days?" Quinn asked. "Murder? Human trafficking? Secret drug cartel working out of Mrs. Olansky's nail salon?"

"Nope. Not even another bike theft. How 'bout you?"

"Well, it's a hotbed of infamy at the Chestnut Diner. Yesterday I told someone we had lemon pie, but we didn't. Got me an old-fashioned tongue-lashing."

"Wow. Scary."

"Plus, there was a kerfuffle when Jake forgot to put a fresh pot of coffee on before the Retireds got there."

"You be careful over there," Rico said with mock horror. "Keep your eye on those notorious Retireds."

Rico said his goodbyes. Quinn leaned her backside against the table and counted the men in her vicinity wearing socks with their sandals. When she ran out of those, she counted all the sun hats she saw, grouping them into large-brimmed, visor, and baseball cap categories. Then she saw one of those canvas Australian ones and had to start over.

"Quinn? You in there?" Wilbur said in his gruff, gravelly voice.

Herman and Wilbur, two of the Retireds she waited on regularly at the diner, stood in front of her.

"Gathering wool, my granny used to say." Wilbur's voice was three notches too loud.

Herman's face was arranged in its normal quizzical manner. He was a true literalist, analyzing and parsing every word and deed so he always looked puzzled, no matter what was happening, for at least ten seconds longer than was reasonable.

"When's the diner opening today?" Wilbur asked.

Quinn took in Wilbur's socks-and-sandals combo. "After the parade."

Right on cue, the wobbly strains of the high school fight song wafted over the park.

Wilbur handed Georgeanne a dollar and picked a cupcake with red frosting from the center of the display, making Quinn wince. As he passed her, he gave her a head-to-toe glance. "You should be the one eating this. You're scrawnier that the puniest side of nothing...and then whittled to a point."

Herman stopped mid-stride and frowned, trying to unpack Wilbur's folksy aphorism.

"I'll have you know," she said, "that I maintain this exquisite figure by adhering to a strict diet comprised solely of the wistful dreams of orphans and the obnoxious words of old men. So thanks for feeding me."

Wilbur cackled and led a short-circuiting Herman away. Quinn did her best not to smile until they turned and walked away. The Retireds might be obnoxious old men, but they were *her* obnoxious old men.

Everyone headed for the nearest street to watch the parade, led by the school band. The older kids played brass and woodwinds, while the younger kids banged wildly on drums, tambourines, and triangles. Behind them came the animals from surrounding ranches: Shetland ponies, goats, and alpacas, followed by two enormous yoked oxen pulling the mayor and town council in a buckboard wagon.

The pooper-scooper team—Duke McCaffrey from Public Works and the Grand Scooper who drew the lucky straw at the June town meeting—followed with shovels and a large plastic bin on wheels. Over the years, the Grand Scooper had turned into the most coveted position in the parade. Each year the honoree tried to outdo Grand Scoopers past. Last year, newly retired Silas Simmons, another of the Retireds, raised the bar exponentially by wearing his powder blue tuxedo, pink feather boa, and pointy magician's hat. This year it was someone Quinn didn't know. Whoever it was couldn't hold a candle to Silas.

Next came the town volunteers, practically the entire population of Chestnut Station. Scout leaders. Church organists and choir directors. The team who delivered meals to shut-ins and new parents, overwhelmed by the ordeal of feeding themselves. Larry the cabdriver, who never charged. Youth sport coaches. A small town like Chestnut Station couldn't survive without neighbors helping neighbors.

By the time the pooper-scooper team traveled three-quarters of the way around the quarter-mile route—south on Gordon's Gin Flat, west on Buckingham Palace Way, north on House of Parliament Avenue—the marching band kids had time to get back to the school and hop on their bikes, decorated so heavily with red, white, and blue streamers, it was somewhat of a miracle their wheels could turn.

In twelve minutes the whole thing was over and everyone was free to wander the fundraising booths and games of the festival.

As soon as the cheering died down, Quinn said, "Mom, I'm going to head to work now."

Quinn waved at her dad and Abe as she passed them.

The town of Chestnut Station was spread thick with creamy sunshine, fragments of music from the marching band settling over the festivalgoers while Quinn walked the few blocks to the diner. She had to detour around a couple of town dogs sprawled across sidewalks, including bloodhound Jethro, the unofficial mascot of the Chestnut Diner. He made it his job most mornings to trot through the diner when Jake unlocked the door, checking out all corners. For what, nobody knew, but when he finished, he'd always wait patiently for his paycheck, a strip of bacon. Then it was back to lolling on the sidewalk.

After Quinn greeted Jethro, then wiped drool from her hand, a man wearing a knit cap and sunglasses turned abruptly and ran into her, knocking her off-balance. "Sorry," he mumbled. Quinn saw a large mole on his right cheek she had at first mistaken for a dimple. He pointed at the handwritten sign hanging on the door. "No website. These the real hours?"

"As opposed to the fake hours?" When he didn't laugh, she said, "Yep, seven to seven every day."

He pushed past her and hurried down the sidewalk. Probably already drunk on festival libations and trying to figure out how to use Jake's restroom without buying anything, Quinn thought. Must not be from around here. All he had to do was ask.

Chapter 2

Quinn pulled open the door to the diner, jingling the chime. Coffee and French fry grease assaulted her nostrils, but just for a minute. She'd only worked for Jake a few weeks, but it was already a comforting odor she came to expect.

She glanced around, surprised by how busy it was. She greeted the customers, promising to be right back with refills.

Jake passed her carrying a coffeepot. His tight T-shirt stretched smoothly over his equally tight torso and biceps. This must be what they meant when they talked about guys keeping it tight. The coffeepot looked puny in his hand. "I've got it, Quinn."

"Morning, Jake. I didn't think you'd be open yet." Quinn felt like a slacker and picked up her pace. She also felt like a creeper, noticing her boss's T-shirt like that. He had to be in his forties. And her boss. Not that she had anything against older men or bosses, but that felt like a Venn diagram without intersecting sets.

"No worries. I got bored, so I unlocked the door."

Quinn crossed the dining room toward the hallway in back, where three time cards hung on the wall: hers, the weekend cook's, and the weekend waitress's. She pulled out the card with her name written at the top in Jake's blocky hand. She glanced at the clock, wrote the time, then shoved the card back in her slot.

As she did, Jake passed by on his way to the kitchen. "Remember to use the exact time when you clock in."

"I always do."

"Yesterday you clocked in at six-forty-five."

"Because that's when I got here."

Jake shrugged, flashing his signature smile, all white teeth, reaching up to his eyes. "I guess I'm a little bit OCD too."

Quinn wasn't thrilled that he knew about her obsessive-compulsive disorder, but it was no different than telling her employer she was diabetic or had allergies. She wondered if he knew, or guessed, about the related depression she was fighting. Full disclosure from the get-go was best, she had decided, at least about the OCD, at least up to a point. Since she would be spending so much time here, if she got stuck in a loop again she wanted someone who understood what was happening.

However, Jake should know what he was talking about. Quinn followed him into the kitchen, dropping the neck strap of a bib apron over her head.

"If I got here at six-thirty-eight but clocked in at six-forty-five, would you feel compelled to go home and restart your day?" Quinn brought the apron ties around her waist and tied them in front.

"No, of course not. I just want to pay everyone for the time they work, no more, no less, and when I see a time like that, I think it's been rounded off and one of us is getting cheated. Money is one of the few things I feel very strongly about." He narrowed his eyes at her. "I'm not accusing you of anything."

"Can you leave your house if a picture frame is askew? Do you check to make sure the oven is off twenty-seven times before you can leave?" She looked around the kitchen. "If the power blips, will you convince yourself all the food has spoiled and you've poisoned your customers?"

"Yep, nope, and maybe, now that you mention it." Jake dumped some hash browns on the grill, where they sizzled pleasantly.

"Then you're not OCD and you shouldn't say you are. People who have OCD aren't just über-efficient neat freaks. Checking to see if your oven is off before you leave your house makes perfect sense. Straightening pictures on your wall when they get crooked makes perfect sense." Quinn pinned her name tag to the front of her apron. "What doesn't make sense, though, is when *efficiency*"—she used air quotes—"turns into an all-consuming obsession with order that makes you create some compulsion to check or clean or organize or wash your hands and you literally can't think about anything else."

Jake flipped the hash browns, cracked four eggs, and poured two pancakes. "Is that what happened to you?"

"Something like that." He didn't need the particulars.

The diner doorbell chimed. Jake leaned to peer out the pass-through window. "It's Chief Chestnut. Better get out there."

Ugh.

When she reached the doorway of the kitchen, Jake said, "I didn't mean anything by saying I'm OCD. Not trying to make light of your... condition. But I take your point. Persnickety is different from obsessive-compulsive disorder."

Quinn gave a crisp nod while a slight smile formed on her lips. Transforming the world, one person at a time. "It's adorable you think you're persnickety." She glanced pointedly around the kitchen, raising her eyebrows at the dirty dishes piling up, the prep containers in various states of emptiness, the haphazard heaps of hand towels, cooking utensils, and order tickets stashed around.

"It's my own personal brand of persnickety. Persnickety lite. Persnick, I guess I'll call it."

Quinn grabbed the coffeepot and was still grinning until she saw Police Chief Myron Chestnut, descendant and namesake of the founder of their town, glad-handing and greeting all the customers in the diner with a bony handshake or clap on the back. His thin-lipped smile turned into a sneer when he saw her.

Quinn knew that Chief Chestnut was the same age as her mother, because he and Georgeanne went to school together. But that's where the similarities ended. He was bony where Georgeanne was soft, brittle where she was delicate, strident where she was compassionate. He was all angles and knobs, giving him a slightly sinister air. It didn't help that he was also sharp-tongued, routinely strafing unwary bystanders like he was a Luftwaffe pilot over Britain.

Quinn made the rounds of the tables to see if anyone needed a refill, all the while racking her brain once again to try to determine why Chief Chestnut hated her so much. He'd been this way since she was a kid, but he never seemed to show such disdain to any other kid. He probably thought she was the one who TP'd his yard that time a thousand years ago. All he had to do was ask Rico; he'd tell him it wasn't her.

Maybe it was her looks. He'd commented on them when she came back to town, making it a point to tell her she took after her dad, something no woman wanted to hear, no matter what her nose and ears looked like. Or maybe it was something entirely different. Whatever it was, even Rico didn't know. She'd asked him every which way she could think of, but his answer remained the same.

When Chief Chestnut got settled at his favorite table in the center of the diner, Quinn poured him a cup of coffee. She felt a little flush of pride when she saw the newspaper crossword puzzle sticking up out of his shirt pocket. He pulled it out and smoothed the wrinkles, then patted his other shirt pocket.

"Need a pencil?" Quinn pulled the collection of writing utensils from her apron pocket, sorting through until she found a mechanical pencil.

"I ain't no sissy." He plucked a pen from her hand with his bony fingers and clicked it at her.

Quinn took it as a dismissal and backed away. *Jerk.* She knew that crossword enthusiasts prided themselves on their ability to do puzzles in ink without making mistakes that needed to be erased. But most of them weren't so snippy about it.

The après-parade crowd picked up and Quinn bustled around taking orders, delivering some Adam and Eves on rafts (two poached eggs on toast), Murphys in the alley (hash browns on the side), and several stacks of Vermonts (pancakes). The only phrase Jake threw at her that she didn't know was a "shingle with a shimmy and a shake"—buttered toast with jam. He didn't use the lingo on a regular basis, but thought all employees should know some diner history if they were going to work in one. Even though it didn't go well with previous employees, he continued the practice with Quinn.

"I get the shingle part, but where did the other part come from?" she asked.

"No idea," Jake said. "You're catching on fast, though."

It was silly, but Quinn felt the thrill of accomplishment, like she was becoming bilingual. Arcane diner lingo wasn't a Romance language, but it was something. She was certainly more fluent in it than the Spanish she took for two years in high school.

After the rush ended, Jake made them two dots and a dash (two fried eggs with a strip of bacon) along with a board (toast) slathered in cow paste (butter), which they ate at the huge booth in the corner. They both stretched out their legs on the vinyl benches.

"Cow paste sounds like something my mom would make." Quinn told Jake about the cupcakes this morning.

"That sounds awful. She's such a sweet lady. I hope she never invites me to dinner."

"She is very sweet. Luckily, she told me when I was a kid that it didn't hurt her feelings when I didn't like what she made. She told me not to complain, though, when I didn't get any of her beef Stroganoff or candied eggs."

"What's wrong with beef Stroganoff?"

"It almost always has marinara in it." Quinn wrinkled her nose.

"Ha! I take it you can cook better?"

"Not to brag, but I've never put marshmallow fluff in a main dish."

"Good to know, because I'm going to need you to do some cooking around here every so often. Starting today."

Quinn's eyebrows shot up. "What? Why can't Chris do it?"

"Because Chris only works weekends." Jake gave a vague wave of his hand. "Don't worry. It'll just be a limited menu: burgers, fries, BLTs, breakfast stuff. Nothing you can't handle. Nobody will be in anyway, off having their own barbecues. The only reason they'd come in here for dinner is if they burned their burgers and they were starving."

"So if I only half-burn them, they'll be happy?"

Jake grinned. "Unless you think I should hire your mom."

"That would be hilariously bad for business." Quinn began gathering their dishes. "Can you imagine what the Retireds would do?"

"She'd charm them so much they'd never complain again."

"Probably."

Jake went to his office while Quinn loaded all the breakfast plates, silverware, and mugs into the dishwasher racks, where she rinsed them with the power hose. The power hose earned her respect the time she used it on a cutting board after Jake had chopped habaneros. When that hot spray hit it, she'd created a toxic cloud that made her choke for twenty minutes. She shoved the trays through the dishwasher, checking it was filled with plenty of soap, disinfectant, and rinse aid. She waited a couple of minutes for it to finish, then stood back from the steam when she opened the door.

Quinn heard the door chime and went to the front to see Rico, who had come in for his daily lunch. He usually tried to come at the end of the lunch rush so Quinn could sit with him for a bit. She brought him a glass of ice water. "Need a menu?"

"Nope. Got my taste buds set for a burger with mushrooms and Swiss cheese."

"Well, unset those buds," Jake said from across the diner. "Mushrooms are gross. They'll be in my kitchen over my dead body. And I'm out of Swiss."

"Bacon burger with cheddar?" Quinn asked.

"I don't know." Rico raised his voice toward Jake. "Got any philosophical problems with bacon or cheddar, Jake?"

"Nah, you're good." Jake returned to the kitchen.

"You heard the man," Rico said to Quinn.

"Coming right up."

"Oh, and Quinn? Care to go on a date with me?"

Without missing a beat, she said, "I wish you'd come up with some new material."

"I wish you'd say yes."

Quinn pivoted. "Rico, it's a terrible idea, us dating. We've been friends forever and you know darn well it'll ruin our friendship. It always does."

"How can it, if we haven't gone out yet?"

"You know what I mean. Besides, neither one of us has a very good track record with relationships."

"What about Bella?"

"Your dog? That doesn't count. And, as I recall, you had to keep the gate locked so she wouldn't escape."

"Quinn, you're right. We've been friends our whole lives, but isn't that what they say—marry your best friend?"

"So now we're getting married? And you never even gave me a ring?"

"I'm serious."

"So am I," Quinn said. "Jake says all the time that he and his ex-wife had been best friends."

"He told me they only had lust in common. You and I are nothing like them. Jake and Loma were from opposite sides of the tracks, different races, different upbringings. You and I could be the two crusts on a loaf of Wonder Bread."

"Your slice is a bit more toasted than mine, Mr. Federico Lopez." Quinn held her pale arm against his darker one.

"True. I am a delightful shade of whole wheat."

"Delightful."

"Seriously, Quinn. We're nothing like Jake and Loma. We're…us. Give us a chance."

Quinn had to admit—but only to herself—that she was the teensiest bit curious about what it would be like to kiss Rico, now that she was back in Chestnut Station. Neither of them had shown the least bit of romantic interest in the other until Rico brought it up after she moved back to town. But there was nothing to gain from dating Rico and everything to lose. He was right that their relationship was completely unlike Jake and Loma's. But still, if it was true that Jake and his ex-wife had been best friends and now everything she'd heard Jake say made it sound like they were mortal enemies, then she didn't want anything to do with it.

"No, Rico. I'm not going on a date with you." Quinn turned back to the kitchen.

"I'll keep asking."

"I'm sure of it."

"It's part of my charm."

"Less sure of that."

Quinn put in Rico's order. Jake asked, "How come you never go out with him?"

"Oh, please. Rico and I have been friends for a million years. It would not end well."

"If you say so."

"I do say so." Not that it's any of your beeswax, she added silently. Quinn returned to the dining room, wondering why Jake cared. *Jeez, I hope he doesn't hit on me. I need this job.* It was quite literally the only one in town.

After a bit, Jake brought out Rico's lunch. Quinn jumped up, expecting to be reprimanded for not hearing the order bell. Jake waved her back into her seat. "It's not busy. Take a load off." Jake set Rico's burger and fries in front of him. As he pulled out a chair and sat with them, he said to Rico, "Hey, guess who I saw the other day?"

"Who?"

"Your favorite waitress—"

"Rita?"

"I thought I was your favorite waitress." Quinn pulled her lips into a fake pout.

"*One* of my favorite waitresses got a better job at an insurance company in Denver, and Jake replaced her with another one—not my favorite— who married a rich guy and moved to Aspen. I was happy to see the backside of her."

"Kinky." Jake smirked.

"You know what I mean." Blushing, Rico popped a fry in his mouth.

"Well, Rita says hi."

Rico took a bite of his burger. As he chewed, his eyes drew together. He removed the top bun and stared at his burger. "You weren't kidding. I really wanted mushrooms and Swiss."

A look of disgust crossed Jake's face. "Mushrooms will never darken my doorway, my friend."

"Not a fan of the 'shroom, eh? Makes me wonder what other dark secrets you're hiding." Rico replaced the bun on his burger. Halfway to his mouth he stopped. "Jake, remember that cook of yours who joined the Navy?"

"Years of therapy couldn't pry him out of my mind. Why?"

"You reminded me of him. He refused to make me a chili dog once." Rico changed his voice to sound like Jack Nicholson in *Five Easy Pieces*. "You can have chili. You can have dog. But you can't have a chili dog while I'm cooking." He returned to his normal voice. "You've had a lot of disgruntled employees come through here." Rico took a big bite of his sandwich.

"Not all of them were disgruntled. Some were perfectly gruntled when I fired them." The phone in Jake's office rang and he went to answer it. The other table of diners stood to pay their bill. Quinn met them at the register. The credit card reader flashed irritated yellow numbers across the display and wouldn't accept their card. They pooled their money and scraped enough together to cover the bill and a bare-bones tip. After Quinn's short tussle with the cash drawer, they left in a huff, muttering about small towns.

"Tourists," Rico said. "Pfft."

She filled glasses of lemonade for herself and Rico, then sat back down. Rico finished his lunch and pushed his plate away. They sipped their lemonade alone in the dining room.

Quinn's eyes drifted to the *Help Wanted* sign that still hung in the front window. She'd hoped Jake would have taken it down by now. "Why *does* Jake have so many employees come through here?"

"I don't think you need to be concerned about your job, if that's what you're worried about. You'd serve me a chili dog, right?" When she didn't smile he said, "That *Help Wanted* sign is a permanent fixture around here. It's true Jake has had a revolving door of bad employees, but you're not one of them." Rico reconsidered. "Not *bad* employees. Just ones who couldn't deal with Jake's ... way of doing things. Like learning what he wants and how to do stuff, even when he doesn't quite know himself."

Quinn pursed her lips. That was certainly challenging. He had told her two contradictory ways to deal with the dishwasher and then got mad when she tried to clarify. She'd figured it out the next day while he was at the bank.

"And some employees didn't take to the lingo lessons very well," Rico added.

"That's what I love the best!" Quinn shook her head. "Some people..." She trailed off with a glance at the *Help Wanted* sign.

* * * *

Later that afternoon Jake hauled a huge tray into the front of the restaurant and set it down on the counter by the register where they kept the desserts. "Replace the pies with these beauties."

Quinn walked over and peered at the tray. "Wow. Those are stunning." She inspected the fancy strawberries dipped in white chocolate, swirled delicately and precisely into a facsimile of the bodice of a beaded wedding dress. Each berry was embellished with a different design. Perfect shimmering dots of white chocolate and pearl-colored nonpareils made up a unique necklace for each dress. The only common element was a dark chocolate dagger sticking into the bosom of each. "What is all this? What's it for?"

"Today was my last alimony payment to Loma." He gestured at the strawberry confections. "Give one free to anyone who wants one."

"Your ex-wife is getting remarried?" Quinn hadn't met Loma, but had heard plenty about her.

"No, this was contractual. We put this date in. She probably only agreed because she thought she'd be married long before this." When Jake saw Quinn's eyebrows lift, he shrugged. "Loma and I used to do everything together. Until she lost her mind."

"Literally?" Quinn sampled one of the strawberries. A little moan of pleasure escaped her lips and she blushed.

"No. But she did her level best to make me lose mine. Literally. She was like a human Ebola virus, planting herself in my spleen until I was able to shake her loose."

"That's dark. And not how Ebola works." Quinn retrieved an empty tray and set about removing the day's individual slices of pie from the three-tiered glass display. "I thought your trash talk was just a joke. You guys aren't friends at all?"

"Define *friends*. If it's someone who's always bringing up every little transgression from your past, then absolutely we're friends."

A customer sauntered up next to Quinn as she arranged the fancy chocolates. He pointed at a slice of rhubarb pie. "Hey! I wanted one of those."

"Have one of these instead. They're on the house."

He studied the strawberries and gingerly reached out to touch the tip of the chocolate dagger. "Nah. I'll stick to rhubarb. Less stabby."

A solidly-built black woman with curves galore yanked open the door and cut left, making a beeline for the fancy chocolate-dipped strawberries. She stared at them while she continuously snapped a rubber band encircling her wrist.

Quinn assumed her to be in her early forties like Jake, but with her tight, stylish clothes and hair, she could pass for a decade younger.

Loma spoke loudly. "Hey, Jake! I heard a rumor you made fancy desserts to celebrate our beautiful divorce. You know a big girl can't resist those. Make yourself useful and bring me a plate. I'll just sit in the corner and eat them quietly."

Quinn wondered how she had heard a rumor if the strawberries only came out of the kitchen a few minutes ago.

Jake hurried from the kitchen carrying a bowl overflowing with plump blackberries, round blueberries, and the most perfect raspberries Quinn had ever seen. He stepped between the woman and the strawberries. "Loma, you've never done anything quietly in your life."

"Whose fault is that?" She waggled her eyebrows at him.

"Don't be gross. People are trying to eat."

"Nothing gross about physical declarations of love between a man and his hotter-than-hot wife." Loma selected one of the strawberries, sucked slowly and pointedly on the chocolate dagger, then delicately bit it off with her front teeth.

"Ex-wife." Jake held the bowl of mixed berries in front of him like a shield. "I've never known another soul who liked to hear the sound of their voice as much as you do. You could talk the skin off an entire kielbasa."

She curtsied, then bit into the fancy strawberry. Shards of chocolate coating rained down upon the floor. "The Fourth of July seems very appropriate to put the final exclamation point on our marriage, what with the fireworks show scheduled tonight."

Jake handed Loma the berries and used the towel over his shoulder to clean the floor. "Why are you here, anyway?"

"You know you have a magnetic pull on me." Loma placed the bowl of berries on the nearest table. When Jake rolled his eyes she said, "Plus, I have a consultation for an interior design job."

"In Chestnut Station?" It was obvious to Quinn by his voice and narrowed eyes that Jake didn't believe her.

"Out at the old Maynard place. Some crazy rich Texans bought it and are redoing it with the help of little ole Loma." She picked up a napkin and piled four strawberries on it. She waved at Quinn, leaning against the counter. "Hey, doll—can you get me a to-go container? That'd be awesome."

Quinn brought a small Styrofoam clamshell to Loma, but before she could hand it to her, Jake plucked it out of her hands.

"You never loved me," Loma said, snapping her rubber band.

"You wouldn't know love if it showed up in your fridge, ready for dinner."

"It goes *Love is patient, love is kind*, not *Love is bossy, love is overcritical*." Loma reached for the clamshell, but Jake held it above her head out of reach.

Loma narrowed her eyes at Jake as she passed him, but then took one step backward and planted a deep kiss on his lips.

"You'll be sorry," she said to him before stalking out the door.

Chapter 3

Before Jake left for the afternoon, he'd given Quinn some last-minute instructions about her cooking duties. "There's a pot roast in the slow cooker. It'll be ready before dinnertime. Make it the special. Add some lumpy mashed potatoes and undercooked green beans and nobody will know I'm gone. I also left some redeye gravy simmering. All you need to do is slice a biscuit and pour it on."

"Biscuits and gravy? Not burgers and fries tonight?"

"Oh, you might cook up a couple of burgers, but the drunks will be in for biscuits and gravy after the festival. It's a Chestnut Station tradition." Jake smiled.

Quinn didn't.

"Don't worry. Everything will be fine. Business as usual and probably a lot less of it. You got this."

Quinn took a deep breath. "I hope so."

After he left, she took a minute to make sure the salt and pepper shakers were full and the individual packets of jelly evenly filled each container on the tables.

Late in the afternoon, the crowd picked up. Quinn bustled around, making sure everyone knew she was handling the diner alone. Subconsciously she wanted word to get back to Jake that she did a great job under trying circumstances, but she didn't want to tell him so herself. It was always better when other people tooted your horn. Maybe then he'd get rid of that *Help Wanted* sign.

She lowered a ridiculous number of batches of French fries into the hot oil and when she thought she had enough for the rest of her shift, stuck them in the oven to keep warm. She made a BLT with a side of coleslaw for Mrs. Chavez at table three and delivered it.

"Where's my burger?" Mr. Chavez asked.

"Coming right out." Quinn hurried back to the kitchen to start his burger. She heard the door chime twice while she watched the burger sizzle on the grill. She kept checking to see if it was still too pink. When she was satisfied, she lifted it on to a bun and scooped a mound of fries next to it.

When she placed it in front of him she noticed his wife had already finished her BLT. Quinn offered an "Enjoy!" that sounded much cheerier than she felt.

She looked around to see whose order she should take next. "Where'd that couple with the two kids go?"

"They left half an hour ago," Mr. Chavez said. "Said they were afraid they'd miss the fireworks show."

"It's not even dark out!" Quinn said.

Mr. Chavez smirked and someone at a table nearby giggled.

Quinn spent the rest of the dinner hour racing from dining room to kitchen to cash register. She knew if she just hustled, she could get everyone's food served almost before they complained. Only once did people at the same table order the same thing. When she was able to carry out two plates at once, she felt like kissing them full on the mouth.

Everything was a blur of charred burgers and fries. She'd made so many combinations of breakfast food she started to get fuzzy about what time of day it was. She sold out of Jake's pot roast. She ladled gallons of redeye gravy over biscuits for the drunks, just as Jake predicted. He was wrong, however, that it was going to be slow.

At one point she raced into the kitchen to find Wilbur flipping two burger patties on the grill.

"What are you doing? You're not supposed to be back here!" Quinn tried to shoo the ringleader of the Retireds out, but he wouldn't budge.

"Larry wanted his burger rare and Silas wanted his well-done. You screwed up both orders." Wilbur's voice was gravel.

Quinn grabbed the spatula away from him. "Why didn't they just switch plates?"

Wilbur stared at her. "Because they didn't. That's why."

"Get out of here before I use this spatula on *you*!"

"I was just trying to help. You're running around like a blind dog trapped in a smokehouse." Wilbur untied the apron he wore and shuffled out of the kitchen. Quinn felt bad about her outburst until she heard him say loudly to the entire restaurant, "She won't even admit she screwed up your orders, boys! Tried to say it was your fault for ordering the wrong thing."

Quinn leaned halfway out the pass-through window. "I did no such thing!" Her shrill voice embarrassed her.

By the time the dinner rush ended, even without the burger debacle and the recalcitrant credit card machine, she had to admit it didn't go very well. Everyone got food eventually, often what they had ordered, but it wasn't pretty. Those who stuck it out were patient with her and generous with their tips to reward her effort, but she knew word would get back to Jake that she wasn't quite up to the task. The *Help Wanted* sign was here to stay.

Quinn was glum, clearing and wiping tables when she heard the tinkle of the door chime. She glanced at the clock for the forty-seventh time. It was still eighteen minutes before closing. There were only two tables still occupied—one by a couple in the middle of a quiet but highly charged political debate, and the other by a couple so in love with each other that they probably thought their food was cooked and delivered by Cupid himself. Quinn wished they'd all continue their activities at home, so she could too. She looked forward to snuggling up with Fang and teaching him all about Netflix binges.

"Sit anywhere, but I've got to warn you the menu is very limited tonight. And I'm getting ready to close soon." She watched as a man helped another man, clearly drunk, across the restaurant to the big corner booth. Quinn was glad she still had some biscuits and gravy left for him. Both men wore costumes. The drunk's head bobbed, but Quinn saw his black fake beard-and-mustache combo. He looked like a cartoon Italian Santa. The other man wore a huge fake walrus mustache that covered his cheeks entirely, black bowler, and round eyeglasses.

The sober one poured Drunky into the large booth and wedged him in, his back to the diner. Drunky dropped his chin to his chest, fast asleep. His friend slid in across from him and exhaled hard.

"Costume party?" Quinn set two glasses of water in front of them.

"Wrong. Murder mystery party."

"How fun! Were you the detective? You look like Hercule Poirot."

"Wrong again. I am the victim."

"Looks like your friend isn't much better."

"We need coffee."

"I can do you one better. I've got one serving of biscuits and gravy left. Best cure on the planet."

"Sold."

Quinn went to the kitchen. If Jake was here she'd call out, "Heart attack on a rack" and he'd reply, "Comin' right up!"

She brought the men their coffee and one large order of biscuits and gravy. The man in the bowler took the plate from her and slid it in front of Drunky. He nudged him. "Eat this. Best cure on the planet."

Quinn thought the man might have smiled at her, but his fake facial hair obscured everything but his eyes. She left them to their hangovers while she dealt with her remaining customers.

It had slowed down enough that she could organize the diner and clean the messes from earlier. She finally felt more in control and realized it had been so busy she hadn't had time to square corners or line up ketchup bottles. Now she did and it soothed her.

Finally, all the customers had gone, except for the guys in the back booth. She wanted to shoo them out like bartenders did. "Last call, boys. You don't have to go home, but you can't stay here." But she didn't want word to get back to Jake that she'd been rude. Not like drunks would remember, but still, this job was the one thing she had going for her.

Quinn moved toward a table near their booth, loudly stacking chairs upside down on it, hoping they'd take the hint that it was long past closing time. She was dismayed to see the sober one had slipped out without paying while she wasn't looking. Drunky had half his face in his biscuits and gravy.

Rapping her knuckles on the table in front of him, she said, "Sorry. I've got to close. You're going to have to sleep it off somewhere else." He didn't stir. "You want me to box this up?" She tried to pull the plate away, but even that didn't rouse him. "Mister, I'm calling you a cab." With one knee on the vinyl seat, Quinn reached for his shoulder and shook him, hard. "Wake up!"

He didn't.

She looked again at his plate of heart attack on a rack with wide eyes. She felt his wrist for a pulse. Then the carotid artery in his neck.

Scrambling backward out of the booth, she covered her mouth with one hand. Her eyes darted around the diner for help, even though she knew she was alone.

She called Rico and told him what happened. He told her to stay put and not to touch anything. She dialed 911. Rico answered. "I'm just leaving. I've already called the paramedics. Go sit down. I'll be right there."

She tried Jake, but he didn't answer. She didn't leave a message. A dead man in your diner was something to hear about in person.

A dead man. Quinn gave an involuntary shiver. She'd never seen a dead person up close before, much less needed to touch one. Her knees wobbled and she dropped into a chair as far away from the corner booth as possible. She wanted to flee but knew she had to stay. The poor man deserved someone to keep vigil until the authorities arrived to deal with everything. How sad that his friend left him, probably so he could get home to his loved ones. Or maybe out of annoyance. Maybe this kind of overindulging was a regular occurrence for the dead man. People could only do so much for their friends, but Quinn knew as soon as his murder mystery friend heard about this death, he would mourn and feel so guilty. Her eyes filled and she brushed at them with the back of her hand. At least his last night seemed fun. Before his heart attack, that is. She took some solace in that and it calmed her the teensiest bit, but she needed to do something, not just sit there staring at the deceased.

She didn't know what was appropriate, though, so she shoved the tables and chairs closest to the booth out of the way, so Rico and the paramedics would have room to work. When she'd cleared an area, one eye always on the dead man, she placed the chairs upside down on the rest of the tables, exactly at right angles, one inch from each corner. She was counting the taps of her foot as she leaned against the wall by the front door when Rico and the paramedics arrived. They checked the man for a pulse. None. One of them officially declared the man dead.

Rico took a couple of photos of the man before maneuvering him enough to pull a wallet from his pocket. "Emmett Dubois." Rico looked at Quinn and the paramedics. "That name ring a bell to anyone?" The three shook their heads.

"What's with his getup?" Rico asked Quinn.

Quinn had to clear her throat twice before she could get any words out. "The guy he came in with said they were at a murder mystery party."

"Around here?"

"I don't know. I didn't ask."

"Did you know the guy he was with?"

"No. But he had a big fake mustache too. Covered his whole face." Quinn's gaze turned to the upturned chair legs on all the tables. One, two, three, four. Two, two, three, four. Three, two, three, four.

"Quinn. *Quinn.*" Rico snapped his fingers in her face. "Where's Jake?"

She squinched her eyes tight until she saw stars and not chair legs or dead men. "Not back yet. I haven't seen him since, like, two this afternoon."

Rico dialed his phone. "Jake, when you get this, call me immediately." He turned back to Quinn. "Who else ate biscuits and gravy today?"

Quinn's hand fluttered to her throat. "I—I don't—I'll have to... Do you think that's what killed him? Did I—?"

"No." Rico put his arm around her shoulders and steered her to the Retireds' table on the opposite side of the diner. "Just sit. I'll call your parents to come get you. We can talk more tomorrow."

"No! I don't want to worry them."

Rico stared at her, ready to argue, but Chief Chestnut arrived. He barked, "Secure this crime scene! What are you doing just standing around?"

The paramedics and Rico jumped into action.

"It's not a crime scene." Quinn spoke in a whisper that yearned to be a roar. "It can't be."

"What's that?" Chief Chestnut stepped in front of her face.

"It can't be a crime scene." Her voice quavered.

"It ain't a junior prom," he snapped.

Quinn recoiled, both at his voice and the sudden boom of the fireworks show. Glancing out the window, she saw it was full-on dark. She hadn't realized how late it was.

Chief Chestnut gestured at the plate of biscuits and gravy. "Get this tested, Rico." Then, turning to Quinn, he said, "Give me a list of everyone you served this to."

Rico said, "Can it wait until tomorrow, Chief? She's had a day."

Quinn didn't wait for an answer, fleeing the diner as a flurry of fireworks lit up the sky and split the night.

She pounded across streets and through Square Park, dodging the *ooh*-ers and *ah*-ers in camp chairs watching the fireworks show. When she got home she found herself blessedly alone, her parents still at the festivities. She flung herself into the bathroom, where she retched into the toilet. She felt a little better after spewing and flushing the day's stress and bile.

When her parents got home, they found her sitting at the kitchen table hugging Fang's bowl.

"Quinn? Are you all right?" Dan dropped to one knee next to her and she buried her face in his shoulder.

Georgeanne stroked her hair. "That Jake," she fumed. "I knew working for him was a bad idea. Tomorrow I'm going to march right over there and give him a piece of my mind. How dare he make you work so late and—"

"No, Mom. It's nothing like that."

"Then what?"

Quinn told them the whole story. "And now I have to make a list of everyone who had biscuits and gravy."

Georgeanne jumped up and tore a sheet from her shopping list notepad. She scooped up a pencil too. "That shouldn't be too hard. Let's make a list while it's fresh in your mind."

Quinn placed both hands over her face. "It was crazy there. I'm not even sure I looked everyone in the face. And there were people I didn't recognize."

"You don't worry about that. I'll put the word out tomorrow. But for now, just tell me everyone you can remember and I'll write them down."

Quinn closed her eyes and tried to rewind the clock. She rattled off names of people she could remember. When she got to the Retireds she said, "Silas was there and ...the guy whose wife died? Drives the cab but never charges anyone?"

Georgeanne nodded and added to the list. "Larry."

Suddenly Quinn dropped her hands from her face. "And Wilbur. I found him in the kitchen at one point."

"Doing what?" Dan asked.

"Flipping burgers."

"That Wilbur," Georgeanne said. "Always willing to pitch in and help."

More like stick his nose in where it doesn't belong, Quinn thought.

They worked on the list until Quinn said that Beyoncé had ordered a chili dog. Georgeanne gave her a hug and shooed her off to bed.

Chapter 4

Quinn tossed and turned the rest of the night, finally giving up and going to the diner earlier than normal. She needed to talk to Jake about all this. The sun had barely cleared the horizon by the time she reached the diner. Her shadow stretched all the way across the street, making her look like a macabre marionette.

Jethro was sprawled across the sidewalk in front of the door, all sad eyes and droopy face. When he labored to his feet, Quinn saw a puddle on the sidewalk. He gave his head a mighty shake, long ears flapping much too loudly in the silence of the hour.

Quinn rubbed his head, then yanked on the diner door. Locked. Stunned that Jake wouldn't be here yet, she fished out her keys, calming when it occurred to her that he probably had the door locked because he wasn't ready to open yet. She could appreciate that. Maybe they shouldn't open at all today.

She got the door open and followed Jethro into the dark diner. Jethro headed straight for the big corner booth. Before she could stop him, he had wedged his big body under the table and was investigating all the odors from last night. Horrified, Quinn called him back. She watched as he then continued on his regular rounds, sniffing into all the nooks and crannies of the restaurant. He veered abruptly to the back booth again, nose sniffing the air and the linoleum.

He must smell all the extra people who were here last night. Quinn gave a shudder. Could Jethro smell death? She was thankful someone had cleaned up everything. "Jake?" She checked his office. Empty. Kitchen too. She even opened the back door to see if he was in the alley. He wasn't.

Jethro ended his tour of the diner by planting himself in front of Quinn. He stared at her with his woebegone face.

Quinn felt like he was accusing her of something and she felt a pang of unidentified remorse. Where was the unconditional love dogs were so famous for? Was Jethro's hiding under all that loose skin and wrinkles?

She called Jake's cell for the eighty-seventh time since last night. Still not answering. "Where are you?" she said to herself. She dialed again, this time leaving a message asking him the same question. Chestnut Station was a small town. Surely by now he would have heard what happened.

Quinn made a pot of coffee and listened to the refrigerator make weird noises. Had it always sounded like that? She wasn't sure. Everything was upside down today. She sat on a stool in the kitchen sipping coffee, waiting for Jake.

Jethro forlornly waited for his bacon paycheck.

"Sorry, dude. Can't help you."

Can't or won't, he seemed to say, staring at her with bloodshot eyes.

Quinn poked around half-heartedly and found a raw carrot for him. He accepted it, but was not happy about it. Carrying it in his mouth without eating it, he left the kitchen. Quinn heard the door chime and she knew he'd pushed the door open and left. She wondered if she'd find the carrot carefully placed across the threshold, like some kind of Don Corleone–style warning. She tiptoed through the dining room and locked the door.

After her third cup of coffee, a rattling on the front door made her jump from the stool in relief. She didn't want to startle Jake, so she flipped the light switch and hurried out to meet him. But it wasn't Jake. Instead, old Mr. and Mrs. Carver peered inside with cupped hands around their eyes.

Quinn twisted the dead bolt, intending to tell them the diner was closed, but they pushed past her.

"Hello, dear. We're so glad you're open. Jeb here needs to get to Denver for some testing at the hospital and we wanted a nice breakfast before we go." Mrs. Carver removed the sweater draped around her shoulders and settled into a nearby table.

Jeb leaned toward Quinn. "Got a bad ticker, they say. Guess we'll find out soon enough. Gonna have me a plateful of bacon today, just in case they say I can't have no more."

Quinn looked into their expectant faces, choking back the fear of another possible heart attack at the diner on her watch. "Okay, let me just get you some coffee, then I'll see what I can do."

She returned with the pot and two mugs, expecting to see Jake at any moment. After she poured, she handed them menus, but Jeb waved them away.

"I know what I want. Three scrambled eggs, more bacon than seems right, a slice of sourdough, heavy on the butter—and I mean heavy."

"Same for me," Mrs. Carver said. "And maybe some fruit? For both of us?"

"Coming right up." Quinn admired their appetites and silently blessed them for ordering the same thing. She found the bacon, feeling a bit guilty about Jethro, and cracked some eggs. She hoped nobody else came in so she could lock up again after the Carvers left. It didn't feel right to have the diner open after everything that happened. And where was Jake? Had something happened to him too? She wished she knew where he'd gone yesterday. What if he'd had a car accident? But surely Rico would have received word about that and would have told her. Unless it had happened out in the boonies, loosely defined as a ten-mile radius from any point in town, a vast area with more scarecrows than people.

Halfway through making the Carvers' breakfast, she heard the door chime. She looked expectantly out the pass-through, but no Jake. Rather, the Retireds.

"Don't you guys get tired of this place?"

Wilbur, Herman, and Bob all shuffled to their regular places with their backs to the wall at the rectangular table with a view of the entire dining room. Silas limped to his seat at one end.

Quinn and Larry did a little dance while they tried to get out of each other's way. Larry had a slight stoop, but he still towered over her. His ears, like all of the Retireds', had grown long and dangly in the way of old men. He was completely gray, except for his hair, which was the color of ginger. He took his seat at the other end of the table. It always looked to Quinn like they were trying to re-create a geriatric Last Supper painting.

Quinn handed out menus even though she knew they had them memorized. "Why do you guys always sit like that?"

"On our butts, you mean?" Silas couldn't resist a joke, bad or otherwise.

Gregarious Bob said, "We don't want anyone to miss seeing our handsome mugs." He smoothed his movie star hair and flashed the smile she knew served him well during his long career on the stage.

"Well, little missy, you of all people should know the Chestnut Diner is the place to see and be seen." Wilbur's words tumbled through his cement-mixer voice. "We like to do both."

Before she could even pour their coffee, two more groups came in. It was just as well, she figured. Jake needed his business to run, especially since after all this—if she wasn't fired—she might ask for a raise. Besides, she needed something to keep her mind occupied. Since her OCD diagnosis she realized that if she could point her anxiety at something else, it wouldn't boomerang back into her brain and sizzle in there like an overcharged battery. She may as well obsess about bacon and eggs until Jake showed up.

She was busy in the kitchen when Rico poked his head in. Quinn stopped what she was doing. "Have you talked to Jake? I haven't been able to get ahold of him. I'm starting to worry." She scooped the Carvers' scrambled eggs and bacon onto plates and set them aside.

Rico pointed to the toaster. Smoke swirled toward the ceiling. Quinn jammed up the button and the sourdough slices popped up. Burnt black. Still smoking. She plucked one of the slices from the toaster and promptly dropped it on the floor. "Ouch!"

"Who ordered Cajun-style toast?" he asked.

"Ha-ha. You're hilarious." Quinn scooped the toast from the floor and tossed it into the trash. Using a pair of tongs, the rest followed. She pulled more bread from the bag and popped slices into the toaster. That would teach her to get cocky and try to do more than one thing at a time. "Have you heard from Jake?" she repeated while squinting at the knob, finally turning it from brown to light brown. At least that's what she thought she did. The toaster was so old the writing had faded away.

"Not yet. I came over hoping he was here. You really haven't heard from him?"

"Not a word."

An order of fried eggs on the grill started smoking. Quinn lunged for them before they went the way of the toast. Rico handed her a plate and she slid the eggs to it, just in the nick of time. She'd hide the lacy edges under some bacon and keep her fingers crossed.

The diner door jingled and Quinn's shoulders slumped.

"I'll get their menus and pour them some coffee, but then I've got to go," Rico told her. "I know you've got your hands full, but when you hear from Jake, let me know."

"Roger that. And same with you." Quinn flipped pancakes and almost wept when they were the right color. She buttered non-Cajun-style toast for the Carvers and dropped it on their plates. She started to run it out to them when she remembered they wanted fruit too. No time to slice anything, so she grabbed two bananas and laid them across the top of their eggs.

She delivered the plates to them.

"That's an interesting presentation, dear." Mrs. Carver lifted the banana from Jeb's plate and set it aside, then did the same with hers.

Quinn straightened, but didn't move from the Carvers' table. She hadn't realized how many people were in the diner. It seemed like twice as many as usual. Seeing them sitting there, looking at her so expectantly, made her heart beat faster. She focused her attention toward the floor and began counting all the shoes in the diner. She started with sandals. Six women's, two men's. Then she started on the sneakers. She only got to three before Mr. Carver touched her elbow.

"I said heavy on the butter. Barely any on here." He lifted his sourdough to show nearby diners. "Would you call that heavy butter?"

A couple people nodded, a couple shook their heads. Clearly an agree-to-disagree situation.

The great butter debate was enough to shake Quinn from her ritual counting. Or maybe it was the smoke she smelled from the kitchen. She raced back to find a griddle full of pancakes beautiful on one side, but blackened on the other. She piled them up on her spatula and dropped them into the trash. Making sure no food was near a heat source, she took a deep breath and returned to the dining room.

"As you can see, I'm here by myself today. So, here's the plan for breakfast. It's all-you-can-eat pancakes today. I'll make them and set them on the pass-through and you just come up and help yourself."

"As long as it's not what Jake made that guy last night!" someone said.

A few people giggled nervously.

So that's why the diner was so crowded this morning, Quinn thought. Word already got out and people were morbidly curious. "The man who died last night simply had a heart attack," she said. "Doesn't have anything to do with the diner. Or Jake." Yesterday she'd wanted kudos for running the diner alone, but today she didn't feel it necessary for everyone to know she was in charge last night too.

"How much?" a man called out.

"How much what?" she asked.

"How much for all the pancakes I can eat?" The man patted his ample belly.

"Jake's gonna go broke with you, O'Shea," Silas hollered.

O'Shea and the crowd laughed good-naturedly.

"Five dollars?" Quinn knew Jake charged $7.59 for eggs, toast, bacon, and hash browns. Five bucks should work for everyone. A nice, round number. She saw some shrugs and nods and nobody left, so she headed back to the kitchen. She poured what was left of the batter into small circles on the griddle, then dumped water and more of the mix into the bowl, whisking it smooth. God bless pancake mix. She poked her face through the pass-through. "Feel free to help yourself to coffee too. And let me know when I need to make more."

Quinn got a rhythm going with the pancakes—pour, flip, plate, pass-through—enough to feel comfortable to step away and make more coffee.

Jeb Carver stuck his head in the kitchen. "We're ready to pay."

"Okay, one sec..." Quinn plated all the pancakes on her griddle but didn't pour any more. She'd developed new respect for a hot grill. She wiped her hands on her apron. "I'm sorry about the butter."

Jeb followed her out to the cash register. "Nah. You made up for it with that mound of bacon."

Quinn began to punch numbers on the register. "I don't want you to blame me when you have a heart attack." She wanted to claw back her words.

"Nah."

When she hit the final button, the register tape was barely legible. The ink was faint and the paper had the telltale thick pink color that signified the roll was empty. Jeb held out a twenty-dollar bill. But the cash drawer hadn't popped open like it should have. Quinn started jabbing buttons on the ancient machine, but it wouldn't budge.

She glanced at the credit card reader. The irritated yellow numbers scrolling across it yesterday had been replaced by angry red letters demanding she *call for service now.*

Mrs. Carver came over to see what was going on.

Quinn looked up at them helplessly, then around the diner.

Mrs. Carver opened her purse and pulled out a small coin purse. She fished around until she came up with six quarters. She plucked the twenty from Jeb's fingers, placing it next to the register and piling the quarters on top. "That's all right, dear. Thank you for a lovely breakfast."

The Carvers stopped by a couple of tables and carried on short, whispered conversations with the diners on their way out.

"Folks, there seems to be a problem with the cash register," Quinn said. "Can you all just pay with exact change today until I get a chance to fix it?"

"When's Jake coming back?"

"Soon, I hope," Quinn said. "But until he does, I'm all you've got. So if you want pancakes, I'm happy to make them until you tell me to stop or until I run out." She glanced around the diner. "And the cash—"

Three or four people spoke at once.

"Don't worry about it."

"Cash works."

"No problem."

"Not a big deal."

The folks in Chestnut Station might be a morbidly curious bunch, but they were easygoing and tolerant and Quinn wanted to hug each one of them. She went back to the kitchen to make more pancakes. Everyone seemed to be handling this fiasco just fine, so Quinn began to calm down.

The rhythmic movements of repetition soothed her and she achieved a sort of Zen state, brain fully zeroed in on pancakes. The diners were busing their own tables, pouring their own coffee, and eating pancakes like they were actually enjoying themselves.

Whenever she had a few seconds, she dialed Jake. Where was he?

Quinn caught snatches of conversations from disembodied voices wafting through the pass-through. As she listened, it became very clear that everyone wanted to talk about the events of last night, even though they had no idea what had actually happened. A man dropping dead in public was certainly a novelty in Chestnut Station.

Nobody seemed to know who the dead man was. Nor did they know Jake hadn't been here. The conversation became less guarded, as everyone realized they weren't the only ones with prurient interest in what happened. The entire diner became one big coffee klatch. The customers were so comfortable with the accommodations and the conversation that they could have been sitting in someone's living room.

"I bet he choked."

"Maybe. But wouldn't someone have noticed?"

"And I know Jake can Heimlich people, because he did it on me once. Laughed too hard once and sucked a cough drop down my windpipe."

"It was a heart attack. Have you seen the way we eat around here? Jeb Carver just ate an entire pound of bacon before he went to his cardiologist appointment this morning."

"I heard he got into a brawl in the parking lot and his face got smashed with a brick."

"Jeb?"

"No. The dead guy."

"That's the dumbest thing I ever heard," Quinn heard Silas say. "Ain't nobody brawling in Chestnut Station."

Quinn set out more pancakes and scooped up the pile of cash that had accumulated in the corner of the pass-through. People piled it up there before calling out goodbye and thanks to her before leaving the restaurant. It was full of tens and twenties. Quinn hoped everyone was overtipping for their pancakes and bottomless coffee. If Jake thought five dollars was too little to charge, she'd just hand over her tips for the day.

The conversation died down and Quinn glanced up. Wilbur stood in the middle of the diner, holding court the way her grandpa used to.

"There was no brawl, no choking, no heart attack. And no Jake." Wilbur waved a hand toward Quinn. "This little lady was cooking last night too. Just like now," he added ominously.

The only sound in the diner was the last gasp and gurgle of a new pot of coffee finishing its brewing cycle.

"Lie down with dogs and you'll get up with fleas is all I'm sayin'."

Quinn froze. Was that an accusation? The image of Wilbur in the kitchen last night materialized in front of her. She moved away from the pass-through and leaned against the prep table where nobody could see her. Heat waves shimmered above the stove, but Quinn made no move to pour more pancakes. It seemed to her the air suddenly felt heavier. She had trouble filling her lungs.

Wilbur's voice rumbled through the air. "You ask me, you're taking your life in your hands here."

Quinn couldn't breathe. She thought she belonged here. These were her people. Her hometown. But if they thought she could—

"Don't be a ninny, Wilbur. Quinn no more killed anyone with diner food than…than…you did," Larry said.

The crowd laughed and rallied to her defense. Relief flooded Quinn's body. She poured coffee into a carafe, but before stepping into the dining room with it, she dialed her phone. "Rico? Talk to Wilbur. He was alone in the kitchen last night. He acted like he was trying to help me, but it seemed bogus. Maybe he did something to the gravy."

Chapter 5

By the next morning Quinn was sure she'd worn out the contact buttons on her phone for Jake, and still she hadn't heard from him. She sat at the kitchen table creating another crossword puzzle.

The puzzle wasn't due to Vera at the *Chronicle* for a few days, but it calmed her. The theme she'd chosen was Murder, which had been on her mind since she'd remembered Wilbur in the diner kitchen.

Quinn normally enjoyed choosing themes, as they set the tone of the puzzle. They could be anything: A broad subject like *murder*, a multipart quotation or poem, hidden words, protest songs, cartoon dogs…the list was infinite. The more obscure the theme, the harder the puzzle. But whichever theme she chose, there were some common principles. In Quinn's typical 15x15 puzzles, she tried to have four theme entries with a minimum of 40 letters. The theme entries were usually the longest words in the grid, ideally with a letter count of 10, 11, 12, or 15. If a theme entry was 15 letters, it could only go in the center of the puzzle. All the theme entries must be symmetrical in length and have the same number of letters, so they could be paired together.

She looked at her brainstormed list of words related to murder: *poisoning, homicide, slaying, conspiracies, manslaughter, premeditated, crime of passion, with malice aforethought, pump full of lead, bump off, triggerman, hired gun*. She narrowed it down to four 12-letter words and one 15-letter word, wondering if she was a skilled enough constructor to use all five as theme entries.

She wouldn't know until she tried. Quinn pulled up a blank grid on her laptop. The house was quiet and still. Unlike Quinn, Georgeanne and Dan slept. The hum from her computer would normally be so quiet as to be inaudible, but in this magical time before sunrise, it might as well be a jackhammer.

It didn't stop her from jumping out of her skin when she heard a quiet tap at the kitchen door. She used an index finger to part the curtains and look out, even though she knew it was Rico.

"I saw the light on," he whispered.

"Yeah. I'm not sleeping much." Quinn sat down again at the table. When Rico remained at the door she popped up out of her seat like a jack-in-the-box. "What's wrong?"

Rico stepped across the threshold and automatically slung his duty cap between his elbow and ribs. He stood at attention with his cap under his arm. His mouth worked, as if he had practiced the words he wanted to say, but couldn't budge them loose.

"What? Is it Jake? What happened? Did you...find him?" Quinn braced herself with one palm flat on the table.

"Yes."

You knew it was bad when there was a one-word answer to a multipart question.

"Is he okay?"

"Yes."

"For Pete's sake, Rico! Tell me!"

Rico took a deep breath and his police training kicked in. Just the facts, ma'am. "I arrested Jake a few hours ago for the murder of Emmett Dubois."

"You did what?" Quinn collapsed into her chair with a thud.

Rico's professional bearing wobbled a bit. "Arrested Jake for the—"

"I heard you the first time. Now sit down and tell me what you're talking about." Quinn gestured to a chair at the table.

Rico placed his hat on the table and sat. As soon as he did, he turned back into Rico the person instead of Rico the cop. "I caught him going into his house around midnight—"

"Is that illegal?"

"No, but he knew we were looking for him and he was...there's no other word for it...sneaking into his house."

"Sneaking?"

"Yes. It was obvious he was trying not to be seen."

"But why?"

"That's what we want to figure out." Rico drummed his fingers on the table. "Have you talked to him since the...you know?"

"You mean, since that man had a heart attack in his diner?" Quinn's voice rose.

"*That man* was a guy Jake used to work with in some fancy restaurants. And he didn't have a heart attack."

"What? Of course he did!" The alternative made no sense.

"Quinn. It was no heart attack."

"Then what?"

Rico picked up his cap and stood. "I'm not at liberty to say."

Quinn stood too. "Where is he? At the station?" She was already opening the door.

"You can't go over there."

"Watch me." Quinn hurried through the door.

Rico had no choice but to follow her. His longer legs caught up to her. He grabbed her elbow but she shook him off.

"Don't you dare try to stop me!"

"I wasn't. I was going to ask if you wanted a ride."

"Oh. Yes. Yes, I do want a ride. Since you offered." She detoured to the patrol car and thrust her arms out impatiently, but Rico ignored her. He opened the back door, gently placing his hand on the top of her head and pushing her into the seat.

Quinn knew the rules. Courtesy rides from the police also came with frisks and locking of purses or backpacks in the trunk. Normally she appreciated this procedure to keep Rico safe. This morning, however, she appreciated him ignoring the frisk.

Even though everyone in town knew she and Rico were best friends, she hoped nobody was up this early to start a rumor that she was arrested.

They didn't speak on the short ride. Quinn had a million questions, but couldn't settle on any of them.

When Rico pulled into the parking lot, Quinn frantically searched for the door handles until she remembered there weren't any. She had to wait like a child for him to open the patrol car door. When he did, she burst past him and flew into the police station.

Donnie Garfield, the junior cop, startled out of his pose, feet up on his desk, hat tipped forward. Clearly he'd been sleeping. "Wha—"

"I'm here to see Jake Szabo," Quinn said.

"You can't—I just got him processed." Donnie looked at Rico, who followed at a slower pace. "She can't, can she?"

Rico shrugged. "I don't see why not."

Donnie began to stand, but Rico waved him back down. "Finish your beauty rest. I'll take her down."

Rico pulled keys from his pocket and Quinn followed him through the reception area, past the desks where he and Donnie worked. Rico paused near the dark conference room and Quinn thought they'd talk with Jake in there. But Rico unlocked the door next to the conference room. Quinn had never been past it. As they stepped through, she saw Chief Chestnut's office with its lights off. To the right she saw the break room and a couple of dark rooms farther down. Past the chief's office, Rico stopped to unlock another door. He swung it open and she saw a staircase. He motioned her down.

When she got to the bottom, she stood in a large rectangular basement, lit up with harsh fluorescent lights. Along the right side, there was a glass-walled room with some rickety chairs scattered near an old metal table. Quinn noticed it was bolted to the floor.

A wide, open area separated the two halves of the basement, at the back of which stood a water cooler, pointy paper cups peeking from the bottom of an attached silver contraption. To Quinn it seemed like it was guarding the space.

Along the left side were two cells with a brick wall separating them. Jake sat in the first one—elbows on knees, face covered by his hands—on a metal cot attached to the wall, a thin rolled-up mattress next to him. He looked up when he heard Quinn's intake of breath.

He stood and grabbed the metal bars with both hands. "Am I glad to see you!"

Quinn didn't know what to say. "Then why didn't you return any of my calls?"

"Rico, man, you've gotta get me out of here!"

"You'll recall it was I who put you in here," Rico said.

Quinn saw Jake staring at Rico. "Oh. I thought you were glad to see *me*," she said. "What's going on, Jake?"

"What else do you need to know, aside from the fact he arrested me for killing Emmett?" Jake jabbed a finger in the air directed at Rico.

"Well, first off, tell me who this Emmett is," Quinn said.

Rico opened the door to the interview room and dragged a chair into the center of the open space that he then sat in, facing the cell.

"Emmett Dubois is a guy I used to work with in some four-star restaurants he owned. I haven't seen him in forever, then he shows up poisoned in my diner."

"Poisoned!" Quinn's hand fluttered to her throat. She turned to Rico. "The redeye gravy? I told you Wilbur did something he shouldn't have in the kitchen."

"The diner kitchen? Why was Wilbur back there?" Jake asked.

"Said I screwed up the burger orders. Larry wanted rare and Silas wanted well-done, so he snuck back there and made new ones."

"Why didn't they just switch plates?"

"That's what I said!"

Rico shook his head. "It wasn't the gravy, Quinn."

"It was bad mushrooms." Jake made a face as he spoke.

Quinn whirled from Jake to Rico. "I didn't cook any mushrooms and Jake never has them in the diner, anyway."

"Never." Jake shook his head vehemently, then took a giant step to the side so he was more directly in line with where Rico sat. "Listen, Rico, pal. You've known me a long time. You've got to let me out of here. I've got a business to run."

Rico stood. "I'll do my best, Jake. You know I will. But when Chief wants something, he usually gets it. I tried to talk him into letting you go on your own recognizance—business owner, house in town, pillar of the community and all—but he wouldn't listen to me."

Jake took another giant step in the opposite direction to stand in front of Quinn again. "Please get me out of here. Please! You've got to!"

"That's Rico's job. I'll do my job *and* yours at the diner, but I'm not a cop. We've got to leave this up to Rico. He'll get you out of jail while I run the diner for you."

"If I don't get out of here, there won't be a diner anymore. No offense." Jake craned his neck to see the clock on the wall above the water cooler. "Hey. It's after six. You've gotta get over there and start prep! Hungry people will be banging on the door."

"Really? That's what you're worried about right now? Hungry people?" Quinn bugged out her eyes.

"I can worry about several things at once. I'm gifted like that."

"Besides, I handled it yesterday."

"How?"

"I found the pancake mix and created all-you-can-eat pancakes day."

Jake stared at her. "That's it? Pancakes?"

Quinn stared at the floor; couldn't answer him. She knew she'd screwed up.

"How much did you charge?"

"Five dollars," she said quietly, without looking up.

Jake threw his hands up in the air and turned his back on her. Quinn heard him mumble something about profit and loss and insolvency.

Quinn began counting the bars on the cell, starting over twice when she lost focus.

"C'mon, Quinn. Let's go." Rico gently held her elbow and steered her back toward the stairs. "Jake, you're just going to have to sit tight while I figure this out. Quinn is doing a great job at the diner. It'll be fine."

"Sure it will." Jake was back in his original pose: elbows on knees, face in hands.

Quinn had no words and followed Rico silently up the stairs. She knew running the diner was serious, but *profit and loss* and *insolvency* felt like bricks on her shoulders. This wasn't just her job, or Jake's. This was his livelihood, his life's work. Presumably, everything he had was tied up in this business. She thought about the Retireds and all those people she had been serving. The diner was important to Chestnut Station as well.

When they got to the top of the stairs and Rico locked the door behind them, she looked up at him. "Does he have an attorney?"

Rico shook his head. "Said he doesn't want one."

"That's crazy!"

"I know. But he says he's not guilty and doesn't want to look like he is."

"Getting an attorney doesn't make you look guilty. I'm gonna go—"

Rico grabbed her arm. "I already tried, but he's adamant. If this is still going on when the courts open after the holiday, I'll try again. Submit the request myself if I have to."

Quinn glanced at the door to the lockup and then at Rico.

"For now he's fine. Completely safe."

"Really?" She knew the answer before she even asked.

"Really."

"You know this is all some kind of big mix-up, right? Arresting Jake is ridiculous. He wasn't even there last night. If anyone should be in jail, it's me, and I shouldn't be either because I didn't serve anyone mushrooms. That guy had a heart attack. Nobody was poisoned at the Chestnut Diner. It's insane to even think it."

Quinn saw Rico's cannot-tell-a-lie face and knew she had to ask him point-blank. She made sure Chief Chestnut's office was still dark. "What evidence do you have?"

Rico sighed. "Emmett Dubois was poisoned by mushrooms that Jake cooked."

"Again," Quinn said impatiently. "Jake wasn't cooking and I know for a fact I didn't serve anyone mushrooms."

"Jake was cooking at a fundraiser that day in Denver. Donnie had the foresight to collect the leftovers and we tested them."

"Already?"

"It was a fundraiser for the governor. Wheels of justice turn faster for some people than for others."

Quinn's head swam. None of this was making sense. "Why was Donnie there?"

"The governor is his stepfather."

"Who else got sick?"

"Nobody."

"Then why do you think it was the mushrooms?"

"Emmett was the only one who was served them."

"Says who?"

"Says Donnie."

Quinn hadn't worked for Jake for very long, but had already seen Jake's disgusted face many times whenever somebody tried to order mushrooms. Rico saw it just yesterday. "You know Jake hates mushrooms. Why would he cook some at this fundraiser and why only for Emmett?"

Rico raised his palms.

"And isn't it more than convenient that Donnie happened to be at this fundraiser and just happened to save the leftovers? You told me yourself that Donnie isn't the sharpest knife in the drawer. *Never going to be detective material*, I think is how you put it."

"I don't know what you want me to say. We have some facts. Not *all* of them—"

"Then you shouldn't have arrested him."

"—because it's early days. But the facts we have aren't looking that great for Jake. Maybe things will change Chief's mind. But right now, this is what I have to work with."

Quinn studied Rico's face. When he wouldn't meet her gaze, she narrowed her eyes. "You have something else. What is it?"

Rico's nose twitched and he pinched the bridge of it, squeezing his eyes shut.

"Tell me."

He opened his eyes and looked directly at her. "We got an anonymous tip. The caller said Jake was seen carrying the bag of mushrooms into the governor's mansion."

"Seen by who?"

"That's all we know. The caller's voice sounded male to Donnie, but that doesn't mean anything. Could have been a woman with a deep voice, or a man calling on her behalf, or it could have actually been a man. We have no way of knowing."

"Can't you trace the call?"

"This isn't TV, Quinn."

"Have you talked to the murder mystery guy who came in with Emmett Dubois?"

Rico shook his head.

"What about those two couples in the diner, the lovey-dovey ones and the ones arguing?"

"We found them, but they didn't see anything other than the two of them coming in the diner and sitting down. They didn't even notice the costumes you reported."

"I *reported*? Don't you believe me?"

"Of course I believe you. The bottom line, though, is that right now nobody knows who the man is who came in the diner with Emmett Dubois."

It was too much for Quinn to process. "I've got to get to the diner. Gotta keep it running while Jake's in here, even though he clearly doesn't think I can."

"I'll walk you over."

"No. You stay here and figure out how to get Jake off the hook." She locked eyes with Rico. "You know this is insane."

Rico opened the door to the lobby. "I'll see you later for lunch."

Quinn walked through the police department lobby with her eyes on Donnie. If he was somehow involved in this, could the cops, even Rico, investigate fairly?

Chapter 6

The short walk back to the diner felt like a forced march. Quinn expected to hear "Dead man walking!" with every step. She began counting her footsteps out loud, but in a whisper. Quinn had compulsively counted many things in her life, but counting her steps was new. She found it soothing.

As she neared the diner she saw a small crowd had congregated, the Retireds in front of the pack. Their chatter stopped abruptly when they noticed her. News about Jake's arrest had clearly arrived already.

Vera Greenberg pulled off her slouch hat and ran a hand through her choppy hair, mussing it more than the hat had. She stepped aside to let Quinn unlock the door. After Quinn waved Jethro in to make his rounds, she let the crowd of humans surge after him.

Vera stopped Quinn from following by placing a hand on her forearm. "I hate to do this, but—" Vera pulled out her reporter's notebook. "Can I ask you some questions about Jake for the *Chronicle*?"

Quinn paled and staggered a bit on the sidewalk. "Vera, I know you're my boss and have been for a long time, but—"

Vera waved away Quinn's words. "This has nothing to do with crossword puzzles."

"It's not that I don't want to say anything about Jake…" Quinn blinked twice. "No, actually, it's exactly like that. I don't want to say anything about Jake or that poor man who died."

They stared at each other for a few moments, then Vera nodded slightly.

"Maybe after the breakfast rush." Quinn's voice was weak, knowing that was undoubtedly not going to be the case.

"Whenever you're ready." Vera jammed her hat back on her head.

Quinn held the door for her. "You hungry? I think I've figured out pancakes."

"Not today. I've got a story to investigate." Vera trotted off the direction Quinn had just come, probably off to the police station.

Quinn watched Vera until she turned the corner, then moved her concrete feet into the diner. Again, all chatter stopped when she walked in. She counted her steps across the dining room. She was dismayed to see Jethro once again sniffing around the big corner booth where Emmett Dubois had died. She called to him several times, but he was hypnotized by some odor, only padding toward her when his nose was satisfied. She expected him to follow her into the kitchen for his bacon paycheck, but he veered into Jake's office, where he circled the desk, nose to the floor.

She dropped to one knee and intercepted him. "Oh, buddy. He's not here. He won't be back for a few days."

Jethro's sad, droopy eyes looked like they got sadder and droopier, if that was even possible.

"*Lie down with dogs and you'll get up with fleas* my foot. What was Wilbur talking about, anyway?" she muttered.

Quinn hugged Jethro around his neck and he plopped his big head on her shoulder. They had a moment. When they pulled away, Quinn felt the slobber soaking into the back of her shirt. She didn't care. Remaining on one knee, facing the big dog, she took his head in both her hands. "Don't you worry. Rico will figure this out and get Jake out of jail soon." Jethro lifted his eyes, but not his head. "Very soon. I promise." Quinn straightened up. "Let's get you that bacon."

She fired up the griddle. By the time she fished out two slices and dropped them on it, they sizzled. She looked at Jethro, sitting in the doorway. A long string slid from his mouth and made its way to the floor.

She barely cooked one strip and left the other to get crispy because she didn't know which he preferred. She plated each one and let him choose. He gobbled down the crispy one, then sniffed suspiciously at the other. Quinn took the hint and threw it back on the grill.

Once Jethro was satisfied and left the diner, Quinn knew she had to focus on all those people waiting in the dining room. She couldn't avoid them any longer. She'd heard the door chime several times while she was with Jethro, so she knew it was even more crowded now.

What to say? What to do?

She took a deep breath before stepping into the dining room. She saw familiar faces from breakfast yesterday. "I'm not very good at this, as some of you found out yesterday, but I think I've figured out how to make pancakes. And bacon. So if you want—"

"We don't care about breakfast," a voice in the back said.

"Speak for yourself!" The portly Mr. O'Shea already had a paper napkin tucked into his shirt collar.

The crowd laughed.

The voice said, "Okay, fine, we care about breakfast, but we were also hoping for some news."

Quinn recognized him as a friend of her dad's. She shook her head and held her palms to the ceiling just like Rico had done with her. "I don't know what to tell you."

"Is it true Jake's been arrested for that guy's murder?" he asked.

Quinn's face answered the question and everyone began speaking at once. When she realized they weren't actually speaking to her, she tuned out the noise and began counting chair legs. It soothed her enough that she could process what had happened at the jail. Her earlier idea that Rico couldn't or wouldn't investigate Jake's case thoroughly or properly seemed ludicrous now. He was a good, honest cop who would do his job, even if Donnie was involved, even if Chief Chestnut pressured him somehow.

Besides, there wasn't a thing she could do about it.

She looked up from the chair legs. "All-you-can-eat pancakes for five—I mean seven—dollars coming up. Cash only. If you want fried eggs and bacon, line up at the pass-through in five minutes. Three bucks extra."

Quinn tied on her apron. *Rico will investigate. Not me. My job is to make pancakes and keep the diner in business until Jake gets out.*

Chapter 7

Quinn couldn't believe it was possible for things to get worse at the diner, but they did. The constant stream of lookie-loos never abated. She ran out of pancake mix, eggs, bacon, and was running dangerously low on coffee. She searched for something, anything, she could make quickly that could feed a crowd. Rummaging her way through the pantry, she found a giant-sized container of marinara sauce and some bags of various types of pasta. As she checked her watch to see if it was too early for spaghetti, she spied a large container of quick oats and almost wept with relief.

She manhandled the biggest pot she could find on to the stove, then filled it with the correct proportion of water to oats. She knew it was correct because it took her three tries to fill the liquid measuring cup to the precise level. As she waited for it to boil she went into Jake's office and looked in the file cabinet for the employment files for Chris and Kristi, the weekend cook and waitress, who were also husband and wife. She'd only met them once, but they were her best hope. Not knowing their last name, she had to search through half the drawer before she found a folder with Chris's name on it. She scanned his application to see if he'd listed Kristi anywhere, thus verifying it was his file and praying she was not deeply violating some privacy law. She added Chris's number to the contact list on her phone, fairly certain she'd need to call him again before this ordeal was over.

When he answered, she blurted, "You guys have to come in. Jake's not here and I'm *dying*!" Quinn immediately regretted her wording. "I'm running out of everything and I don't know what to do. Can you swing by the grocery store and get some stuff, then come in and help me?"

"Who is this?" Chris asked.

"It's Quinn."

No response.

"At the diner?"

Still nothing.

Then: "I'm just yankin' you."

Quinn was so relieved, she forgot to be annoyed by his prank. She returned to the kitchen and glanced into the pot of water. Not even close to boiling. "When can you be here?"

"Can't. We already have plans."

"Can you break them? This is kind of an emergency."

"Well, darlin', it might be an emergency, but it's your emergency, not mine. My emergency today involves tubing down the river with an ice-cold six-pack, maybe with some fried chick—"

"Seriously? You're not coming to help me? Neither one of you?"

"Kristi can't come neither. She's my DD."

"Your what?"

"Designated drinker."

"You mean designated driver."

"I know what I said."

Frustration boiled up out of Quinn. "Have a nice day, then!" She disconnected and refrained from throwing the phone against the wall. Nothing else was boiling, so she hurried back into the office and yanked open the file cabinet drawer with all the employee files.

Even though she, Chris, Kristi, and Jake were the only employees right now, the drawer was full. Clearly, Jake never weeded ex-employees from the file cabinet.

Quinn pulled as many as she could from the drawer and plopped them on Jake's desk. Then she ran out to the dining room to make sure everything was okay—or as okay as possible—under the circumstances.

"There you are. Are you going to take our order anytime soon? I've got to get the salon opened soon."

"I'm trying, Mrs. Olansky. I should have some oatmeal ready in a bit." Quinn was glad to see someone had taken the initiative to make coffee.

"Oatmeal. Yuck." Mrs. Olansky plucked her purse from the back of her chair. "C'mon, Henry. We'll come back for lunch instead. Maybe there'll be some news then too."

Before Quinn could respond to her, someone called out, "This is the worst coffee I've ever had. It's too weak."

"No, it's too strong," another called.

Quinn fled back to the kitchen, where the pot of water was finally boiling. She picked up the container of oats and dumped them into the water, then turned to find a big enough spoon to stir. By the time she turned back, the oatmeal was bubbling over, spilling on to the burner. Without thinking, she grabbed the handles of the pot to slide them off the heat. When they scalded her hands, she let out a shriek and dropped the pot. She watched helplessly as it teetered in slow-motion on the edge of the stove, then toppled to the floor. It landed with a loud crash.

Quinn was rooted to the spot, shaking her hands in front of her as if she could wave away the pain. People crowded into the kitchen, and some peered in the pass-through window. Someone clicked off the flame under the burner. Silence reigned as everyone assessed the impressive display of oatmeal coating most available surfaces. A few wrinkled their noses at the acrid smell of burning oats.

Finally, a woman in her forties wearing a skirt suit and sneakers steered everyone from the kitchen. "Show's over, folks. You all run along home and eat your breakfast there today. And your lunch." She flapped her hands in front of her. "Shoo. Go along now. Unless you're going to stay and help clean up this mess." The group shuffled backward out of the kitchen, with the woman herding them all the way out of the restaurant. "If you already ate, don't forget to leave your cash. And give that poor girl a generous tip for going above and beyond."

The door jingled as everyone left, a few complaints hanging in the air of the suddenly silent diner.

Quinn realized she was still shaking her hands. She held them close to her face to see how badly she'd burned them. She jumped when the woman touched her elbow.

"Let's get some cold water on those. Did you grab the pot without mitts? Why didn't you just turn off the gas?"

Tears filled Quinn's eyes because of the pain, the stupidity, the unfairness, the humiliation, and the woman's act of kindness in taking care of everything.

"Never mind." The woman steered Quinn toward the sink and gently placed her hands under cold running water. After a bit, she lifted one and inspected it. "That doesn't look so bad. I don't even think they'll blister. You were lucky." She placed Quinn's hand back under the water.

"Thank you. I don't even know your name."

"Cynthia. I'm Abe the handyman's daughter. Looks like you got yourself a doozy of a cleanup."

Quinn turned off the water and dried her hands. "And I better get to it before the lunch rush." She glanced toward the pass-through window. "Or anyone else looking for breakfast."

"Don't worry about that. I locked the door. People can do without the Chestnut Diner for a while until you get yourself squared away."

"Thank you so much for taking charge like that. My brain just shut down completely. I couldn't even count."

"Count what?"

"Never mind."

"I wish I could stay to help you clean up, but I've got to get to work myself."

"You've already done enough. Thanks again."

"How are those hands?"

Quinn opened and closed her fists a few times. "I think they're okay." They both inspected her palms closely. "See? It's just red. No blisters or anything."

"Your instincts were good to drop the pot, even though you knew it would make a mess. But maybe next time just turn off the gas under the burner. And wear oven mitts!"

"Thanks." She studied the mayhem forlornly. "Better get to it."

"Walk me out and lock the door behind me. You don't need customers for a while."

"Jake's gonna kill me if he hears I closed up the diner."

Cynthia cocked her head.

"Not kill me…just be real mad…but not real mad, just the regular, appropriate amount of mad." Quinn winced.

"Close the diner. Jake will understand."

Quinn twisted the dead bolt behind her and hoped that was true. Twisting the dead bolt caused her brain to rev. A battery pack of intensity ramped up to *overload*. A cascade of worry wove its way through her. She felt like the needle of a sewing machine. She'd always liked when her mom let her press the foot pedal on the machine to create perfectly even and straight stitches in the fabric. Today, however, each rhythmic *thunk* of her anxiety signaled another catastrophe.

Jake will be mad.

Jake will yell.

Jake will fire me.

The diner will fail.

Jake will be bankrupt.

He'll lose his house.

Jake will sue me.

Mom and Dad will be disappointed.

They'll try to pay Jake and lose their house too.

They'll kick me out.

I have no money.
I'll be homeless.
I won't be able to afford my meds.
I'll never get back to normal.

Chapter 8

It took Quinn more than an hour to stop her cycle of catastrophizing. From her research about OCD, she knew that's what was happening, but nowhere did the research tell her how to end the cycle. She stopped it by letting her mind go blank while she cleaned up the oatmeal, spoonful by spoonful.

One thousand and fifty-six of them.

When she was done, she collapsed in Jake's office chair and felt sorry for herself for a few minutes while she gulped ice-cold lemonade.

Exhausted but calmer, her palms only throbbed a little from the burn. But this would not do. She could not keep working like this, especially since she was definitely not a short-order cook.

The employee folders were still on the desk, and she pulled the one on top toward her and opened it. She found the section of the job application where it asked what position they were applying for. After sorting all the files into *cook* or *waitress* piles, she started making calls to the ex-cooks of the Chestnut Diner, all men. Maybe she could persuade one of them to come back temporarily.

The first guy she called told her he'd moved to Chicago.

The second one said, "Absolutely not. That job was hard! I work at a print shop in Denver now. Much easier."

The third one said, "I'd love to—you sound cute—but I've got a sweet gig mooching off my girlfriend."

Eww.

The next dozen were all variations of the same.

Quinn dialed the last one, hopeful when she saw it was a local prefix. "Is this Michael Breckenridge? I'm calling from the Chestnut Diner and—"

Click.

Quinn dialed back. "I'm sorry, I just called you but the call must have dropped."

"No, it didn't. I hung up on you." Which he did again.

"Well, I guess there's no love lost between Michael Breckenridge and Jake." She decided to try the waitresses too. Maybe one of them had cooked on occasion. Or might be willing to try. But all the responses were the same: they didn't live here anymore, got another job, didn't want to, *really* didn't want to, and a new excuse, pregnant.

With a sigh, Quinn surveyed the contents of the refrigerator and pantry areas and made a list. Then she dragged the erasable sandwich board from the storage room into Jake's office, gathered some colored markers, measured and marked out evenly spaced lines, and wrote on both sides, *Hot dogs, hamburgers (no cheese), salad, fries, chili. While it lasts. Cash only.*

When she was satisfied, after wiping off any stray marks and erasing one side completely three times because it seemed crooked, she unlocked the door and manhandled the heavy sign to the sidewalk in front of the diner.

She'd only closed for a few hours and was open for lunch, so Jake couldn't complain too much. Plus, his kitchen was probably cleaner than it had even been before. Thinking about Jake getting mad at her made Quinn's heart race. She pressed her right thumb to each of her fingers in turn, then did the same with her left hand. Soon, her breathing slowed.

Customers wandered in right away, some not even aware she'd been closed.

The Retireds, on the other hand, shuffled in complaining, Wilbur the loudest and most annoyed with her.

"What do you think you're doing, little missy, closing the diner like that?" Wilbur grabbed the Panama hat off his head and slapped it against his thigh, making Quinn jump.

"For the ten-thousandth time, Wilbur, my name's not Little Missy. And you should be happy I closed. There was a ... kitchen mishap."

"Mishap." Herman stared at her, as if he was hearing the word for the first time. Quinn didn't know if he was asking a question or just checking the mouthfeel of the word.

Larry put a hand on her shoulder and asked quietly, "Is everything okay?"

"Everything's fine, Larry, thanks." Quinn patted his hand. Ever since he lost his wife just after Quinn started at the diner, he'd been desperate for company and human touch.

"At least the diner's open now, eh?" Bob did a little soft-shoe before he sat down at their regular table.

When Bob finished his dance, Silas said, "A little song, a little dance, a little seltzer in your pants."

Quinn placed two full pots of coffee on their table. "Go nuts, boys," then she went into the kitchen and dumped a bunch of hot dogs into water to boil. She readied buns, organized condiments for do-it-yourself fixins, tossed a huge bowl of salad, dumped cans of chili into the huge pot she'd just cleaned oatmeal out of, placed oven mitts nearby, and said a prayer to the fryer.

Lunch went much better than breakfast. People seemed happy enough to order from the limited menu, except for the Retireds, who peppered her with a million questions, all of which she answered with "No."

By simplifying the menu and streamlining her prep, Quinn easily kept up with the demands of the kitchen and the front of the restaurant. Generally, she wasn't wild about having OCD, but if it was her albatross, sometimes having something to obsess over—like the diner—was useful. As long as she was obsessing about something external, she could keep her compulsive rituals at bay.

As she was in the kitchen between customers, eating a hot dog herself, Quinn heard the door jingle, then Loma's voice. "Jake? Hey, Jake, I need to talk to you."

Before Quinn could finish the last bite, Loma was in the kitchen, snapping the rubber band on her wrist. "Where's Jake?"

Quinn held up one finger while she swallowed.

Loma snapped the band fast and rhythmically, eyes darting around the kitchen. "Is he in his office? I really need to talk to him."

What is she so guilty about? Quinn wondered, following Loma into Jake's office. "He's not here."

"When will he be back?"

"I don't know."

"Would you tell him to call me? I have something important to tell him."

Quinn debated for a hot minute not to tell her about Jake, but decided she'd find out soon enough. "Loma, Jake's been arrested."

"Makes sense. It's criminal how good he still looks after all these years."

"I'm not joking. He's been arrested."

Loma choked off a laugh. "For what?"

"Murder."

Loma narrowed her eyes. "You're playing with me."

"I'm not."

"Who'd he murder, then?"

"A guy he used to work with. Emmett Dubois."

Loma wobbled and grabbed the desk for support. Quinn could see she wanted to ask more questions, because her mouth kept opening and closing.

"Sit down. I'll get you some lemonade." Before Quinn got through the doorway, Loma had pushed her aside and was running through the dining room.

As Quinn watched her go, she couldn't help but wonder what Loma needed to talk to Jake so desperately about. She couldn't quite put her finger on why she thought Loma looked so guilty. Maybe the nervous snapping, coupled with her warning yesterday to Jake: "You'll be sorry." Sorry about what? Loma seemed surprised that Jake had been arrested, but maybe she was a good actor. Or maybe she wasn't surprised about Jake—maybe she was surprised that Emmett Dubois had been murdered. She probably knew him too, if Jake had worked with him back in the day.

"Stop. Just stop it." Quinn put her hands on either side of her head, as if that would choke off the thoughts swirling around in there. All of Quinn's questions were unanswerable right now. Easier not to ask anything.

Not much was happening with the late-lunch crowd, but she kept her brain occupied by refilling drinks, accepting a couple payments, and wiping off tables. As she did, she thought about the murder. It just didn't make sense. Why would Jake serve mushrooms only to Emmett? And why did Emmett come to the diner afterward? She wondered about the guest list for the fundraiser. Who else was there besides Jake, Donnie, his mom, and the governor? The murder mystery guy.

Finally, she called Rico. "What's happening with Jake? Did his ex-wife show up?"

"Show up where?"

"At the station. To see Jake."

"Nope. She hasn't been here."

"Weird. She rushed out of here and I just assumed she was going to see Jake. She came in the diner all hot to talk to him."

"About what?"

"I don't know." Quinn paused. "What else is going on over there? Any leads? Is Jake getting out soon?"

"Doesn't look like it."

"Tell me more about this fundraiser thingy that he was at."

"Quinn, I can't. I gotta go."

Rico disconnected and Quinn stared at her phone. She knew she couldn't close the diner again, but she had questions. *Maybe the fiasco with the oatmeal and the cash register refusing to open was a sign that instead of running the diner, I should help Jake by getting him out of jail. I'm sure there's something I could help Rico with.*

She dialed the police station and asked to speak with Donnie. "Hey, it's Quinn over at the diner. Have you had lunch yet?"

"No."

"Come to the diner, then."

"I've heard you're not a very good cook."

"Don't be silly. I'm a perfectly adequate cook. To prove it, it'll be on the house."

Apparently Donnie thought free food that wasn't very good was an acceptable trade-off, because he said he'd be over in a bit. Quinn barely knew anything about Donnie, but if he was somehow involved in this, Rico might not be able to get at the truth. Donnie was, after all, a fellow cop and the governor's stepson. Perhaps even a nepotism hire.

When he got to the diner, Quinn served him a burger only slightly pinker than he wanted ("people pay extra for steak tartare"), fries that were hardly burned at all ("just a good, rich brown"), and a cup of chili he agreed wasn't terrible. Quinn didn't tell him it came out of a can.

Between customers, she sat with him. "How come you don't come in the diner for lunch every day like Rico does?"

"Mom said my uniform was getting tight." He shoved French fries in his mouth. "Don't tell her I was here, okay?"

"I don't even know your mom." With his mouth full, he bugged his eyes out at her so she added, "Fine. Your secret is safe with me." Quinn fiddled with one of the place settings of silverware wrapped with a napkin. "Speaking of secrets…tell me more about that fundraiser."

"It's not a secret, I don't think, but I don't know if I should…"

"I have some ice cream in the freezer."

"What kind?"

"Chocolate, vanilla, and pistachio."

Donnie leaned in. "Can I have all three?"

For someone in his mid-to-late twenties, he sure acted like an eight-year-old. "Of course. Be right back."

After clearing a table and taking payment for the last diners, Quinn slid a bowl with three heaping scoops of ice cream in front of Donnie. "So tell me about the fundraiser." She hoped the ice cream would act as truth serum.

"Not really much to tell," he said, digging in. "For most of it I was hanging out in the kitchen away from all the hoopla. Mom kept introducing me to people I didn't want to talk to, so I was hiding. She made me come in uniform, can you believe it?"

"She's just proud of you, I bet."

A man held an empty glass in the air and Quinn jumped up to give him a refill. When she got back to the table she prodded Donnie to continue his story. "So...you were hanging out in the kitchen?"

He slurped a hunk of pistachio ice cream off his spoon. "Yeah. And one of the waiters asked if I'd do him a favor and bring a plate to one of the guests, a Mr. Dubois. Said it was a special diet request and very important. Told me the cook himself asked for it to be delivered. I was just standing around, so I did him a solid."

"You knew Jake was the cook?"

"Of course. I'm not blind. He was standing eight feet away from me."

"Who was the waiter?"

"Don't know."

"Could you identify him if you saw him again?"

"Doubt it. It was a guy, though."

A woman with twin boys came in the diner. Quinn called out, "Sit anywhere you want. I'll be right there." They chose the big corner booth. She turned back to Donnie. "Didn't you think it was weird that he asked you to deliver the plate and that those were the only mushrooms in the place?"

"I didn't know until later that those were the only mushrooms served. And why wouldn't he ask me to help? I was just standing around."

"Didn't you say you were in uniform? If I saw a cop in a kitchen at a fundraiser for the governor, I'd assume he was on duty, not an extra pair of hands for a lazy waiter."

Donnie shrugged and shoved the last bite of chocolate ice cream in his mouth.

Quinn had more questions, so she didn't want to annoy him by arguing about something that this unknown waiter did that they'd probably never know the answer to, anyway. Assuming Donnie was telling the truth, that is. To Quinn, that seemed like a gigantic assumption. "You told Rico right away about the mushrooms, and even thought to preserve the leftovers from Emmett's plate?"

"Yeah, well, believe it or not, I'm not just another pretty face. I'm actually an officer of the law." He plucked at his uniform. "I was still at the fundraiser, because my mother would not let me leave, when I heard the call about the dead guy—er, victim, here at the diner. I remembered his name and scooped up the plate before it got washed. Police one-oh-one."

Quinn cut her eyes to the corner booth.

Donnie added, voice dripping with sarcasm, "Even a lowly plebe like me was able to put two and two together."

"Lady? Can we have some root beer?" one of the twins asked.

As Quinn poured two root beers, she studied Donnie stabbing at the last vestiges in his ice cream bowl. He couldn't identify the waiter who handed him the mushrooms, but jumped to the conclusion that they were poisonous just by hearing the chatter about Emmett Dubois at the diner? Quinn ran through the events after finding the body. She couldn't remember Rico or the paramedics saying anything about mushrooms or poisoning. Everyone was thinking heart attack. At least she was thinking heart attack and assumed everyone else was. But she had run out of there while Rico, Chief Chestnut, and the paramedics had stayed.

Quinn delivered the root beers and took their food order. Before going into the kitchen, though, she stopped in front of Donnie. "Pretty lucky you were still at the fundraiser when that call came in." *I wonder if he has a grudge of some kind against Jake.* "Who else was at the fundraiser?"

"Jake's ex-wife. Emmett Dubois's ex-wife. Bunch of people who used to work with him."

"Him who?"

"The victim … Emmett Dubois."

"How do you know they used to work with Emmett?"

"Um…because I'm investigating his murder?" Splotches of color appeared on Donnie's face and neck. His jaw tightened. "We got a list right away of everyone working that night. Governor's party, remember? Stuff happens fast when my stepfather, the governor"—Donnie's face puckered like he ate a lemon—"wants it to." He made a noise that could only be described as a *harumph.*

It was obvious to Quinn that Donnie had a challenging relationship with both his mother and his stepfather. She excused herself and hurried into the kitchen to scoop up a salad for the woman and place hot dogs in buns for the boys. She pointed out the condiments.

"Where are my fries?"

"Yeah. You forgot our fries!"

She stared at their petulant eight-year-old faces. "We're out. Sorry." She had a momentary pang when she thought how disappointed Rico would be with her if he knew she told two lies in three words. Too bad, she thought, she was in the middle of an important interrogation. "Fries aren't good for you."

"Neither is root beer, but you gave us that."

"True. You want me to get you some water?" She loomed over them.

"No, ma'am," they both stammered.

Slightly ashamed of her lack of customer service, Quinn glanced at their mother and visibly relaxed when she saw the woman stifling a smile.

Just as well, she thought, heading back to Donnie. *I have more important things on my mind than French fries.* Maybe a disgruntled employee of Emmett's poisoned him. They had to get someone else to deliver the mushrooms so they wouldn't be recognized—either by Emmett, in case it didn't work, or by the other waiters, in case it did. "Tell me about that anonymous call you took."

"It was a call. And it was anonymous." Donnie narrowed his eyes at her. "Why do you want to know all this?"

"I'm trying to help Jake—"

"Why don't you just leave it to us." He said it as a statement, not a question. More like a verbal head pat, which was annoying enough, but he was younger than she was, which really peeved her.

She wanted to say, *Why don't I leave it to you? Because I don't trust you.* But she didn't. Before she could ask him anything else, Donnie suddenly pushed back from the table, grabbed his duty cap, and bolted down the hallway, and out the back door of the restaurant.

Quinn was still staring in the direction he'd gone when Rico pulled up the chair next to her and said, "Wanna go on a date with me?"

She jumped and spewed some choice words strung together in a way her grandmother had probably never heard before. "Jeez, you scared me!"

"Sorry."

"Did you see Donnie? He ran out of here just now like he was on fire."

"Nope." He glanced at the remains of Donnie's lunch. "Maybe it was something he ate."

"Very funny." Quinn's smile vanished when she saw Rico's truth-telling face. "His lunch was perfectly fine. Aren't you here to eat?" She stood and reached to clear Donnie's place, perhaps with a bit more force than was necessary because Rico placed his hand on her forearm.

"No, I don't have time. Sit down for a minute." Rico glanced around the tables. "It doesn't look too busy. You've probably been at it all morning."

Quinn sighed and returned the plate to the table. "You don't know the half of it."

"How are you doing?"

"I've been better." She ran her fingers through her hair, then re-clipped her messy bun. "How's Jake? How's the investigation going?"

"Chief still thinks Jake killed Emmett."

"You'll just have to prove otherwise."

"It's not that easy, Quinn."

The thirsty man again waved at her from across the restaurant. When he caught her eye, he raised his empty glass.

She nodded at the man as she stood, then asked Rico, "Why not?"

"I can't talk to you about this."

One of the twins called to her, "Hey, lady. Can we just get our own refills? You're too slow."

"Sure. Go ahead. If it's okay with your mom."

The woman shrugged. "Knock yourself out. The lady's clearly got better things to do." As the boys jumped up, she grabbed one of them by the arm. Dipping the corner of her napkin in her water glass, she wiped a smear of mustard from his face.

Quinn hoped this wouldn't get back to Jake. She whispered in Rico's ear. "Why can't you talk to me?"

He whispered back, "It's unethical. And even if I wanted to, this isn't the time or place."

"Was it unethical when I helped you solved that bicycle theft?"

"Well…no. That was just friendly conversation."

She felt anger and frustration bubbling up, at Rico, at the twins, at customers in general. Before she made anything worse, she refilled the man's iced tea and placed Donnie's dirty dishes in the plastic busing tub. She calmed herself further by adjusting everything on the table into its proper place. She was aware of Rico's eyes on her. Square container of single-serve jellies in the center of the table, grape packets on the left side, strawberry on the right. She plucked out a container of grape and dropped it into her apron pocket so each side had the same amount. Salt and pepper centered against the right side of the jelly container. Tabasco centered on the left. Fake flower in a short vase in the back. Napkin dispenser at the front. She pushed on the napkins, alarmed at the amount of play in the mechanized spring. She'd have to deal with filling it later. She'd have to deal with everything later. But right now, without looking at Rico, she grabbed the tub and carried it into the kitchen.

He followed her. "Have you been sleeping?"

She flung the dishes into the dishwashing tray. "Not really."

"Taking your meds?"

She stopped and glared at him.

"Quinn, I just—"

Leaning against the sink, she sighed. "I know. I'm fine. It's just that…I really want to help Jake."

"You are. You're running the diner for him."

"I want *him* to be running the diner."

"So do I."

Quinn heard the customers talking to each other. The woman said, "Do you think we can just leave the money here? I promised these boys I'd take them to a movie."

"That's what I'm going to do," the man said. "But I wanted some pie first."

Quinn called through the pass-through, "Be right there!" She looked at Rico, then back toward the pass-through. Rico was absolutely right. *This is not the time or place to have a real conversation. If I'm going to learn anything about the investigation, we'll need to be away from the diner and away from the police station.*

"Wait here," she told Rico.

As Quinn handled the customers, she assessed Rico. That unfortunate hair, but at least he kept it short. Tall, lanky, no bulging muscles, but he could probably carry most people out of a burning building. What would she say to someone to sell them on a blind date with Rico? He's funny. He's gentle and kind. He would absolutely never lie to you, guaranteed. He was nice to old people and animals, and she'd seen him go out of his way to calm a red-faced, squalling baby by speaking soothingly and letting it latch on to his finger with a tiny fist. Quite endearing, actually. A person could do worse. Way worse.

He even deflected praise at the police station, despite the fact he did all the work over there.

Dating her best friend still seemed like a stupid idea. Dating her best friend to get information about a police investigation seemed ridiculously stupid. But she couldn't shake the niggling thought that Donnie was somehow involved in this and that Rico and Chief Chestnut were rallying behind him as one of their brothers in blue. She couldn't really see Rico covering up a crime or even bending the rules for a fellow officer, but she had been extolling the virtues of a well-placed white lie for quite some time now. She'd argued that there were many circumstances where telling the truth was not a very good idea, and in fact, even dangerous. Lies could be necessary. Like when a woman said she had a gun to scare away a burglar. Or a *Beware of Dog* sign with no dog on the premises. Maybe Rico finally learned the lesson.

At any rate, Rico was absolutely right that the diner wasn't a good place to have a meaningful conversation, since she was jumping up every three seconds to refill sodas or take orders. A quiet place to talk was exactly what they needed.

Quinn returned to the kitchen to find Rico with his face above the pot of chili and a Styrofoam container in his hand.

"Changed my mind about lunch. Think I'll take some of this chili to go."

"Oh, you won't want that."

Rico cocked an eyebrow. "Because..."

"Because it may prove embarrassing on our date tonight."

He grinned wide and handed the to-go container to her. "Bring me the blandest thing you can find. Do you have any oatmeal? And make it snappy—I need to get a haircut."

Yep. Way worse.

* * * *

Rico sat in Mrs. Olansky's chair while she gave him a trim. He let the drone of hair dryers, clippers, and voices wash over him. He closed his eyes.

He knew going on a date with Quinn was probably stupid, but he couldn't help it. Ever since she got back to Chestnut Station he couldn't stop thinking that it might be their destiny to be together. They had all that history and neither one of them had many prospects here in town.

Apprehension nipped at him, though. He knew Quinn was going through a rough patch, rougher than anything he'd seen before. He felt honored that she trusted her diagnosis with him. The way she described her OCD was vivid and compelling, but completely unlike anything he'd ever experienced. She told him that it felt like she constantly carried a fully charged battery pack in the back of her head. She explained that if she didn't aim it at something—whether it was at her counting or organizing or solving crosswords—or something else, she'd burst. After her interview with the Denver police, she told him all that anxiety and obsessive thinking got pointed back at her and that's why she couldn't function. She told him the resulting depression was like wearing one of those weighted x-ray vests their dentist made them wear.

Watching Quinn today, he'd noticed her counting and organizing, but he also noticed when she was talking to those twins she was doing something with her fingers he'd never seen her do before, touching each finger to her thumb. He wondered if she was even conscious of it. Was it just something to do with her hands or was it another compulsive ritual?

He'd ask her about it on their date tonight.

"What are you grinning about, Rico?" Mrs. Olansky brushed the hair off the back of his neck.

"My date tonight."

She unsnapped the cape draped around him and handed him a mirror. "I'm not going to ask how you like it because I'm never sure I want to know."

Rico held the mirror up to catch his reflection in the large mirror over her station. "It's perfect, Mrs. O."

And it was.

* * * *

The rest of the afternoon passed without too much kitchen drama, but Quinn was wrung out by 4:00 when she looked up at the sound of the door jingling and saw Chief Chestnut's bony frame striding into the diner. He held the newspaper folded to the page with the crossword puzzle.

"Coffee," he barked at her.

What is his problem? Quinn grabbed a mug and briefly considered making a fresh pot before deciding he wasn't worth the effort. She placed the mug next to the puzzle and filled it, sloshing a bit out.

"Watch it!" He yanked the puzzle away and blotted it with his napkin.

Quinn stood by the beverage station and watched him sip his stale coffee and work the puzzle. Chief Chestnut was an odd duck. He did the downs before the acrosses. Quinn had never heard of anyone doing that before. Was it some sort of strategy? Was it easier that way? Harder? Does he just like going against the grain?

She sauntered over with the coffeepot. "Interesting. You do the downs first."

"What of it?"

"Nothing. I've just never seen anyone do that before." She topped off his mug.

"Just like changing it up."

Quinn stared at the answers he'd filled in and wondered if she should tell him 18-down was wrong.

"Do you mind?" He shooed her away.

"Can I ask you a question?" She didn't wait for an answer. "When's Jake getting out of jail?"

"Never, if I have anything to say about it." His lips disappeared as he smiled a joyless smile, showing his crooked teeth. "Oh, yeah. I do have something to say about it."

"Chief Chestnut, sir, you know Jake didn't kill anybody."

"I know nothing of the sort." He returned his attention to the puzzle and Quinn knew she'd been dismissed.

She cleaned off tables and squared up corners. The diner was quiet except for her occasional scraping of a chair leg against the linoleum, so she was startled when Chief Chestnut mumbled, "Oh…eighteen-down was wrong." She smiled to herself.

That was the beauty of a crossword: There was only one right answer. If you made a mistake, you had several chances to fix it, as long as you weren't completely pigheaded to think your first answer was always correct. The reason they said crosswords were good exercise for the brain was because they forced you to make connections that you might not normally make. Like, if the clue was *cheers*. You needed to decide if they meant the sitcom or a toast. Or if *rib* referred to a barbecue entrée, a body part, or teasing.

And you always knew by a question mark in a clue whether the answer was going to be a pun or a little joke. Place for a retired soldier? *Cot.* Do business? *Salon.* Wheels of fortune? *Limo.*

Exercise for the brain.

Chief Chestnut was pigheaded about many things, but the crossword was not one of them. He could admit mistakes and change his thinking in a puzzle grid, at least.

Change his thinking. Quinn's eyes lit up. Of course! *Chief Chestnut does every single one of my puzzles, but has no idea I make them. What if I sent him some subliminal messages through the crossword? What if I got him to think about investigating someone other than Jake?*

But who?

* * * *

Rico picked her up that evening and they finally escaped the hugs and knowing glances from Quinn's parents. Quinn knew they'd wanted to see this date materialize for quite some time, but… sheesh.

"I'm sorry about all that." Quinn was relieved to be buckling herself into Rico's Toyota rather than the backseat of the police cruiser.

"About all what?" Rico winked at her.

After insisting that he swing by the diner so she could check the locks and make sure everything was shut off, they decided on the busy Chinese restaurant out near the highway, usually filled with cross-country travelers who didn't want fast food, but who also didn't want to come the three miles into town. Quinn appreciated Rico suggesting it, wondering if he, like she, knew that few locals ate there. It wasn't like she was embarrassed to be seen eating dinner with him, since they did that quite often. But it would be nice if nobody pegged them as being on an actual date, which they would if they saw Quinn in a sundress with her hair styled in something other than her struggle bun, and Rico wearing khakis and a dressy shirt.

On the way to the restaurant Rico said, "How was work today? Are you managing okay?"

"You too?" Quinn sighed. "Mom and Dad grill me constantly. I wish you guys would quit worrying." He started to say something but she cut him off. "I know you mean well, but everything's fine. Like I told them, I'm just trying to get my sea legs. As soon as I organize stuff better, I'll be great. You should see how far Jake keeps the knives from the prep table. And none of the containers are marked! I'll take my label maker over there tomorrow and fix it all up." Quinn quickly chose a new subject and put this one to rest. "How are the Rockies doing?"

"Terrible. No pitching, no fielding, no hits. They're barely playing baseball."

Quinn let Rico bellyache about his team the rest of the way to the restaurant.

After they were seated, Quinn glanced around. Rico noticed and said, "I don't recognize anyone. Do you?"

"That's not what I—"

"It's nobody's beeswax what we do."

"Except my family, of course."

"Of course. Should I have asked Fang for permission to escort you to dinner?"

"You could have. But he probably wouldn't give you a straight answer. He's very koi."

Rico grinned. "It's understandable. You know, he used to have a girlfriend but then he lobster."

"Sad."

"Yes, but then he flounder."

"He has a lox on his plate now."

"Some people don't like fish puns, but these are kraken me up."

"If you think of any more, let minnow."

"Nah, I've been telling too many. I'll have to scale down."

The server brought them both a Tsingtao beer, interrupting their pun war. She left them to peruse the menu.

Rico raised his glass and Quinn clinked hers against it. "Here's to first dates," he said.

"And fishy puns," Quinn added before taking a sip. "Why'd you give me Fang, anyway? Was it really just to thank me or was it because of"—she waved her hand across the table—"all this?"

"Flowers felt too personal, especially after all the times you turned me down, and I knew what would happen with your parents if I suddenly showed up with a dozen roses."

"Pretty much the same thing that happened tonight."

"Pretty much. And a kitten or a puppy seemed like too much work, but a goldfish seemed just right. Are you feeding him okay? Not too much, remember."

Quinn flushed at his condescension. She immediately let go of her annoyance, though, because she was, in fact, overfeeding Fang. And she knew it. It was difficult knowing he was only to receive twenty flakes, which she counted into her palm, then watch as so many of them drifted down, settling into the colored gravel she'd added at the bottom of the bowl. Did the fish food people know how many flakes would sink to the bottom and take that into consideration? Did they have a complicated algorithm that calculated *flakes pinched* minus *flakes lost* to equal the correct amount of food per goldfish? Was Fang normal for a goldfish? She knew he'd gorge himself on the new flakes she dropped in and probably hoover up whatever had fallen earlier, but the entire process was almost more than she could handle. What if she starved him? Why couldn't he just eat the twenty flakes before they fell? Then they'd both be happy.

"Fang's fine." Quinn picked up her menu, lightly touching each appetizer description. "What shall we order?"

Dinner was delicious and she enjoyed herself, beginning with the egg rolls and wontons, all the way through the cashew chicken and kung pao beef. But when Rico ordered red bean buns and lychee ice cream for dessert, Quinn began to get nervous. This was a date, after all, not just dinner with Rico. All too soon it would be after dinner, with all the potential land mines to navigate. Quinn tapped each finger to her thumbs, once, twice, three times.

Quinn realized Rico was getting nervous too because he dropped both his credit card and the leather check presenter, then practically gave the poor server a concussion when he dove for them.

She was ready to leave, but knew that meant driving home and some sort of awkward kiss. But maybe it wouldn't be awkward, she thought. Maybe it would be perfectly natural, sparks would fly, and they'd end up happily ever after. They'd set up at Rico's tiny house, give Fang his own room, and invite her parents over for Sunday brunch.

Quinn tapped her fingers again. Once, twice, three times. Four.

At a stoplight she watched a trickle of sweat run down Rico's temple. He caught her looking and wiped it away with the back of his hand.

Twice they spoke at the same time. Quinn held up her hand, stop-sign style. "You first."

Rico pointed at the park as they drove past. "I was just going to ask if you remembered when Carla Mason broke her arm there."

"Man, that was revolting. Elbows shouldn't bend that way."

He turned a corner, tipping his chin toward the steps of the Catholic church. "And that's where you made out with Jimmy for the first time."

"Also revolting. He was a wet one." They passed the Tastee Q. "And that's where you stalked that poor girl every afternoon when she was just trying to earn an honest day's minimum wage scooping ice cream. Whatever happened to her?"

"She couldn't control herself in my presence. Finally her family had to move away to give her some semblance of normal life."

"Oh, I remember. Her dad sold their ranch and they moved to Denver."

"Isn't that what I said?"

Quinn relaxed her grip on the armrest, hoping Rico had calmed a bit as well.

In the middle of the next block, he made an abrupt U-turn, flinging her against the car door.

"Whoa. What are you doing?"

He cleared his throat. "I wasn't thinking and started driving to my house. But you probably want to—you don't—your parents—"

"I'm over thirty, Rico. My parents don't get to—"

"I know. I just…"

"Me too. Yes, to my house."

Rico looked as relieved as she felt. She knew they certainly wouldn't be getting intimate tonight, but it was definitely better not to be at his house, just in case. She popped a mint in her mouth and crunched it nervously, seven times, turning her face toward the window so Rico wouldn't hear.

They pulled up to the curb in front of Quinn's house. The lights were out, but she wouldn't put it past her parents to be sitting in the dark, watching for this moment. Hopefully, Mom wouldn't come running out in her robe taking pictures she'd post on Facebook of "the happy day Quinn and Rico began their lives together."

She started to tell Rico about her mom's hypothetical Facebook post, but the second she turned toward him, he leaned over and kissed her. Quinn let it happen at first, then joined in.

It didn't take long, though, before her brain took over in two-part harmony. The melody sang the words: *I'm ruining everything. He's too nice for me. We're so different. We'll fight about everything. This is more awkward than I anticipated. What do I do if his hands start moving?* But then the bass began beating a rhythm: *This isn't good...this isn't good... this isn't good.* All thrummed louder and louder until she closed her eyes and pulled away.

Her breathing was ragged.

His eyes were wide.

In unison they said, "I'm sorry!"

Rico scooted back toward the driver's door. "Quinn, that was like kissing—"

"My brother!"

"You don't have a brother."

"I know. But if I did, it would be icky — just like that. Probably."

"Icky?" Rico gazed at his hands.

Quinn took them in hers. "No. Not icky. Not at all. Just not...for me." The last thing she wanted to do was hurt his feelings. Her eyes welled.

They locked eyes. Then Rico smiled sadly. "Not for me either." He squeezed her hands. "No sparks over here."

"Oh, thank goodness! Rico, I was so—"

Rico leaned in for another kiss, pulling away fairly quickly. "Nope. Nothin'. You?"

Quinn shook her head. "Three out of five?" She leaned forward and they tried again. After a bit the kiss dissolved into giggles.

"You can't say we didn't try," Rico said.

"We can both report back honestly to my parents."

They sat in comfortable silence.

"I'm glad we tried, though." Quinn spoke softly.

Rico nodded.

Quinn said, "I saw me ruining everything. Fighting constantly—"

"About me being sloppy."

"And me being...me."

"And the logical conclusion?" he asked.

"We'd have an ugly breakup and wouldn't be friends anymore."

"And I'd cry," Rico said. "You know how I hate to cry." He looked her in the eyes. "You've come a long way, Quinn."

"Have I?"

They sat quietly, watching miller moths flit around the streetlight.

"I feel bad for you that things didn't work out in Denver with the DPD like you wanted, but I gotta say, I'm glad you're back in town," Rico said.

"I'm glad we decided to be friends and that this horrifying little experiment didn't blow up in our faces."

"I don't know what I was thinking. It was like kissing my grandma, my sister, and my cousin all at once."

"Your sexy grandma-sister-cousin, you mean."

"Ew."

"I'm glad I'm back too. I sure don't miss waitressing at that skuzzy Denver truck stop or living in that awful motel."

"What? Places you rent by the week aren't posh?"

"Don't tell my parents, but what finally sent me back here wasn't Mom's begging—although she had really upped her game—but when some junkie kicked in my door." Quinn cut Rico a sidelong glance. "What am I saying? Of course you're going to tell my parents."

Rico was quiet for a moment. "So what if you can't be a Denver cop. Lots of people wash out in the early stages."

"Before they even get to the academy?"

Rico didn't answer. "Now that you know what's expected to get into the academy, you could try again. I whipped you into good physical shape, didn't I? Taught you all those tactical holds? You definitely should try again. Then apply here in Chestnut Station."

"No openings. Besides, that's not my calling anymore."

"What is your calling?"

"Working at Jake's diner. For now."

"And apply to the Chestnut PD in the future?"

"Chief Chestnut would never hire me." Quinn turned sideways in her seat, glad Rico had swung the conversation in her direction. She'd almost forgotten about Jake's investigation. "How 'bout I just help you with your cases? You're always saying you need someone to bounce ideas off of since Chief Chestnut and Donnie aren't interested. You could use my stellar skills."

Rico thought about Quinn telling him she needed something to obsess over that didn't include her anxieties. He had noticed again at dinner she was doing the finger thing, so he asked her about it.

"Yeah. That's something new I started the other day."

"Is it subconscious?"

"No. Absolutely not. I do it because it calms me. That's what the compulsive part of OCD does—gives some control."

"But I thought you did the counting and the organizing for that."

"And now I do this too."

"Because of the Jake thing?"

"Probably."

Rico tried touching his thumb to his fingers. It didn't make him feel anything. He stopped and they stared at each other. Finally he said, "You did help me solve that bike theft when I was stumped."

"It's a deal, then. You tell me all about your cases and I'll help you solve them."

"I can't tell you everything, but I do have a tiny budget for freelance investigative work."

"You're going to pay me? Awesome! What if Chief Chestnut finds out?"

"I'm actually not going to pay you and the chief won't find out, because you'll do it pro bono and not tell anyone."

"Then why'd you tell me you had a budget?"

Rico frowned. "Because I do. Let's just hope nobody asks me anything about it."

"Why, Rico, I think that's almost like telling a fib!"

His nose twitched. "Don't remind me."

Quinn held her pinky in the air. "Partners?" Rico caught it with his pinky. They finished their exchange by dancing their entwined pinkies while making the Three Stooges noise—*woo woo woo* up toward the roof, then *nyuk, nyuk, nyuk* coming down.

They were both quiet for a moment, letting their brains catch up with everything that had happened this evening.

Finally Quinn broke the silence. "Donnie told me he was given that plate with mushrooms by one of the cater-waiters, who he says he can't identify."

"Yeah?"

"Well, Jake hates mushrooms—"

"So I've heard."

"He never cooks with them, obviously never eats them, and I'm sure doesn't know anything about them. If they were the poisoned kind, he'd never even know." Quinn shifted in her seat, pulling her leg up under her so she was turned toward Rico. "We have to figure out who brought those mushrooms to the fundraiser."

"An anonymous caller said Jake did."

"Do you believe that?"

"No."

"Then we have to find out who did."

"Don't you think we've been trying? They just came in a plastic bag you can get at any grocery store."

"Can you just buy poisoned mushrooms at a grocery store? Are they like those puffer fish that are such a delicacy in Japan that can kill you if they're cooked the slightest bit incorrectly?"

"No." Rico shook his head emphatically, then reconsidered. "At least I don't think so. But these types of mushrooms have reportedly been found all over Colorado. In Denver, in the suburbs—Aurora, Castle Rock, Monument, Colorado Springs. Anywhere there are oak trees."

Quinn chewed her pinky nail. "Any idea why Donnie sprang into action and had the presence of mind to get those mushrooms tested? You said he's never shown initiative before."

Rico drummed his thumbs on the steering wheel. "I've been wracking my brain about that since this started." He looked at Quinn with lips pressed into a tight slash. "I just don't know. It's really not his MO."

Quinn fiddled with her necklace. "Maybe someone told him to."

"I've been thinking the same thing."

"Maybe you should keep a close eye on Donnie. Up until now you've always talked about him just being green. Maybe you can't trust him."

Rico grabbed the steering wheel with both hands. Even in the glow of the distant streetlight Quinn saw his knuckles turn white. "The idea of not being able to—he's part of the—you have to be able to trust—"

Quinn put her hand on his forearm. "I know. And maybe we're wrong. But until we know...." She squeezed his arm. "But you can trust me. You know that, right?"

Rico nodded and smiled at her.

They let that hang in the air a minute. Then Rico perked up. "At least the gravy at the diner tested okay. Jake and you are both off the hook for that, at least."

"So Wilbur wasn't up to anything nefarious in the kitchen that night either?"

"Nope. Says he was trying to help you, and I quote, 'Not screw up anyone else's order' end quote. Corroborated by Silas and Larry."

"Well, isn't he just a prince among men. I still don't understand why they just didn't switch burgers."

"I asked them all that. They honest-to-goodness didn't think of it." At Quinn's skeptical face, he added, "You said yourself they're complainers. Clearly they're not problem-solvers."

"Wilbur snuck into the kitchen pretty readily."

"True. But I doubt he'll be doing that again anytime soon. Said helping was for the birds."

"Sometimes I gotta agree with him." Quinn untangled herself so both feet were on the floor.

"Having second thoughts about helping me?"

"Absolutely not." She picked up her purse. *I need this*, she wanted to add.

"Remember, though, that this is my job," Rico said sternly. "There's stuff I won't be able to share with you."

Quinn smiled. She knew how to frame questions just right to make Rico answer her. "Sure. I get that. But I may think of things you haven't thought of. And since you don't have anyone over there to help talk things through, I'm happy to be your sounding board." She already knew she wouldn't be telling him everything she did in order to protect him and his job, if necessary. She didn't want him to get in trouble if she bent any rules.

Quinn leaned over and kissed Rico on the cheek before getting out of the car. As she made her way up the sidewalk to the front door she whispered to herself, "Thanks, Rico."

When she walked in the house, Georgeanne was arranging herself on the couch next to Dan. The TV was tuned to an old *Murder, She Wrote* episode. Quinn thought Georgeanne seemed a bit out of breath.

"Were you spying on me?"

"No." Georgeanne's hand fluttered to her face.

Quinn cocked her head.

"Maybe a little."

"I tried to stop her, Quinn," Dan said.

Georgeanne whacked him on the arm. "Who was the one who dug those out of the closet?" She pointed to a pair of binoculars on the windowsill.

"Dad!"

"Just doing a little bird-watching."

"At night?"

"We were just worried about you, sunshine."

"How much did you see?"

"There was more to see?" Georgeanne's eyes opened wide.

"Mom! Gross. And no, there wasn't. Just enough kissing to make us realize we're just friends and never going on a date again. Definitely no more kissing."

"I guess it's good you figured it out." Georgeanne looked like she might cry.

Quinn laughed. "Jeez, Mom. You look like you'll never see him again. He's not going anywhere. We're still friends. Nothing has changed."

Dan slung his arm around his wife's shoulder, but addressed Quinn. "We just really like Rico. Always have. We kinda hoped—"

"I know, Dad. I kinda did too. But it's way better this way. Trust me."

* * * *

After the episode of *Murder, She Wrote*, Quinn said good night to her parents. "Oh, Mom ... have you heard of anyone in town hosting or attending a murder mystery party on the day of the murder?"

Georgeanne considered the question. "I don't think I do, Quinn. But I can ask around, if you'd like."

"That'd be great. Thanks."

In her room she watched Fang navigate around his bowl while her laptop powered up.

"Seems like you've settled in okay," she said to him.

Fang stopped swimming and opened and closed his mouth a few times. His billowy fins and tail delicately rippled the water, keeping him in place.

"You just let me know if you'd rather be closer to the window instead of here on my nightstand."

A bubble escaped Fang's mouth and drifted to the surface.

"I'm happy to hear you say that, but the offer still stands. Just say the word."

Quinn watched as he took a leisurely lap. When he came back around, she asked, "You hungry?" She picked up her tweezers and the fish food. She counted twenty flakes into her palm then dropped one in the bowl, making sure it was in front of Fang so he could see it.

After he gobbled it down she gave him another. She fed him one flake at a time. The eighteenth one he let fall to the gravel. And the nineteenth. "You're full?" She offered him the last flake, which he nosed, then let drop.

Quinn placed her index finger against the bowl, relieved to know how much he actually ate. Maybe she could do this.

She settled against her headboard and did a search for any local Meetup groups who might have had a party. She wasn't surprised to find there were no Meetup groups of any kind in Chestnut Station. She searched *murder mystery Colorado July* and got nothing. She deleted the *July* and tried again. Still nothing.

She clicked away from the Meetup page and searched *poisonous Colorado mushrooms*. The first item that popped up was an article from a couple of years ago about poisonous mushrooms found in someone's yard in Aurora, just like Rico said. The article cited the Denver Botanic Gardens, but offered a link to the Colorado Mycological Society website.

They had loads of information and Quinn clicked on a map of all the places the poisonous mushrooms had been found in the state. None anywhere near Chestnut Station.

She scrolled and clicked around some more and found nothing Rico hadn't already told her. She watched a short, embedded video of a newscast about those mushrooms found in one of the Denver suburbs. They cut away to an expert who explained it wasn't dangerous to touch the mushrooms, but went into some detail about what could happen if any of it was ingested. Quinn placed a protective hand on her belly. *Gross*. Cut back to the reporter with the poor, unfortunate couple in whose yard the mushrooms were found. They seemed as scared as if they'd uncovered an unexploded bomb. "What if a child or a dog had eaten one?" the woman asked. "We're lucky we found it before anything bad happened," the man said. They didn't report how they'd found the mushrooms.

Why, Quinn wondered, whenever she finished watching a news report or reading an article in the paper, did she have more questions than when she started?

Chapter 9

When Quinn got to the diner in the morning, after she gave Jethro his payment and ushered him back outside, she called Chris, the weekend cook, to beg him to come help out.

"It's Thursday. I don't work 'til Saturday," he said.

"I know, but this is an emergency."

"But it's not Saturday."

Quinn assumed any further conversation would travel this same roundabout. "What about Kristi? Is she there? Can I talk to her?" At least that way there'd be another set of hands. Quinn wasn't wild about having to cook, but she would if she had to.

"She don't work 'til Saturday neither."

"Can I talk to her?"

"Yeah. On Saturday when she comes in."

Seriously? He just hung up on me? Quinn looked at her phone in disbelief. Jake would hear about this.

Quinn looked around Jake's office. Tattling to him wouldn't help anything, although he would definitely hear about this.

The neat pile of ex-employee files remained exactly where Quinn had left them yesterday, an inch from the bottom edge of the desk and an inch from the side. The top file was centered, but at a quarter-turn from the rest. She plucked it off and opened it.

"Michael Breckenridge. The guy who wouldn't talk to me," she muttered.

She used her cell to call the number again. She recognized his voice. "Don't hang up on me! My name is Quinn. I work at the Chestnut Din—"

Seriously? Again? She angrily punched in the number. It went immediately to voice mail. She picked up Jake's desk phone and dialed. Same thing. "He blocked me? On both phones? What is his problem?"

Quinn dropped the receiver into the base and leaned back into Jake's chair. Clearly, this guy does not want to talk to anyone from the Chestnut Diner. Could he carry an old grudge against Jake? Enough to set him up for a murder?

She called Rico from her cellphone. "Do you know of any ex-employees of Jake's who might have a grudge against him?"

"All of them? But I can't talk now, Quinn. Call you later."

She texted him. What kind of partnership is this if you give me the bum's rush? She inserted a tears-squirting-out-of-the-eyes-laughing-face emoji so he'd know she was joking. Kinda. I wanted to tell you there's an ex-employee of Jake's I want to look at closer. She deleted the last few words and retyped I want you to look at closer. Call me when you can.

Of course, none of this got her any closer to opening the diner or having a more successful day. She slapped her head, remembering she hadn't called the credit card people or the cash register people. She opened Jake's bottom drawer and felt for the manila envelope of cash she'd hidden down there. Nobody would think there was a bunch of money under two empty water bottles and a handful of carryout menus from local restaurants. Hiding the menus was probably a good idea. Wouldn't look good to customers that you craved other restaurants' food. Made sense, just didn't look good. "Bad optics," like they said in politics.

Clever concealment or not, she needed to get to the bank to deposit it. But when was she supposed to do that? Maybe if she could clone herself, at least temporarily.

She remembered that a friend worked temp jobs all through college. She loved the flexibility and likened it to being a substitute teacher, working only when she wanted to.

Quinn typed *temp service for restaurants* in her search engine and after clicking around, found listings for *food service staffing*. She found a Denver phone number that looked promising.

"I'm calling from the Chestnut Diner and I need a cook and maybe a waitress today to help me."

"Today?"

"Yeah, like now."

"That might be difficult. Is this for a permanent position?"

"I don't know. Maybe."

"I'm sorry, we're only working with businesses who are temp-to-hire."

"Then that's what I am."

The woman on the other end paused. "Regardless. I don't think we have anyone available for diner work like now."

"When will you have someone?"

The woman sighed. "Ma'am, this isn't Domino's. You can't just call up and order a line cook to be delivered in thirty minutes. There's vetting. There's paperwork."

"Honestly? I just want a warm body that can flip burgers and has a passing knowledge of a small restaurant kitchen. I don't care if they've been vetted. I don't need their paperwork. I'll accept the consequences." *I'll just get Rico to run background checks on anyone they send me.*

The woman sighed again. "Not vetting for them. Vetting for you. You have to enter into a contract with us. It doesn't happen overnight."

"Oh. How long will it take?"

"A month? Three weeks, at the earliest. The gal who does the contracts is on maternity leave and we're swamped. Do you want me to set up an appointment for an interview?"

"No. Never mind."

Quinn hung up and scrolled through the listings again, this time more carefully. Many companies specified the businesses they worked with: hospitals, universities, senior living places. None mentioned supplying short-order cooks for a diner whose owner was sitting in jail and whose waitress was in over her head. Way over her head.

The front door rattled and Quinn jumped up. She should have had the coffee going and breakfast prepped long ago. At least she remembered to stop at the grocery store and buy an industrial-sized box of pancake mix.

Here goes nothing, she told herself as she pasted a welcoming smile on her face for the breakfast rush.

* * * *

The morning went predictably poorly. The regulars—especially the Retireds—were getting tired of fetching their own coffee and the novelty of paying cash for pancakes, scrambled eggs, and bacon had definitely worn off. Especially because there weren't any eggs or bacon left. She should have bought more when she bought the pancake mix, but she could have sworn there was plenty. How in the world did restaurants know how much to buy? Was there some formula, like with the fish food? Some egg-to-person ratio everyone but her knew? Quinn tried to talk people into breakfast chili, but she got no takers.

And when one starving lady who claimed to be "over carbs" finally agreed to have breakfast salad, Quinn had to return to tell her that it had wilted. She couldn't, in good conscience, even serve it for free. The woman left in a huff.

Since when do people get tired of pancakes so fast? This is a diner, for pete's sake.

Word was clearly getting around that there was no good gossip at the diner, nor was there good food. Or any service.

Quinn had mixed feelings about having fewer customers. On the one hand, it meant less work and fewer people complaining about... well, everything. On the other hand, it meant Jake was surely going to lose his diner and Quinn was going to lose her job. And if she lost her job, she'd never be able to move out of her parents' house, since there were no other jobs in Chestnut Station. And because she had no savings, she couldn't go back to Denver either. Not that she wanted to.

She didn't have a choice. She had to figure out this diner thing at the same time she'd work to help Rico get Jake out of jail. If she could just figure out which direction to point Chief Chestnut, she could get busy on her crossword puzzle plan.

She'd start with learning more about the dead man. Between customers she searched Emmett Dubois's name online. The first hit was a testimonial he wrote for Loma's interior design business: *Loma worked closely with me and my team. She readily accepted our input and carefully explained the entire process to us every step of the way. Ours was a large project and we couldn't have been happier with the final results. I heartily recommend Loma and Partnership Design! —Emmett Dubois*

A link to Loma's website was included, so Quinn clicked it. She scrolled through pages and pages of luxurious design jobs Loma had done. The work was eye candy and it made Quinn long for a place of her own to decorate.

She returned to the search page for Emmett Dubois and found his name linked to a restaurant in Denver called the Crazy Mule. She checked their hours. She'd have plenty of time to get there after she closed the diner. Who better to talk to her about Emmett than his employees?

* * * *

It took her about an hour—technically an hour and a quarter, if you included the time she spent checking all the locks, making triple-sure everything was shut off, and verifying the refrigerator continued to work—

but she found the Crazy Mule in a semi-industrial part of town, not too far from Interstate 70. She found a space right up front in the parking lot. It was a big, sprawling place, but wasn't busy. Quinn was seated quickly, near the beverage station toward the back. Her waitress promised coffee.

While she waited, Quinn glanced around the interior, comparing it to the Chestnut Diner. Where the Chestnut Diner was clean, bright, and cozy, the Crazy Mule had certainly seen better days. This decor did not match the opulence shown on Loma's website. *I must have the wrong Emmett Dubois.* The carpet was threadbare and stained, and most of the vinyl seats had at least one spot repaired with duct tape. It seemed vaguely familiar to Quinn, but the restaurant wasn't really in a part of Denver where she had hung out when she'd lived here.

The customers seated near her covered a wide spectrum of demographics—hipsters, young parents with kids, a few men in suits, and at least one family with a couple of bored teenagers traveling through Colorado. The map spread on the table and the exhausted adult faces were a dead giveaway.

The waitress brought coffee in a chipped mug with a faded crazy-looking mule logo on both sides. "Know what you want, hon?" She pulled a pen from behind her ear.

"Actually, can I talk to the manager?"

"I'll ask him to come out."

"That would be great. Thanks." On the drive to Denver, Quinn had already decided that her cover would be to ask about Loma's interior design work, since Emmett's testimonial referred to "his team." It didn't seem right to come right out and ask about Emmett, but an in-person testimonial might work. She hoped the manager wouldn't ask her a boatload of questions. She didn't want to keep track of too many fibs. It wouldn't be a lie to say she'd love to hire Loma and she was intrigued by Emmett's reference. Short and sweet. And completely true.

If the manager talked with her, then Quinn knew she might get some good information on both Emmett and Loma.

Finally, a pudgy man in a cheap suit stepped up to Quinn's table. "I'm the manager. Vince Koneckny. I understand you wanted to talk to me. Is something wrong?" His voice had a tinge of world-weary resignation, with a soupçon of trepidation. Like Quinn was just one more ingredient in the dreadful stew of his life.

"No, not at all." She spoke a bit too cheerfully, as if to make up for his gloominess. "Emmett Dubois said the Crazy Mule was being renovated?"

"Emmett's dead. If he owes you money—"

"No, nothing like that. And I'm sorry for your loss."

"Did you know him?"

"No. I wanted to talk to you about Loma Szabo's interior design company. Emmett wrote a reference for it and I was hoping you were part of the team that worked with her."

"Ah, Loma." He immediately brightened. "I'd recommend her in a heartbeat. I love that woman." He slid into the seat next to Quinn. "What do you want to know?"

Quinn was caught off guard at his helpfulness. If someone had come to chat with her at the diner, she would not have been so helpful. Of course, she also didn't have employees like he did to handle things. She took a sip of coffee to buy some time to think. She put the mug down and looked at him. "What kind of work did Loma do for you?"

"She designed the interiors of some restaurants Emmett used to own." He glanced around the Crazy Mule. "Not this one. This here's a chain. Can't make any upgrades without an act of Congress."

"I'd love to see the other restaurants."

"Sadly, they're all out of business now. Emmett and I both ended up here." He waved the waitress over for more coffee. She topped off Quinn's and set down a mug in front of Vince and filled it. "Thanks, Kelli." He took a sip and made a face. "Loma was great to work with. The project took quite a long time, but she held our hands through the entire process. I was point man on several things. I got to know her pretty well. Kinda felt bad for her, though. She put everything on hold—her own career, having kids—because her ex-husband promised as soon as he was settled in his restaurant career, he'd support her in her interior design business."

Quinn was confused, but pretty sure he was talking about Jake. "But it sounds like she *was* doing interior design. And had her own business."

"Yes, but we were her only client. I'm sure her ex thought he was being magnanimous by letting her do it."

"You're definitely not her only client now. Her website has tons of pictures of work she's done."

"I'm delighted to hear it. I always thought she had a good eye for that kind of thing. In fact, one time—"

"Excuse me, Vince," Kelli said. "I'm sorry to interrupt, but there's another grease fire."

"Oh no!" Quinn started to get up, but he waved her back down.

"Don't worry. Happens all the time." He stood. "Thanks, Kelli." He turned toward Quinn. "I hope you hire Loma. If you need anything else, give me a call. And tell her hi from me when you see her." He walked through the restaurant without picking up his pace in the slightest.

Kelli poured more coffee. She wasn't exactly fat, but neither was she thin. Instead, she was that pleasing plumpness that middle-aged women grew into. Everything was now directed forward, confident and solid, outward evidence of years of being in charge—almost always behind the scenes. If she stood in the rain, the drops would politely withdraw, content to dampen a less capable person.

"Does that happen often?" Quinn asked her.

"Kitchen fires? Yeah."

"That must make it interesting."

Kelli snorted. "I suppose. But it never happened at Emmett's other restaurants." She cut her eyes in the direction her manager had gone. "I'm sorry. I didn't mean to eavesdrop. But I heard Emmett's name and couldn't help myself." She held out her hand. "Kelli Mahan."

"No worries. Pleased to meet you. I'm Quinn." She was thrilled her plan to get intel on Emmett was working out so well. "You were saying?"

"Just that Emmett ran a tight ship, once upon a time. Kinda lost his will when he came to this corporate catastrophe. All kinds of rumors started flying. People said he bribed a health inspector, hadn't paid his taxes, had a gambling problem. I never believed any of it, though."

"You worked for Emmett too?"

Kelli nodded. "A long time. Especially long in the food biz. I started out at his restaurant in Manhattan, but then he and this guy, Jake, had a falling-out. We were all screwed when it went out of business, but at least Emmett helped a bunch of us get new jobs. I landed in Denver." She shrugged. "Emmett was a good guy."

"I'm sorry for your loss." After a respectful pause: "He got you this job?"

Kelli swept an arm out to the side, acknowledging the Crazy Mule. "Yep. In all its glory." She set the coffeepot on the table.

"What was the falling-out with this Jake guy about?"

Kelli waved her hand. "Long story."

"So he was a jerk?"

"No, not at all. He was super-sweet, a really good boss."

"Jake was your boss?" Quinn made a mental note to add a ten-dollar tip for Kelli for all the information.

"Not technically. Emmett was the boss, but Jake was…well, he was the guy who could get things done for everybody. Help with health insurance coverage, get us extra vacation days, that sort of thing. Plus, he was a better cook than Emmett, made much more interesting food. Everyone loved him. I feel terrible for him." She lowered her voice. "I heard he's been arrested. Terrible. Don't get me wrong, Emmett was a good guy and definitely didn't deserve to get murdered, but he had a chip on his shoulder. And all his shenanigans annoyed the investors. I heard a rumor once that the majority shareholder was ready to pull out."

"Who was the majority shareholder?"

"I don't know. Emmett only referred to him as his silent partner."

Partnership Design. Loma's business. Quinn clarified, "Him? The silent partner was definitely a man?"

"Hm. Now that you mention it, I'm not sure. I always assumed, but maybe not."

"What kind of shenanigans was Emmett involved in?"

"Emmett always said that Jake ruined his business and that he was a thief." As Kelli spoke, she glanced around the restaurant. When it was clear nobody needed her, she sat down at Quinn's table and let out a tired sigh.

"Jake stole money? Like embezzlement?"

"No, recipes."

Quinn wrinkled her brow. "I thought you said Jake was the better cook. Why would he steal recipes?"

"He wouldn't. People say weird stuff. For a long time there was a rumor about Jake's wife and Emmett, but I never believed it. Until Emmett told me it was true, that is."

"An affair?"

"Not exactly. According to Emmett, one time Loma—that's Jake's wife—came to him and said they should have an affair to get back at Jake and Emmett's wife, Margosha."

"Jake and this Margosha were having an affair?" Quinn's head was spinning. This was the best ten bucks she ever spent.

"They were sure spending a bunch of time together, if you know what I mean. Margosha was from Bulgaria or someplace. In her fifties, but absolutely gorgeous, with no work done, or so I've heard. But anyway, when Loma suggested that she and Emmett have this affair, Emmett said 'Gross!' and laughed right in Loma's face!"

"Ouch."

"Exactly. And he told the story to everyone, over and over again, laughing every single time."

Quinn was puzzled, picturing Loma's perfect skin, long, manicured nails, and wide, ready smile. "Loma is beautiful, not gross at all."

"Agreed. But Emmett was gay. Emmett and Margosha had a green-card marriage."

"Emmett told you all this?" *And you're telling me? Bless your heart!*

"It's no secret. And it was years ago. She got her green card. They've been divorced for a few years now. Had a huge happy-divorce party. Best party I'd ever been to before or since. It was at their premier restaurant in New York." Kelli got a faraway look in her eyes. "Fell in love with caviar that night."

"What happened to the restaurants?" Quinn asked.

"I don't really know, but a bunch of people lost a bunch of money. And Emmett ended up here. It's not much of a job, but if you hang around long enough, they give you a week of paid vacation and a five-hundred K life insurance policy. I'd rather have double the vacay, but the life insurance is cheaper for corporate. And they cancel it as soon as you quit. Literally, it's the very least they can do."

"Are you going to stay, now that Emmett..."

"I don't know. I have a couple of side gigs, but you know how it goes. I'll probably drop dead here." Kelli blushed at her poor choice of words. She stood and smoothed her uniform. "I should get back to work. Sorry I was such a chatterbox. Normally nobody wants to talk about anything other than the condiments on their burger or the weak coffee." Kelli picked up the coffeepot and tilted it toward Quinn, who shook her head.

"The coffee was just fine and I appreciate you taking the time to talk to me, Kelli. But if I drink any more I won't sleep for a week."

"Coffee's on the house. Thanks for not complaining about it."

Quinn changed her mind about the tip, slipping a twenty under her coffee cup for Kelli. As she headed for the exit, Vince Koneckny was walking away from her. Quinn watched as a folded magazine slipped out of his back pocket. He didn't notice, so Quinn picked it up. She almost followed him to return it to him, but he suddenly found himself being squalled at by some unsatisfied diners. Quinn looked at the magazine and saw it was, instead, a colorful catalog. *FUNdamental Restaurant Products*, it screamed in large letters, all in different colors. The *FUN* was in a silly font, all in fire engine red. Below that touted their June knife sale, complete with several exclamation marks and photos of every type of knife a restaurant might use. She placed it on top of a pile of newspapers near the unmanned hostess stand and hoped Vince could get back to it soon.

Chapter 10

The next morning, Friday, Quinn got up early and talked Donnie into letting her see Jake in the lockup.

"I have questions about the diner. C'mon...please?"

After staring at her for an uncomfortably long time, Donnie slowly got to his feet. "What do I care if you talk to him?"

"Is that rhetorical?"

"Leave your purse here." She squinted at him, trying to decide if that was a good idea. His bored stare told her she had no choice. She dug around until she pulled out a pen and a mini–spiral notebook, then dropped her purse on Donnie's desk. She followed him downstairs, where he left her alone with Jake. She made a mental note to ask Rico if that was protocol, but just as quickly abandoned the idea in case it wasn't. She might need Donnie to let her talk to Jake again. Almost certainly, in fact.

Jake's face lit up and he shot a barrage of questions at Quinn.

She held up one hand. "Me first." She turned back the cover on the spiral and clicked her pen. "The credit card machine isn't working. Who do I call?"

"There's a sticker underneath it with the company and the eight-hundred number to call for service."

"Same with the cash register? It's stuck."

"No idea. It's never broken before."

Quinn listed all of the kitchen staples she'd run out of and Jake told her how to replenish everything. With a sigh, he even described how to find his secret stash of emergency cash cleverly hidden in the desk in his office under some to-go menus and empty water bottles. Quinn debated whether to tell him it wasn't so cleverly hidden.

"Now if only I could find time to go shopping or call those vendors."
She started to close the notebook where she'd jotted down the instructions.
"Oh. And the fridge is making a funny noise."

"Describe it."

Quinn did, a cross between clanking and wheezing that hurt her throat
but was a fairly good imitation.

"Nope, that's normal. Now if it starts going"—Jake proceeded to trill
and whistle—"then call Abe. Other than all that, how's it going over there?"

"It's chaos." It slipped out before she knew it. She couldn't take it back,
so she went all-in and told Jake everything. "There are too many people
to disappoint, too many orders to get wrong, too much toast to burn, too
much oatmeal to spill—"

"That's what makes it fun! It's a challenge to juggle all those balls."
He paused when he saw the look of horror on her face.

"I'm not good at juggling. I need to throw one ball and catch it. Then
set it aside and throw another ball and catch it." It was Jake's turn to look
horrified. "It was easy when I was just waitressing. Bring food there, fill
those waters, clear that table. One thing, then another."

"It's exactly the same now. You're just cooking the food first."

"It's not at all the same. Now, I'm supposed to be chopping onions
while I'm cooking fried eggs while I'm trying not to burn the bacon while
I actually *am* burning toast while I'm grating potatoes while I'm cooking
scrambled eggs while I'm chopping tomatoes while I'm looking for an
omelet pan while I'm—"

"How else would you do it?" Jake looked bewildered.

"I want to chop vegetables for Silas's omelet, then cook the eggs, then
fill the omelet, then fry the potatoes, then toast the bread, then bring it to
Silas, *then* do the next order."

Jake stared at her, trying to process her words. "Are you telling me you
take care of one customer completely before you handle another one?"

"It's so … chaotic," she said meekly.

Jake ran his hand through his already messy hair. "Quinn, you have
got to make this work."

She didn't want to make promises she couldn't possibly keep, so she
changed the subject. "Did you know there was an eyewitness who saw you
bring a bag of mushrooms into the governor's mansion?"

"So Rico said."

"How do you explain that?"

"I can't." He slumped on to the edge of his bed.

"What's your attorney say about it?"

"I don't have an attorney."

"Still? Why not?"

"Because I have you."

"That's not funny, Jake. You need an attorney."

"I don't trust public defenders. They're all overworked and underpaid. And my corporate attorney is on safari in Kenya somewhere, completely off the grid. I couldn't call him even if I wanted. And I'm not guilty, so I don't need him anyway."

"That's ridiculous. You're in trouble here."

He shrugged. "So what are you doing to get me out of here?"

"Jake, I'm trying, I swear, but I'm still baffled by those mushrooms. Did you really cook them? Why would you bring them only for Emmett?"

"Yes, I cooked them, but I didn't bring them or order them. They were already there in the kitchen when I got there. They had a note attached that said *special request* on it with Emmett's name. I remembered how much he liked mushrooms, so I bit the bullet and sautéed them for him."

"Didn't you think it was weird?"

"Honestly? I thought he'd made some kind of big donation to the governor's campaign and that gave him special dispensation or something."

Quinn raised her eyebrows. "You think quid pro quo for campaign donations are sautéed mushrooms?"

"No. Well, maybe. I don't know about politics." Frustration caused Jake's voice to notch up.

"Was it the only special request?"

"The only one with mushrooms. I've been over this a hundred times with Rico. Two gluten-free, one vegan, and four vegetarian."

"See? Those make sense." It was Quinn's turn to notch up her voice. "Didn't you think it was weird that—"

"Quinn. In retrospect, a lot of this has turned out to be weird. Give me a break."

She took a deep breath, then changed the subject.

"I went to the Crazy Mule."

Jake's eyes widened. "And?"

"And I spoke to a waitress named Kelli Mahan. Remember her?" Jake nodded. Quinn proceeded to tell Jake about their conversation.

When she finished, Jake nodded again. "Emmett's been saying for years that I ruined his business. He told anyone who'd listen that I stole his recipes and ideas. He couldn't stand that I was the more talented chef. And then someone wrote an article about me that irked Emmett. He thought it was going to be an interview about him, but it turned into a bigger thing about the restaurants and my involvement."

"Do you know how I can reach Margosha, Emmett's ex-wife?"

"Why?"

"Because I want to talk to her about all this—why do you think?" Quinn wasn't able to keep the irritation out of her voice.

"Her number's in my Rolodex. Do you know what that is?"

"Of course I do," she snapped. "It's—" She almost let it slip that it was on her list of rare words to try to use in a crossword. Instead she said, "It's something I've seen Jessica Fletcher use."

"Who? Never mind. I don't care. Margosha's number is in there. The last one I had for her, anyway. We haven't talked in a while."

"Quite a bit of sour grapes between you and her, as well?"

Jake shrugged. "I don't know."

"And between you and all those old employees of yours?"

He gave her another shrug in response. They stared at each other for a moment.

"I tried calling some of them to come in, but I couldn't get anyone to help. I even called a temp service, but they wouldn't help."

"Employees are the worst part of owning a business."

"Ouch."

"You know what I mean. They always have so much baggage. So many issues. So many reasons not to do their jobs."

Quinn bristled at the suggestion. Is that what he thought of her? Did he consider her OCD baggage? Or maybe it was baggage that she was doing everything in her power to keep his business running.

She was still trying to decide whether to say anything when she realized he was still talking, unaware she hadn't even been listening.

She interrupted him. "How'd you get the job cooking at the governor's fundraiser?"

"Headhunter."

"What's that?"

"Glorified temp service."

"Can I get employees there?"

"Doubt it."

She told him about her conversation with the temp agency yesterday.

"You can't just go hiring people willy-nilly so you can run out and get a pedicure or something."

"A *pedicure?*" Quinn's voice got shrill. "Is that what you think I'm doing?"

"Well, no..." Jake dropped his head into his hands. "I don't know why I said that. Go get a pedicure if you want. It's none of my business."

"You're making it worse. Besides, there's no way I want people touching my feet."

"Have you called Chris and Kristi?" he asked.

"Do they give pedicures?"

Jake sighed.

"Yes," she said. "They're absolutely no help."

Jake nodded. "They're pretty flaky."

"Why do you keep them?"

"See anyone else beating down the door to work there? Besides, they're dependable enough. As long as I never really need them." He pointed at the clock on the wall. "Shouldn't you be getting to the diner?"

Quinn sighed. "I suppose."

Jake's voice took on a softer edge. "I really do appreciate everything you're doing for me."

Quinn wondered if that would be true even after she ran his diner into the ground.

* * * *

Quinn opened the diner and watched Jethro investigate the big corner booth. It creeped her out whenever he snooped around back there, like he was searching for something, or that Emmett's ghost had unfinished business and still hovered around the diner. You know, like ghosts do.

She felt an overwhelming urge to make sure everything was turned to an even number, as if that would cast some sort of protective spell over her and the diner today. The air-conditioning got bumped up from 73 to 74. She waited to clock in at 6:14 even though she had to wait fifty-three seconds to do so. She nudged the volume on the radio. It was odd, but she felt better.

She made coffee before calling the suppliers Jake had mentioned. She had a promise for cheese, eggs, bacon, bread, ground beef, and assorted produce to be delivered as a rush. She even had a tech ticket into the credit card company.

The town's fascination with the murder and Jake's incarceration seemed to die down to mostly nothing, if the smaller crowd trickling into the diner was any indication. Fewer or not, they were still hungry people requiring breakfast, so Quinn quickly inventoried her supplies. She stacked two huge cans of marinara sauce in the center of the work space. She piled all the different types of bread—sourdough, whole wheat, buns, English muffins—next to them. She still had plenty of potatoes, which she sorted in rows of large, medium, and small. If those suppliers actually came through, she only needed to worry about breakfast today—maybe lunch too—depending on the nebulous definition of *rush* they'd given her. After studying what she had to work with, she turned the oven to 450 and placed all the small and half the medium potatoes inside to bake.

She brought her colored markers to the dry-erase board. She cleared the board and wrote, *Friday Breakfast Special—Italian Pain and Hash Browns.* Below that she wrote *Friday Lunch Special—Baked Potato with Butter.* And below that she wrote *$7 Cash Only.*

She wasn't wild about *Italian pain* but hoped people knew it was the French word for bread. *Italian bread* wasn't quite what she meant and it might not seem truthful. *Italian pain* probably was.

It only took her three tries to get the lettering perfectly even. When she was satisfied, she headed back to the kitchen to grate some of the large potatoes. Before she got there, Wilbur said, "What the heck is Italian pain? You trying to kill us?" Wilbur did not pronounce it like the French would.

Quinn smiled what she hoped was her most winning smile. "Picture this, Wilbur: A delicious bread boat covered in a glorious pool of marinara sauce with a side order of crispy hash browns."

Wilbur considered this. "Weird, but don't sound half bad. Make me one."

"Me too," said Larry.

"And me!" Bob nodded emphatically and Silas joined in.

Herman shrugged and Quinn took that as tacit approval. Besides, what else was he going to eat?

"Five Italian pains coming right up." Quinn pronounced it like Wilbur did. "Help yourself to coffee and I'll get busy." She felt a tiny thrill and understood maybe a bit of what her mom felt when she created one of her recipes. Now, to make it palatable. And not painful.

Quinn made a plate of Italian pain for herself to taste, sprinkled a bit of grated Parmesan cheese from a can on top and mentally patted herself on the back. She wolfed it down, then made five more plates for the Retireds.

Silas peered into the plates she held and announced, "That looks good enough to eat!"

Larry murmured his agreement, but Herman wrinkled his nose. "I'll stick to coffee."

An older couple Quinn didn't know sauntered over to the Retireds' table. After watching Wilbur take a bite, the man asked, "Any good?"

Wilbur shrugged. "Could be worse."

Quinn beamed from the faint praise. It could indeed be worse.

The older couple placed their order.

Soon enough everyone was enjoying—or at least eating—their Italian pain, so Quinn poured herself a cup of coffee and headed to Jake's desk. She found the Rolodex that held tiny cards with names and contact information. The black plastic frame was dusty and stained, looking like it had been around for fifty years or more. Quinn wondered if it had once belonged to Jake's dad or even his grandfather before him.

She played with it, twirling it ever faster until it shot off the desk. Grabbing for it, she knocked the phone off the hook. As she struggled to replace the receiver and scoop up the contact cards, she bumped the phone base and the call history lit up. It began scrolling through all the calls she'd made to the ex-employees.

As names flashed past, one caught her eye: Colorado Premium Employment. That wasn't the name of the temp service she'd called. It had to be Jake's headhunter. The call that perhaps started all of this.

The phone continued to scroll and flash despite the buttons Quinn jabbed to make it stop. Finally she gave up and let it do its thing. She picked up her cellphone and typed in *CO Premium Employment* in her internet browser. No hits. She checked her spelling. She spelled out *Colorado*. Nothing. Sheesh. This place must be super-exclusive. Word of mouth only, probably.

Jake's desk phone had finally stopped scrolling through his call history, having gone all the way back to January 1.

Quinn picked up the Rolodex and returned it to the square spot on the desk free of dust. She checked on her customers and got everyone squared away, twitchy to get back to the Rolodex. Those cards weren't going to re-alphabetize themselves. When she'd organized the Rolodex, she spun it to Margosha Dubois's card, which Jake had placed with the other M's.

She really didn't want to call Margosha, though, and was much more curious about Colorado Premium Employment, partly because of Jake's predicament, but also in case they could get her some help for the diner.

Quinn peeked into the dining room and saw everyone happily eating their breakfast, with no new customers waiting for her. She moved back to Jake's chair and held her finger on the *call history* button while it scrolled from January to June, where she began to slow it down. She pressed the button at the number she wanted.

After a pause, a man answered brusquely, "This is Sam."

"Is this Colorado Premium Employment?"

He paused again and Quinn worried that she sounded like a salesperson.

"It is."

"Hi...I'm looking to hire some temporary employees for a diner in Chestnut Station."

"Chestnut Station?"

"Yes, it's east of Denver—"

"I know where it is. Not possible." The man got even more brusque, if that was possible, as if just hearing the phrase *east of Denver* gave him indigestion.

"Yes, it's absolutely possible to have a town east of Denver. There's an interstate and everything." Quinn smiled, hoping her wisecrack would cure his indigestion and deliver him to a pleasant disposition.

It didn't.

"Wrong," he said.

"Wrong? What's wr—"

"It's not *possible* to work with anyone out of the Denver *metro* area, not in the *wasteland* that is Chestnut Station, and certainly not for a *diner*." The way he said it made Quinn think he would run for the shower as soon as he hung up. And hang up he did. Immediately and abruptly. The shower probably followed.

Quinn looked at the receiver long enough for the recording to come on asking if she wanted to make a call or not. The conversation, brief though it was, didn't make much sense to her. After all, this guy got jobs for Jake and *he* was way out in the boonies *and* at a diner. The difference was probably just that he was getting high-end jobs for Jake, not trying to staff a diner. The challenge of working at a diner was surely the same as working at a high-end place. The only difference would be the snooty customers they catered to who didn't think twice about overpaying for their dinner. There was also something about what he said that she was having trouble processing, but couldn't quite put her finger on it. Quinn didn't get a chance to become too indignant about the discrimination in this guy's twisted head, because Wilbur stuck his head in the office.

"Need more coffee." His eighty-year-old legs wouldn't turn as quickly as he'd like so, to punctuate his statement, a three-point turn in the doorway had to suffice.

Quinn rolled her eyes at his back. "Not even a *please* or a *would you be so kind as to*, Wilbur?"

He didn't break stride, just acknowledged her with a wave over his head.

* * * *

After the next breakfast rush died down and the Retireds had their own pot of coffee on their table—their third—Quinn settled back into Jake's office chair.

She hadn't figured out what was bothering her about the brief conversation she'd had with Jake's headhunter, aside from his urban hatred of anything out of a Denver zip code. Maybe it was just his crappy demeanor.

She flipped through the Rolodex again until she found a card that had a scribbled name with *attorney* underneath. Quinn called and got his voice mail saying he was out of the country on an extended vacation and to call another law office in case of an emergency. Quinn called that number and spoke with an attorney who sounded like he'd rather be on an extended vacation too. After Quinn explained the situation he said, "If this guy doesn't want an attorney, there's not much I can do for him."

"Not much?"

"Well, anything."

"You can't do anything for him."

"Not unless he agrees to retain me."

Quinn sighed and said she'd be in touch if things changed.

After checking on the customers, once again she plucked the Rolodex from its dust-free spot and stared at Margosha's card.

She screwed up her courage and dialed. A woman answered on the second ring. "Is this Margosha…Dubois? Emmett's ex-wife?"

"Who may I ask is callink?"

"My name is Quinn Carr and I—"

"I do not this name recognize. Goodbye."

Yet again Quinn stared at the receiver and listened to the dial tone after someone had hung up on her. What was it with people, anyway? She wasn't even sure if she'd been speaking with Margosha or just someone else with an Eastern European accent. A relative, maybe? Where did Kelli say Margosha was from? Belarus? Bosnia? Bulgaria? Was it a cultural thing to answer the phone and always expect to know who was on the other line?

Rico rushed into Jake's office.

Quinn hung up the phone, saying to him, "There's so much about the world I'll never understand. I should travel more. Have you talked to Margosha yet? Or that headhunter who hired Jake to cook at the governor's fundraiser?" While she spoke she was squaring up the corners of the Rolodex contact cards.

"I need to ask you something."

The seriousness in Rico's voice made Quinn's head snap up. "What?"

"I need to know about that online review you gave the Crazy Mule."

"Online review? I never—"

Rico handed her a piece of paper. Quinn studied it with a frown. It was a printout showing photos of food and the particulars of the restaurant at the top. Below that was a one-star review from a Quinn C of Denver. She read the review. With each sentence her eyes got wider and her cheeks got pinker. When she was done, she handed the paper back to Rico.

He read from the piece of paper. "The Crazy Mule makes people Crazy Sick. Someone should tie up the cook and force-feed him his own fettuccine Alfredo until he explodes. One less bad chef in the world." Rico glared at her. "Did you write this?"

"That's why the place seemed familiar," she murmured.

"Familiar? What are you talking about?"

"I went over there to get some information about Emmett. Had a nice chat with one of his waitresses."

"You didn't answer me. Did you write this?"

Quinn nodded. "A thousand years ago. But I didn't mean any of it. I was just pissed off. I went there on a date with a guy I really liked"—Quinn glanced away from Rico—"and got food poisoning. Barfed all over his car and never heard from him again." She looked at Rico. His lips were flat and tight against his teeth. "But so what? There's no law against writing one-star reviews."

"But there is a law against threatening people who wind up dead."

"I didn't threaten anyone!" Quinn blanched at Rico's narrowed eyes and the way he twisted the fabric of his duty cap. "Does this make me a suspect? That's ridiculous. I didn't do anything!" Quinn began touching each finger to her thumb, beginning with her pinkies. She moved her hands behind her back so Rico wouldn't see. "Besides, I thought Chief Chestnut was convinced Jake did it."

"He was, until he saw your incriminating review."

Quinn stopped touching fingers. "And how exactly did he see that?" She already knew the answer and her eyes flashed with anger.

"It was on my desk."

"And?"

"And he asked me who wrote it."

"And?"

"And I told him it was you."

Quinn exploded. "You couldn't tell him it was nothing or you didn't know who wrote it?"

"But I did know."

"Get out of here before I say something I'll regret."

Rico pulled his duty cap from under his arm and wedged it on his head. "Quinn, I'm—"

"Just go. We'll have to talk about it later."

After Rico left, Quinn had to clear some tables, deal with the cash people had left, and make more coffee for the Retireds. How they didn't float right out the door was a question for the ages. Back in the kitchen, she began slamming things around as she loaded the dishwasher and scrubbed the stainless steel countertops. She was winded and finally sat down to catch her breath. "So, now I'm a suspect too," she said to the dishcloth in her hand. "That's just great." The very idea that Rico would suspect her of killing Emmett Dubois enraged her. But wait. It wasn't Rico. Surely he had argued with the chief about this. But that's how much Chief Chestnut hated her. How could she convince him she was not at all involved in this, and neither was Jake?

Quinn tapped one fingernail on the metal counter in a soothing rhythm. She needed to finish that crossword to convince Chief Chestnut to expand his investigation, pointing it away from Jake and now from her too. But not only didn't she know in which direction to point him, she was always so exhausted when she got home she could barely focus on anything. Constructing crosswords took more brain cells than she came home with every night.

She continued to tap her fingernail against the metal, counting each *click*. When she reached twenty-two, an explosion rattled the pots and pans on the sink. She leaped away, eyes darting in all corners.

She crept around the kitchen like she was a member of a SWAT team clearing a building.

Was it the gas line? Sabotage?

Suddenly the pungent odor of burning filled the kitchen. Smoke poured from the oven. She grabbed oven mitts and carefully opened the door.

Sabotage? No. Baked potatoes.

Silas poked his head into the pass-through. "Everything okay, Quinn?"

She stepped aside and showed him the inside of the detonation zone, covered in exploded potato bits, all in varying states of incineration.

"Oh dear." He shook his head. "Didn't you poke holes in them before you started baking them?"

"No. Why?"

"So they don't explode. Everyone knows that."

Quinn glared at him. "Does everyone know how I'm supposed to clean this?"

* * * *

After she removed the unexploded ordnance from the oven and scrubbed the kitchen—again—she served the Friday lunch special to the Retireds. Once again, they came for breakfast and stayed through lunch. They were the only customers who hadn't cleared out due to the stench.

As she had scrubbed the oven, she also solved her problem of being too tired to construct puzzles.

She grabbed her purse and hurried out to the Retireds' table. "Guys, will you keep an eye on things here while I run home for a sec? I'll be back before you miss me." She was halfway to the door. She knew they'd say yes. At least some of them.

"Sure."

"Why not?"

"What else do I have to do today?"

"Do we have kitchen privileges?" Wilbur asked.

"No!" Quinn called over her shoulder. She yanked open the door and looked back at them, comfortable around their table. "You can make coffee, but nothing else." Wilbur started to speak. "I'm serious. Only coffee." As she sidestepped Jethro lying on the sidewalk in front of the door, she turned back. "And thanks, guys! I really appreciate it. Be right back."

Summer midday heat took its toll on Quinn and her sprint home quickly morphed into a stroll, then a slog. She wished she'd driven to work. As she walked, she mulled over potential clues for the crossword.

By the time she'd burst into the kitchen at home and startled her mom enough to raise a spatula in defense, grabbed her laptop, and hopped in her car, she had a plan in mind.

At the diner, she hurried in, hoping the Retireds had done as she asked and stayed out of the kitchen. They looked as if they hadn't moved at all. They still sat in their regular seats around the large rectangular table.

They glanced up as the door chimed.

"Did you miss me?" She hurried past them, noticing by the tall glasses in front of them that they'd graduated from coffee to cold drinks.

"You were gone?" Silas joked.

"Anything interesting happen while I was gone?" She hoped Chief Chestnut hadn't come looking to arrest her or anything.

"Just some guy making a delivery. Told him to come back tomorrow since you weren't here," Silas said.

"Oh no! Was it the produce guy? I needed that stuff—" Quinn stopped when she saw the men trying to stifle laughs. She went into the kitchen and came out holding a plump heirloom tomato. "Very funny, guys."

"Had you going, didn't I?"

"Yeah, you got me. Good one." She flashed a grin, then returned to the kitchen, where she raced to put away all the produce so she could commence working on her puzzle.

It wasn't her first choice to sit in the big corner booth where Emmett had died, but many others had every day since. Plus, it really was the best seat in the restaurant for keeping an eye on everything. People could only see the open lid of her laptop while she worked on the puzzle and if anyone came close, all she had to do was shut it to keep it safe from prying eyes.

She fired up her crossword program and created a new 15x15-square puzzle grid.

The mini–spiral notebook was still in her back pocket, so she pulled it out and dug a pen from her apron pocket. Down the left side she started a list for her very specific theme: Who Else Should Chief Chestnut Investigate? Unknown cater-waiter, Loma, Margosha. She squinched her eyes as she tried to access her memory to pull the name of the ex-employee who kept hanging up on her—Michael Breckenridge. Everyone else she had called had been happy to talk to her. Why wasn't he? After tapping her pen on the pad for a bit, thinking about the things Kelli the waitress had told her, she also added, *life insurance* and *silent partner*.

Those were the directions she wanted Chief Chestnut to take in his investigation, rather than just dwelling on her and Jake.

Crossword puzzles are symmetrical, up and down, and from side to side. You can turn them any which way and the grid remains in perfect balance. Because of the symmetry, however, the black squares need to be in certain places. They serve to break up long words and to make a puzzle attractive to the eye. A 15x15-square puzzle like this one can only have 38 black squares and 78 entries, the words that go in the squares. Puzzles almost always have a theme, even if it's not obvious to the person solving the puzzle, like this one would be. Quinn's puzzles were never titled with a hint to the theme, like in the *New York Times* crosswords, and they certainly never carried her name as the creator.

She looked at her list. Technically, these entries would be the theme of this puzzle, and she really hoped they would wiggle into Chief Chestnut's brain and lodge there long enough for him to get the subliminal message she was sending.

Because of the symmetry of the grid, the theme words had to have symmetry also. She needed the entries to be certain lengths, to fit a certain number of boxes in the grid.

She counted the number of letters in her entries and jotted them to the side.

cater (5)-waiter (6)

Loma (4)

Margosha (8)

Michael (7) Breckenridge (12)

insurance (9)

silent (6) partner (7)

The only thing that jumped out at her was that *Breckenridge* was easy to clue in Colorado, since it was also the name of a popular ski town. Obviously, she couldn't combine it with *Michael*, mainly because it was only a 15-square grid and that was a total of 19 letters. She crossed off *Michael*, but then cocked her head and wrote *Michelangelo* at the bottom of her list. She counted the letters: Twelve. Perfect. She had two of her theme words: *Michelangelo* and *Breckenridge*. Because they'd be the longest entries in the puzzle, maybe—if Chief Chestnut was looking for a theme—this would stick in his brain.

She thought long and hard about *cater* and *waiter*, but ultimately crossed them off as being too generic. She knew that Rico had been trying to locate the waiter who had asked Donnie to deliver the plate with mushrooms to Emmett at the governor's fundraiser. But even Donnie couldn't—or wouldn't—identify him, so without any other information than that, no crossword clue was going to help anyway.

There was always room in a crossword for a 4-letter word, so she kept *Loma*. She knew of a city in California called Loma Linda, because it was where she had to order her fitness gear, boots, and flashlight for police academy training. That was a potential way to clue the word. Theoretically, the Chestnut Station PD ordered items from the Police Clearing House in Loma Linda at some point too. Although, the beauty of a crossword puzzle was that you didn't need to know every single clue. If you knew all the down entries that crossed an across word, you'd automatically filled in the across word. But it would be way better for Chief Chestnut to know all the entries so the subliminal message could stick.

Quinn tapped her pen on Margosha's unique name. She typed it into her crossword database. No other constructor had ever used it in a puzzle. She typed it into an internet search and was stunned to see it pop up as the title of a TV show. She followed the link to the Internet Movie Database and saw it was a Russian TV show. She doubted it was entertainment that Chief Chestnut binged on.

She scrolled and found nothing she could use as a clue. Nobody famous was named Margosha, there was no town named Margosha, no song lyrics singing her praises, no snack foods, no beauty products.

She threw in the towel. There was no possible way to clue *Margosha*. Plus, she realized, it would be way too obvious it was a planted word. The last thing Quinn wanted was for Chief Chestnut to use this puzzle to find out she was the one who created them, especially now that she'd had the brainstorm to fill his gray matter with subliminal messages. Maybe she really could help Rico in his job. Chief Chestnut shut down a lot of Rico's investigations, especially the more serious ones. Quinn had once asked Rico why. He told her that the chief aspired to be mayor, though not necessarily in Chestnut Station. His ego was bigger than that. He believed if he could point to a very low crime rate where he was chief of police, it would go a long way in getting him elected mayor someplace else. As crazy and underhanded as that was, he was probably right. His plan would work as long as some nosy reporter or whistleblower never asked Rico a direct question about it. It seemed distasteful to Quinn, who would love nothing better than to see Chief Chestnut go down in flames, but with him gone, Rico would be the new chief.

She crossed *Margosha* from her list of entries. She could, however, use the entry *wife* as the counterpart to the 4-letter word *Loma*. *Ex-wife* would be better, of course, but those pesky two extra letters just wouldn't fit.

She crossed off *insurance* because she couldn't think of any other logical word to pair with it. Again, Rico had to be on this line of questioning already and if he found something, he'd of course bring it to Chief Chestnut's attention. Even he couldn't ignore that. The names of beneficiaries were always of interest to law enforcement investigators. Who would benefit from someone's death was one of the first questions they asked.

She studied *silent* and *partner*. Because they had differing numbers of letters, they couldn't be used in a symmetrical pattern on the grid. But Quinn was convinced she could make it work, so she left them on her list of entries.

She flipped the page and wrote a clean list of her theme words:

Loma/wife

Michelangelo/Breckenridge

silent/partner

The fact that the last pair had different numbers of letters triggered her OCD, but she had to shake that off. It also went against all the rules of crossword construction. She shook that off, too. Will Shortz would understand, given the circumstances.

Over the course of the afternoon, between the very few customers that came in, she worked on the puzzle. She decided where her longest entries needed to go, then filled in thirty-eight black squares.

She appreciated using a computer program for her grid, because the computer automatically made the puzzle symmetrical. When she clicked on a square five spaces from the left on the top row, the computer also automatically blackened a square five spaces from the right on the bottom row. Back when she used to do it all by hand on graph paper, she'd forget or miscount and it would throw her entire grid off. Since she couldn't stand erasures, she'd always have to start over.

When she was happy with the design of her grid and the black spaces had a pleasing look to them, she filled in her theme words. *Michelangelo* and *Breckenridge* were easy because there was only one place for them to go, filling row four from the top on the left and row four from the bottom on the right. The rest of those rows were taken up with black spaces. She gave *wife* the top right corner and *Loma* the bottom left. She wanted *silent partner* to trigger something in Chief, so she found a place for *silent* at the beginning of the seventh row from the top and *partner* at the end of the row, sixth from the bottom.

Then the hard work began: All the rest of the entries. This was a lot of trial and error. Every so often she'd stop and ask the computer to fill in the grid for her, but until she fixed some entries on her own, it was an impossibility. Quinn knew that professional cruciverbalists would never deign to use the computer to fill their grid. It was a point of pride to fill with as little help from the computer as possible, but Quinn was: one, in a hurry; and two, barely professional. Besides, nobody was going to tattle to the crossword police on her.

She tapped the command to automatically fill the grid and let out a whoop when letters magically appeared in all the spaces. She couldn't believe her eyes when one of the entries smack-dab in the middle of the grid was *ins*. To her, because of her dad, it was an obvious abbreviation of *insurance*, but maybe not conventional, so she wouldn't clue it that way.

Now, all she needed was to write the clues, which she thought was the most fun.

She was pleased by her results and this puzzle might have been completed in record time. She never kept track of how long a puzzle took to create, because she rarely did it all in one sitting, but maybe she should start. She texted herself a reminder.

Quinn checked over her puzzle one last time. She verified some of the clues, like making sure she got the Steven Wright quote verbatim, and that a RONDEL poem actually had 14 lines. She clucked her tongue over some of the more obscure words like EBLIS and ARUI, but she didn't have time for better entries. Besides, she reasoned, crossword enthusiasts knew a lot of obscure words.

She also didn't have time to run it by Vera to edit. Generally, Vera didn't have much to say about the puzzles. Editing was merely a formality to her. As she said many times when Quinn sought her opinion about the puzzle, "Our readers will let me know if there's a problem with it." Which was exactly what Quinn tried to avoid whenever possible. If Vera happened to ask why Quinn had uploaded a bonus puzzle to the website, she'd simply say she got excited about it, which was absolutely true.

The fact that Vera probably still wanted to interview her for an article about Emmett's death also weighed heavily in her decision not to contact her. So far Quinn had seen only a short blurb online about the basic facts: Emmett Dubois died under suspicious circumstances, Jake Szabo had been arrested and sits in the local jail, Quinn Carr found the body. When the next print edition came out, there might be more, but no quotes from Quinn, if she could help it.

She uploaded the puzzle to the newspaper website and sent a quick email to the "Puzzle Corner" subscribers alerting them to the surprise bonus puzzle this week.

Then she waited.

ACROSS
1. Simon and Garfunkel's "A ___ Shade of Winter"
5. Spot of tea, to a Brit
10. Michelle, to Barack
14. One of HOMES
15. Islamic devil
16. Word with rain or rock
17. Type of moth
18. Library transactions
19. Greek sandwich
20. Painter of the Sistine Chapel
23. Dahs' counterparts
24. 14-line poem with only two rhymes
28. Trouble for a tooth
32. Addams family cousin
33. Wade's legal opponent
34. With 45-across, one who provides capital only
35. ___ and outs
36. Campaign funding grps
37. Some campaigns win them
38. Hit the jackpot
39. Book parts
40. Ford contemporary
41. Bud holder
42. Where the chips are down?
43. The beginning of time?
44. Chesapeake or Tampa
45. See 34-across
46. Trout's home
48. Samoan coin
49. Colorado ski town
55. "Not only that ..."
58. Longest river in France
59. Genuine
60. Aquatic mammal
61. All you need in a medical crisis, maybe
62. Leather piercing tools
63. ___ Linda, CA
64. Brother of Jack and Bobby
65. Wall Street Journal subj

DOWN
1. Bridge position
2. North African sheep
3. Sunblock ingredient
4. "Absolutely!"
5. Yo-Yo Ma, for one
6. WWII subs
7. Vague reason for not attending a party
8. Pong preceder
9. Proclaims
10. Prairie schooner
11. Frozen
12. Christmas tree, often
13. Former name of Tokyo
21. Utopias
22. Place to park
25. Come home exhausted
26. Dawn of mammals epoch
27. One receiving a security deposit
28. Fancy ties
29. Bunk assignment
30. Mini hamburger
31. Boardroom bigwigs
32. Holiday or Red Roof
35. Charged particle
36. "Whenever I think of the ___ , it brings back so many memories." Steven Wright
38. "No ___ !"
39. Kitchen gizmo
41. King Arthur's hood?
42. Steinbeck's novel " ___
44. Soap unit
45. Gazed intently
47. Deadly virus
48. What they did in Breckenridge
50. Ice cream ___
51. Persia today
52. Like grass in the morning
53. Guys' partners at square dances
54. "If all ___ fails"
55. Digital communication? Abbr
56. Author Tolstoy
57. Famous uncle

Chapter 11

Before Quinn prepped salad for her new dinner special—God bless produce deliveries—she took water out for Jethro, who was sprawling in front of the diner. She opened the door and the blast furnace that was Chestnut Station in summer hit her again. The petunias growing in the sidewalk planters had been broiled, generating a heavy curtain of cloying sweetness that hung over the entire town. She literally staggered toward the water dish. She filled it, then ushered Jethro into the diner.

"Much too hot out here." She picked up the water dish and placed it just inside the door. Health department, shmealth department.

Jethro ignored the water and plodded over to the big corner booth.

"Rain nor shine nor beastly heat can keep you from your rounds, eh, boy?" Quinn felt twitchy as she watched him duck under the table and snuffle under the seat. He was taking his duties much more seriously this afternoon, maybe because she'd flipped the script on him by letting him in late in the day too. Paying her back with extra diligence?

He backed out from under the table and turned his sad, droopy eyes on Quinn. When she didn't respond, he turned his head back to the booth. When she still didn't respond, he sighed and crawled back under the table.

Quinn bent to see what he was doing. He turned his head as languidly as before from her to the seat, then back again, until finally she crawled under the table with him, fearing the worst.

"Please don't tell me there's a dead mouse back here." Quinn glanced around the diner, but the couple eating pie à la mode were only focused on it and each other. She placed her cheek on the linoleum and peered into the darkness under the booth. No dead mouse lump, thank goodness. Just a bite of hot dog one of those twins must have dropped. It was wedged in with an assortment of trash that had fallen under there over the years. Another duty she'd need to add to her list. She wriggled out and got the broom. Jethro moved out of her way as she swept the detritus into a small pile. She gestured to the hot dog as an invitation to him and he plucked it from the heap, swallowing without chewing.

Paper straw wrappers, foil from pieces of gum, ancient wadded-up napkins, a cootie catcher some kid had made, and a folded sheet of paper. She scooped it all into the dustpan, but plucked the paper out at the last minute, her curiosity winning over neatness. She unfolded it and saw glossy colored letters cut from a magazine glued on it. *I know what you did, Jake.*

Quinn stared at the message, then stared at Jethro, who stared right back, a stringy slip of saliva dangling from his jowls. Quinn turned toward the couple eating pie, who continued to ignore her. She read the note again. And then what seemed like seven hundred more times.

She stumbled toward the storage room, broom and dustpan clattering. At this, the couple startled and scowled at her. Quinn dealt with the dustpan before heading into Jake's office. She read the note again. It was clearly meant to intimidate Jake, but what did it mean? How long had it been under the booth? Quinn sucked in a breath. Did the murder mystery guy drop it the night Emmett Dubois died? It was on the side of the booth where he sat. He must have. What was the note writer trying to accomplish? What had Jake done?

Who *was* this murder mystery guy?

She called her mom. "Hey, did you ever find out anything more about any murder mystery parties around here?"

"Nope. Nobody knows anything. I think I've checked with everyone who might host or attend something like that. I'm sorry I couldn't have been more help."

"No worries, Mom. Thanks for trying."

"Maybe I should have one. I could make a menu like they'd have on the Orient Express."

"Maybe stick a pin in that idea for a while."

Quinn knew she needed to get back into the kitchen. People were going to start trickling in for dinner soon and she had nothing prepped. But hungry bellies seemed less important than the note she held in her hand. She traced her finger over the letters spelling out *Jake*. Black lowercase J. Red capital A. Blue lowercase K and E.

J-A-K-E. She didn't even know this man, not really. She'd worked for him for less than a month. She had been in such a daze when she landed back at her parents' house. She'd never asked anyone about him, just shrugged and took the waitress gig her mom got her, hoping her meds would kick in soon.

Quinn tried to convince herself the note didn't mean anything; it was completely unimportant and irrelevant to everything that had happened. But she couldn't do it. Who would send a message like that? Her concerns that one of Jake's ex-employees had a grudge against him had mushroomed—she winced at the metaphor—into full-fledged blackmail. Was that possible? Had Jake cut corners here at the diner? Maybe the rumors Kelli mentioned didn't involve Emmett at all. Maybe *Jake* was bribing the health inspector.

Her eyes cut to the pile of employee files still on Jake's desk, aligned with precision at the corner of the desk. She heard some noise in the restaurant and went to check it out, almost crashing into the giggling couple standing in front of her.

"Can we pay?" The man opened his wallet, voice dripping with sarcasm.

"Yeah...five bucks?" Quinn stuffed the note in her pocket.

He placed a five-dollar bill in her palm. "Hm. Thought it would be more." His voice sounded much more pleasant. The woman nudged him with her elbow and he dropped a single on top of the five.

Another nudge netted Quinn another single, but she was barely paying attention. "Thanks. See you soon," she said automatically. She stuffed the bills into her apron and turned back to the office. Before the door chime signaled their departure, Quinn was organizing the employee files by termination date.

Logic would dictate that the more recently someone was fired, the more likely they'd be angry enough to send that note to Jake. She couldn't discount anyone, she reasoned, because people did carry grudges. After all, Rico still hadn't forgiven that mean Molly Campbell who started the rumor about his man-perm.

Tapping a pen against her cheek, she formulated a reason to call them. She didn't want to lie, but she couldn't come right out and ask if they were blackmailing her boss. She needed to find an opening gambit that painted the truth with the most delicate brush. *Tap, tap, tap.* Finally satisfied, she picked up the file on top.

Rita Calhoun. This must be Rico's favorite waitress. An uncomfortable twinge of jealousy made her study the paperwork in the file more closely. Why was she his favorite? There was nothing specific to her job performance, just the original application she had filled out and some copies of IRS and OSHA forms with her signature.

Quinn picked up the desk phone.

A woman answered on the third ring.

"Is this Rita Calhoun?"

"It is."

"My name is Quinn and I'm thinking about a job at the Chestnut Diner."
Not a lie. I'm thinking about my job constantly. At this very moment, in fact.
"I understand you used to work for Jake Szabo? Can you tell me about him?"

"Ah, the Chestnut Diner. Funny, I just ran into Jake last week. Still handsome as ever. That man doesn't seem to age." She paused. "How bad do you really need a job?"

"Pretty bad."

"I suppose you could do worse."

"I don't mind waitressing, but I'd rather do it for a good guy."

"Oh, Jake's a good guy, but he's kinda persnickety. And he was always testing me on some stupid diner language. I finally quit—or maybe he fired me, I can't remember. But I kept forgetting to check the chemicals in the dishwasher and he totally lost it."

"Lost it?"

"Well, he didn't scream or anything, but he glared real loud. And then he told me I had to wash all the dishes in the diner by hand."

"That seems a bit harsh," Quinn said.

Rita laughed lightly and Quinn got an inkling of why Rico might have been smitten with her. "It definitely wasn't the first time I forgot. I would have screamed and yelled at me. I mean, I'd worked there long enough to remember, but I just couldn't. Well, I could have, but I chose not to. Truth be told, I didn't really care much about that job. He should have fired me long before that. If you really need a job and you don't mind waitressing, then I say go for it. Learn to use the dishwasher and that stupid lingo and you'll be fine. He's a good boss. Fair-minded. Persnickety, yes, but fair. You could do worse, especially in Chestnut Station. Way worse." She paused. "Plus, he's sure easy on the eyes."

Quinn blushed. She did *not* want to think about Jake that way. "Where do you work now?"

"Insurance company in Denver, for a guy who is not at all easy on the eyes."

"Thanks for talking to me, Rita."

"Good luck with the job."

"Thanks." *I'll need it.*

Between dealing with people who wanted dinner, Quinn called five more ex-employees, waitresses, and weekend cooks. Some of them she had called before when she was looking for help for the diner. Only one mentioned that getting two calls about the Chestnut Diner after all this time was weird. They all relayed some variation of what Rita had told her, that Jake had his quirks but was a good, fair boss. Nobody else mentioned his looks, though.

Quinn delivered a salad to a woman, but was called back immediately. "Is this ranch dressing?"

Quinn glanced down. "Yes, it is."

"I ordered blue cheese."

"Oh. Sorry." Quinn grabbed the bowl from her hand, but the woman didn't let go.

"On my burger."

"You ordered a burger? That's not on the menu tonight." Quinn waved vaguely at the dry-erase sandwich board that still had yesterday's menu on it.

"You let me order it."

Truth be told, Quinn didn't even remember taking their order, yet they all had sodas in front of them. She glanced around the restaurant. She didn't remember any of these people, but many sat with food and drink in front of them.

I am losing my mind, she thought.

She turned her attention back to the woman and her salad. "I don't—I can't—what do you—" Quinn heard the door chime behind her but continued playing tug-of-war with the bowl.

"Wanda, just eat the salad," the man at her table said. "You don't need a burger anyway." He guffawed.

"Aw, mister. That ain't nice." Loma had stepped to the table and was face-to-face with him. "You should apologize."

The two of them had a stare-down, which Loma won. Not only didn't she blink, she didn't blink in a very aggressive manner.

Quinn snapped out of her daze. "If you don't want the salad, I'm sure I can find—"

"Don't bother." The man pushed his way past Loma. Wanda followed, without looking at anyone.

Quinn watched them leave, then hissed at Loma. "I need this job!" Quinn started clearing the table. Loma touched her on the elbow, but Quinn roughly shook her off. "You don't know what I've been up against here, keeping this place running, doing everything, cash register not working, people mad at me. I don't know how many more bad meals I can even make!" Quinn's voice rose into the dog whistle range.

Loma stared at her for a moment, then took a firm grip on her upper arm and steered her into the kitchen. She took the dishes from Quinn's hands, placed them in the sink, then gently pushed her toward the stool. "Sit."

Quinn sat, trying to control the dull roar that echoed in her head. She clamped both hands over her chest, sure her heart was going to burst right out.

Loma returned and held Quinn's face in her hands. "I told everyone that there was a kitchen emergency and sent them all home—"

"You did what? You can't—"

"I can and I did. I turned the *Closed* sign and locked the door too." Quinn started to protest and hop down from the stool, but Loma held her in place. "You, my dear, are coming apart at the seams. And I know why."

Loma held up several pieces of paper. The one on top had colored letters cut from a magazine.

Chapter 12

Quinn gasped. "Where did you get that?"

"Shouldn't your question be, What is that?" Loma crossed her arms, boosting both boobs.

Quinn stared at her. Was Loma blackmailing Jake? *Am I in danger here? Is that why she sent everyone home and closed the diner? So she could murder me?* "Don't kill me…please."

"Kill you? Girl, what are you on about?"

"You're—you're not here to kill me?"

"What in the world is going on in that head of yours?" Loma uncrossed her arms, letting her boobs drop, and leaned against the sink. "Do you really think I'm that badass that I could kill someone?" She picked up a stainless steel bowl and looked at her reflection. She fluffed her hair. "I admit, I'm pretty fierce, but more in the colloquial sense than the literal."

"Then why are you here? And why did you send everyone out of the diner?"

"I sent everyone away before you had some kind of meltdown and stabbed someone with a salad fork."

"I wasn't going to—"

"I've heard what's been going on here. But we have bigger fish to fry. I came here to show you this. I thought we should talk." She held the papers out to Quinn, who reluctantly took them from her.

Quinn read the page with the cutout letters first. "*To keep me quiet, you need to call this number for further instructions.*" She looked up at Loma for answers to her unspoken questions. Loma waved impatiently at the other pages.

The next page was a fax on an office-supply store letterhead with Jake's name scrawled across it. People still faxed?

"*Call the number on the next page and read the statement into the phone.*" She shuffled to the next page. The phone number didn't mean anything to her. She scanned the statement.

"Read it out loud. I want to hear it again."

Quinn read, "*It is hereby acknowledged and affirmed that I, Jake Szabo, did knowingly and purposely hog the spotlight at every opportunity over the course of my career. I, Jake Szabo, consistently put my needs above the needs of the restaurants, as well as above the needs of all the employees and investors. I, Jake Szabo, relegated associates and teammates to insignificant roles, the likes of which proved to be insurmountable for many of them. And I, Jake Szabo, never allowed anyone in my professional orbit to shine, an unforgivable sin in any collaboration. Of these and many other transgressions, I, Jake Szabo, am guilty as charged.*"

"Did you get these from Emmett?" Quinn waved the pages in the air.

"So, you already know about Emmett and Jake."

Quinn didn't say anything, not entirely sure what she knew anymore.

"Remember when I rushed out of here when you told me Jake had been arrested?" Quinn nodded. "I had to go see for myself if my hunch was right, and it was. Jake snuck in and stayed at my guesthouse that night Emmett was murdered. When I finally went in there, I found these and his phone. They must have fallen out of his pocket."

"Or he stashed them there," Quinn said. "But what does it all mean?"

"This is a list of stuff Jake did to Emmett."

"Is it true?"

Loma shrugged.

"Emmett Dubois was blackmailing Jake." Quinn couldn't believe what she was hearing. "We need to take the notes to Rico."

"No. We need to talk to Jake."

* * * *

Quinn shooed Jethro from the diner. He plodded down the street while she locked the door, pivoting back twice to check the lock while Loma marched ahead of her. Quinn wasn't sure if she wanted Rico to be there or not. Donnie said Rico wasn't in, but was expected back in the next twenty minutes or so.

At the station, she tried to introduce Loma to Donnie but he already knew who she was. Donnie led them to the basement. As they passed Chief Chestnut's office, she saw him talking on the phone, his back to the door.

The minute Donnie went back upstairs, Quinn got right to the point with Jake. "Was Emmett Dubois blackmailing you?"

When Jake replied, "Yes" with a calm voice, Quinn got flustered. She had expected him to hem and haw or even deny it, so this was a completely unexpected turn of events.

Quinn couldn't formulate another question from the many that tripped through her brain. Luckily, Loma was there.

"Did you go to the police? What did they say? Who else knows about this? Why didn't you tell me? What does all this mean?" She thrust the pages through the bars of the cell.

Jake glanced at them before handing them back to Loma.

"You must have dropped them at the guesthouse that night." Loma lowered her voice. "I also found your phone."

"It's all true, everything he wanted me to say in that statement," Jake said. "None of it is a secret. I thought if I played along, maybe he'd get bored or at least get what he needed from me. It's just silly vindictiveness. Inconsequential, completely harmless."

"Then why didn't you mention it to me?" Loma said.

"Or me?" Quinn glared at him.

"Because it was inconsequential and completely harmless." Jake sighed.

"Did you tell Rico?" Quinn asked.

"No."

"Even after Emmett was killed?"

"Listen, when I got the first note I thought maybe it was a dissatisfied customer. Remember that guy who wanted shoes on his BLT, but I forgot to make it a to-go order? And that omelet I screwed up last week? Stuff happens and people want to blow off steam. Besides, like I said, there hadn't been any threat or demand. Whoever it was hadn't asked for anything. There was nothing to tell the police."

Quinn started to interrupt, but he continued.

"And I didn't want bad publicity for the diner. This is a small town. I need every customer I get."

A pang of guilt shot through Quinn but she tamped it down. *Focus.* "You said the first note. Have there been more than this?"

Jake sat on the edge of his bed, hands clasped together between his knees. "Only one more."

"Actually…" Quinn stretched out the word. "I just found another note at the diner. Well, Jethro found it."

"Why didn't you tell me?" Loma put her hands on her hips.

"Because I thought you were going to murder me."

"I still might."

Jake interrupted. "What did it say?"

Quinn pulled it from her pocket and unfolded it. She felt a stab of remorse that she didn't treat it as evidence, but, she reasoned, she didn't realize it was evidence until after she picked it up.

Loma lunged for it but Quinn held it out of her reach. "Fingerprints." Loma harrumphed.

"*I know what you did, Jake.*"

His head snapped up. "What did I do?"

"No, that's what this note says." The three of them contemplated for a bit. Then Quinn said to Jake, "You said you got another note? What did it say?"

"It told me to deliver two hundred dollars to a certain location."

"Where?" Loma asked.

"That's the thing," Jake said. "There were a million texts that came through, each one sending me all over creation. It was like a terrible scavenger hunt."

"When did you do this?" Loma asked.

"The night of Emmett's murder." Jake sounded despondent.

"No, that's great! We'll just show Rico your phone with all the texts. It'll prove you were nowhere around when Emmett died," Loma said.

"But Jake still made those mushrooms for Emmett," Quinn pointed out. "And someone told the police they saw him carry the mushrooms into the governor's mansion before the fundraiser."

"Plus, the envelope I picked up at the office store also had a burner phone in it that I was told to leave with the money in the final location."

"Jake, why didn't you go to the police when it first happened?" Loma moaned.

"I know. But it was only two hundred bucks. If he was that hard up..." Jake sighed. "In retrospect, of course things are more clear, but it just seemed like if Emmett was still carrying that grudge and hated me so much, maybe all he needed was to hear that confession from me. We never really had closure. I figured if that's how he wanted to get closure, then what's the harm?"

Quinn was dubious. Nobody went to that much trouble just to hear some bogus ten-year-old confession.

"I think you should tell Rico about it now, Jake," Loma said.

"I don't know." Jake looked at Quinn. "What do you think?"

"What's the worst that could happen?" It was advice Quinn had heard from her dad numerous times over the years, whenever she began a spiral of catastrophizing. Her problems never involved such high stakes or dire circumstances, however.

"But you didn't tell me what you think."

"What I think doesn't really matter right now," Quinn told him. "It only matters what Rico thinks." She didn't verbalize what was really troubling her. It was clear Jake stashed his phone and those notes at Loma's guesthouse, since he didn't ask where Loma had gotten them. He knew both were incriminating, despite what he'd just told them. Emmett was blackmailing Jake and Jake knew it. Jake delivered the money—or said he did, anyway—after Emmett already ate the poisoned mushrooms. Emmett died in the diner when Jake claimed to be on his terrible scavenger hunt. But that last note that Jethro found? *I know what you did, Jake* didn't sound like it was from Emmett. Of course, Emmett would know what Jake had done, whether it was referring to past transgressions or the current ransom demands.

It sounded to Quinn like Jake had another blackmailer. But was it one who knew that Jake did something with the mushrooms, or was it something else?

"You need to tell Rico." Loma went right up to the bars on the cell so Jake could see how serious she was.

"I don't think that's a good idea. This noose is tight enough as it is."

"It gets you off the hook. It shows you weren't even around when Emmett died."

"We've been over this, Loma," he said. "Emmett was poisoned at the governor's fundraiser. His death came later."

Loma and Jake bickered back and forth about the ramifications of telling Rico that Emmett had been blackmailing Jake.

Quinn paid no attention, trying to decide whether the conversation with Rico should be to tell him that Jake had a blackmailer, or that Jake might have two blackmailers. And would he even listen after their little tiff about her online review? Of course, he'd listen. Rico was a professional.

She ran through how she'd expect the conversation to go, but no matter which role she took or which direction the conversation went, it always ended with Rico telling her to bring him solutions, not problems. That was the aphorism he'd heard a zillion times from *his* dad growing up. Maybe that was why he hadn't really conferred with her on this case, despite promising he would. Maybe he didn't want to simply bring problems to her. *Or maybe*, Quinn considered, *maybe he just didn't trust me.*

"Quinn! Are you listening?" Jake bellowed at her.

She snapped to attention. "What?"

"Oh, hush, Jacob Joseph Szabo. There's no need to yell at her," Loma said, flinging an arm around Quinn's shoulder. "She wasn't the one who closed the diner. It was me." Loma stage-whispered in her ear. "He thinks you're slacking off, shirking your diner duties, eating bonbons all day."

"I'm not—"

"I said nothing of the kind! Quinn, don't believe a word she says. I simply asked—very politely and reasonably, I might add—who was handling the diner right now."

"And I told you, nobody is. Because Quinn and I just found out a new twist to your case and we thought it was more important to talk to you and Rico about it than to serve salads to cranky women." Loma clasped hands with Quinn and turned toward the staircase. "So on that note, we will extend a hearty farewell, whilst we go conversate with Rico." She ushered Quinn ahead of her, then added, "And you can apologize to Quinn later. She doesn't need your grief on top of everything else. Shame on you."

Quinn was halfway up the stairs, waiting for Loma. "He doesn't have to—"

"Yes, he does. And he would have if I hadn't hustled you out of there." Loma was grinning at her. "But let's make him stew about it for a bit. It shouldn't even cross his mind to holler at you for closing the diner every so often. You're only human, right?"

"I guess."

Loma laughed. "You guess you're human?"

"Some days I'm not so sure."

Rico was waiting for them at the top of the stairs. "Hello, ladies."

"Are we glad to see you," Loma said, brushing past him.

Rico raised his eyebrows at Quinn, who just shrugged.

"Let's get the big man involved in this." Loma raised her hand to knock on Chief Chestnut's door.

Rico grabbed her wrist and walked her out to the center area. "Involved in what?"

"The big twist in Jake's case."

"How 'bout you run it by me first?" Rico glanced at his desk next to Donnie's. Donnie sat, watching the interaction. Rico crossed the room and opened the door to the conference room. He motioned for the two women to sit down.

Loma began talking before she took a seat. She told Rico all about the blackmail notes Jake had received and what Jake had done about them. She finished with a triumphant, "And that shows you Jake didn't kill Emmett."

Rico and Quinn hadn't said a word the entire time, but now he looked at her with the tiniest hint of a raised eyebrow. Quinn knew that meant he wanted her opinion. Instead, she looked at her lap.

Rico took a moment to formulate his thoughts. "All it shows me is that Jake was being blackmailed by Emmett Dubois and Emmett Dubois winds up dead."

"But Emmett wasn't asking for anything. He just wanted Jake's confession."

"I thought you told me Jake delivered two hundred dollars cash in response to a blackmail note."

"But what's two hundred bucks? It's nothing. That ain't serious ransom. That's just...just..."

"A token," Quinn finished for Loma.

"Right on." Loma flashed Quinn a double thumbs-up. "And that statement Jake was supposed to read. He said every word was absolutely true."

Impatience sounded in Rico's voice. "Look. Here are the facts you just brought me. Jake served deadly mushrooms to the man who was blackmailing him. And he never mentioned any of this to me, despite having many opportunities." He looked from Loma to Quinn. "Does that seem like something an innocent man would do?"

Quinn didn't say that his point was legitimate, but she did feel like she needed to offer an opposing argument. "Rico, what is Jake's motive to kill Emmett? Nothing in the blackmail notes was so outrageous as to ruin Jake's life or send him over the edge of despair. Like Loma said, everything was true and most of it was already public knowledge, or at least public knowledge within Jake's circle of friends. None of this information would harm Jake professionally or personally, and that two hundred dollars was not a hardship for him to pay. It probably came out of the petty cash at the diner."

"Petty cash. You tell him." Loma crossed her arms and boosted her bosom until it flopped over her wrists. Quinn began to recognize this as Loma's I-mean-business posture. She had to admit, it had power.

Rico stared at them. Quinn saw his nose twitch. "I'm not gonna lie—"

"As if that needed to be said."

"—but this twist, as you call it, does not look good for Jake. In fact, it looks very, very bad." Quinn and Loma began to speak at the same time, but Rico held up one hand to silence them. "You've told me what you wanted to tell me and now I have to think about it." Rico stood and Quinn did too. Loma remained seated with her arms crossed.

Quinn left the conference room while Loma stayed behind to reiterate all the same arguments to Rico. Quinn walked over to Donnie, sitting at his desk filling out a form. "Hey, Donnie. Can I ask you something?"

Donnie glanced up, suspicion on his face. "I guess."

"When you were at the diner the other day, why did you race out the back when Rico came in?"

He stared hard at her, jaw working.

It was clear to Quinn he had some important reason to keep the answer to himself. He kept staring at her and she leaned in, anticipating gathering another clue in this mystery. *Maybe this would be the one that cracks it wide open and exonerates Jake.* She tried to arrange her face in an open manner, inviting Donnie to spill his innermost secrets.

Finally, he glanced across the room toward the conference room where Loma was still haranguing Rico, then he glanced to the side to see if Chief Chestnut was around. Assuring himself that his secret would only be heard by Quinn, he leaned closer to her and whispered. "Because he'll tell my mom I'm off my diet. Have you ever noticed he can't tell a lie? Not even for a friend? It's creepy."

Quinn sighed. "You're right, it is creepy."

Even though his door was closed, Chief Chestnut's bellow from his office sailed easily to Donnie's desk. "Garfield! What the hell is a poem that has fourteen lines?"

Rondel, Quinn thought.

"Don't know, Chief," Donnie bellowed back. Then, quieter to Quinn, "He's doing the crossword."

"I thought that only came out on Wednesdays," she said innocently.

"Special edition. He wouldn't shut up about it. If he was a happier sort, I think he would have danced a jig."

Quinn felt the warmth of self-satisfaction radiating through her body. She tamped it down so she wouldn't look smug, then rescued Rico by dragging Loma away from the police station. Back at the diner she kept the *Closed* sign visible and locked the door.

"I think you and me are the only two people on earth who think Jake is innocent. We've got to get him out of the slammer." Loma glanced around the diner and began snapping the rubber band on her wrist.

Quinn wondered if snapping that band was one of those "tells," like in poker where players subconsciously signal what they're thinking. Did it mean Loma didn't think Jake was innocent? Did it mean Loma was hiding something? Quinn couldn't decide, but she did know she wasn't going to mention that she wasn't completely convinced of Jake's innocence. Questions kept piling up and what Quinn was sure of yesterday, she wondered about today.

"I need some tea," Quinn said. "Want some?"

"Sure."

"And we better talk in Jake's office so nobody sees the lights and thinks we're open." Keeping the diner closed made Quinn's palms sweat, but she couldn't focus right now on the diner. These blackmail notes would have to become her obsession.

After they had steaming mugs of peppermint tea in front of them, Quinn said, "Tell me about the fundraiser."

"What's to tell? Boring speeches, big checks, brazen self-promotion for my interior design business. At least the food was good."

Quinn wrapped her hands around the mug, the warmth soothing on her hands. She'd almost forgotten about that boiling pot of oatmeal. She was lucky she hadn't been seriously burned. "Did you know Jake was cooking?"

"Not 'til I got there."

"Did you recognize other people there?"

"Of course, all movers and shakers." Loma rattled off a list of names Quinn had never heard of. "And Emmett, of course."

"Did you talk to him?"

"No. I was busy trying to drum up business from my tablemates and I knew he was broke." A guilty grimace flashed across Loma's face. "I know it was supposed to be a fundraiser for the governor, but I need to raise funds more than he does."

"Is your business…struggling?" Quinn knew this was prying, but she was technically investigating a crime, not conversing with a friend.

Loma blanched. "No! Why, have you heard something?"

"No, not a word. I was just…prying."

"Just between us friends, I'm not doing bad, but I could do better. And now I feel awful laying it on so thick with Margosha to hire me, especially when I was a guest at her table." Loma whipped out her phone. "Look at how lovely it was." She held out her phone to Quinn while scrolling through photos. The ballroom was decorated in silver and teal. Loma paused at a photo of her with her arm around the waist of another woman, all exotic hair and makeup. She had several inches on Loma. "Man, I looked hot that night. On *fuego*."

"Smokin'. Who's that with you? She's gorgeous."

"That's Margosha."

"Wow. I bet she's wearing enough makeup to paint a barn."

"Nope. Not that I noticed anyway. And I don't think she's had any work done either."

"Remarkable. And very unfair." Quinn patted her hopeless bun and plucked at her baggy clothes.

Quinn's fears that Rico's head might be turned roared back. "I've been trying to talk to her but she keeps avoiding me. Any idea why?"

"No clue. Her English isn't so great, even though she's been here a pretty long time. But you can get away with a lot when you're that gorgeous. Maybe she just didn't know why you were calling. Why do you want to talk to her?"

"Her alibi, for one thing."

"Same as everyone else. She was at the fundraiser."

"Yeah, I guess in this case alibis are stupid. What I'm more interested in anyway is whether she's the beneficiary of Emmett's life insurance and whatever estate he has. I want to know if she knows who the silent partner was in Emmett's business." Quinn watched Loma's face very carefully to see if she had any reaction to the words *silent partner*. Loma's face was buried in her teacup. "I also want to know if Margosha knew any of the cater-waiters who were serving at the fundraiser." Quinn looked at Loma. "Did you know any of the servers?"

"None that come to mind." She shrugged. "But I go to a lot of events like that. They all kinda run together."

Quinn nodded, but as someone who never went to fancy events, she was not entirely sure if what Loma said made sense. "And I want to know if Margosha was ever in the kitchen that night." Quinn pressed her lips together, worried she'd said too much, but her brain was working overtime. "Wait. You said her English was bad. Is that a reason someone would cut letters from a magazine for a blackmail note? So they don't have to call anyone on the phone? Or is that strictly to disguise handwriting?" Quinn realized she had been touching her fingers to her thumbs, and slid her hands under her thighs. "Can you get her to talk to me?"

"I can try." Loma pulled out her phone but had to leave a voice mail. "Hey, Margosha. Two things. Have you found Emmett's paperwork about what he wants for his funeral? I mean, if we can't find it we can try and guess about flowers and music and whatnot, but we don't even know if he wants cremation or burial. So let me know. And the second thing is, my friend Quinn needs to talk to you. She has some questions for you about Jake that might help get him out of jail. She'll call you tomorrow." Loma raised her eyebrows and Quinn nodded.

"You know, maybe she doesn't want to talk to me because she thinks Jake's guilty. Why would she want to talk to me if I think he's innocent?"

"Good point."

They both sipped their tea, peppermint permeating the air in Jake's office.

"So, you're helping plan Emmett's funeral?"

Loma nodded. "I've known the two of them forever and I have some experience with funerals. Buried both my mama and pops last year."

"I'm sorry to hear that."

Loma brushed Quinn's sympathy aside. "It is what it is. I try to remember the good stuff." She drained her tea, then crossed her arms.

Quinn stiffened, worried about what was coming next. She relaxed immediately when Loma said, "You know, in cop shows, they always have a big whiteboard or something to write all their clues on. Can we do that?"

Quinn's eyes lit up and she stood. "We can indeed. We don't have a whiteboard, but there's a huge roll of butcher paper and colored markers in the storeroom. We can use the big booth." She checked the time. "It's after closing so it doesn't matter now if anyone sees us out there."

Quinn tore off a tablecloth-sized piece of paper and draped it across the entire table. Loma dropped the markers in the center.

"Let's write down all the suspects." Quinn grabbed a thick black marker and, centered at the top, wrote in all caps: *WHO KILLED EMMETT DUBOIS?* Using a red marker, she began a bulleted list at the left margin by writing *MURDER MYSTERY PARTY GUY*. Then a blue one and wrote *SILENT PARTNER*.

Then a green one, *MARGOSHA DUBOIS*. Yellow for *ANONYMOUS CALLER*. Pink for *MICHAEL BRECKENRIDGE*.

"Who's that?"

"An ex-employee of Jake's who's acting really hinky."

"Hinky?"

"Suspicious. Keeps hanging up on me."

"I hang up on people all the time."

"But all of Jake's other ex-employees have been happy to talk to me and tell me what a great boss Jake was."

"Great?"

"I know, right?" Quinn picked up the purple marker and wrote *DONNIE GARFIELD*. Quinn had held the slanted tip the wrong way and was dismayed to see how different it looked from the way she'd written the other names. It was all she could do to keep from wadding up the paper and starting over, since she'd ruined the entire thing. She would have if she'd been alone.

"Wait. The cop? Why him?"

"I don't know. Just a gut feeling. Don't you think it's weird that even though he never takes initiative—according to Rico anyway—he immediately thought the mushrooms might be important and preserved them? But at the same time he can't identify the guy who gave him the plate to serve to Emmett?"

Loma nodded. "I guess."

She cut her eyes at Loma, who held out the orange marker with an expectant look.

"Who's next?"

Quinn uncapped the orange marker, but hovered it above the butcher paper. She lowered it far enough to make a bullet on the page before lifting it in the air again. She did this three more times before Loma grabbed her wrist.

"Just write it. The suspense is killing me!"

Quinn pulled the face people made when they smelled garbage or tasted a bad clam. Or accused their boss of murder. Then she wrote *JAKE SZABO.*

Loma took a step back from the table. "No way. You're kidding, right?"

Quinn began touching the fingers on her left hand to her thumb. Her right hand still gripped the orange marker. "I don't like it any more than you do, but Rico is right. Jake was being blackmailed and now the blackmailer is dead. That doesn't look good."

"But you said yourself that someone might be pretending to be Emmett blackmailing Jake."

"True. But now that I think about it, it's kind of a long shot, isn't it?"

The two women stared at the butcher paper. Finally Loma said, "You know that's a work of art, right? How do you get everything so straight? And I love the drop shadow boxes around all their names."

All Quinn could see was the terrible purple slant to Donnie Garfield's name. And, of course, the names of potential murderers. To avoid having to talk further about them, Quinn added some more flourishes. She made sure all the T's were crossed with the same-sized line. She added a triangle to the center of the capital A's and a dot in the center of the O's, in contrasting colors.

"Such a lovely list for a terrible project."

"Like all of my reports for school. My teachers loved me. I was very organized." Loma didn't need all the particulars, but Quinn continued: "When I was ten, I got an entire box of *Cagney and Lacey* videotapes from my neighbor's garage sale."

"I loved that show! They were so kickass, and yet those stupid men never gave them the props they deserved." Loma *tsk-tsked.*

"I watched every episode that summer, that's all I did. Then I went back and organized and color-coded them as to season and episode, numbering them from one to one hundred on a complicated scale where I analyzed believability of crime, cuteness of guest stars, and whether I solved the crime before the second set of commercials." Suddenly embarrassed, Quinn quit talking and turned away from Loma. She lined up the markers at the top of the butcher paper in the order she'd used them.

Loma lightly touched her back. "How is your OCD?" she asked quietly.

Quinn whirled around. "How did you—"

"Well, it's pretty obvious right now and the way you checked the lock so many times, but Jake told me when he was thinking about hiring you. And the other day, he told me he was worried about you with everything going on."

"You two talk about me?" Quinn blushed.

Loma shrugged. "We talk all the time. How do you think I knew about those chocolate strawberries? You'd think by looking at me that sniffing out chocolate was my superpower. But really, Jake called and invited me over. After all, it was my alimony day too."

"But…"

"Ain't no big deal."

Quinn didn't know if she meant the OCD or the fact she and Jake talked all the time. Either way, Quinn was shocked. Jake was worried about her? He didn't act like it. Just like he didn't act like he was besties with Loma.

Loma saw the look on Quinn's face and laughed. "Girl, you look like I just ate an iguana, tail first."

"But the way you two talked that day. I thought you hated each other."

Loma waved her hand as if shooing away a pesky gnat. "It's all an act. He worries, but doesn't like to show it. I have diabetes, which is why he was so mad at me when I wanted to eat those scrumptious-looking chocolates. Didn't you see how he kept trying to hand me that bowl of fruit? This rubber band was his idea." She snapped it twice. "He figured when I get tempted by sweets I could snap myself out of it. It's terrible when I come here."

Quinn remembered all the snapping going on when Loma was in the diner that day. "If he didn't want you to eat those chocolate strawberries, why'd he make them, then call you to come over?"

"He's an enigma." Loma laughed. "Why does Jake do anything?"

Like hire someone with OCD, Quinn thought. Or not tell anyone he was being blackmailed.

"And why aren't you snapping now? You're in the diner."

Loma waved her arm around. "Do you see anything to tempt me? No pies out. No Danish. Barely any food at all, from what I hear."

Quinn glanced around the diner. She wasn't wrong. "Be right back," she told Loma. When she returned, she was wearing a rubber band on each wrist.

Loma shook her head. "Won't work. You're just gonna substitute it for that finger thing you do and organizing and color-coding everything."

Quinn felt naked, on display in front of Loma, who'd seen everything.

"Ain't no better than a Band-Aid," Loma continued. "If it worked, would I still be sixty pounds overweight and this close"—she held her thumb and her first finger two millimeters apart—"to needing insulin?"

Quinn didn't respond, but kept both rubber bands on. If counting, organizing, and her finger thing hadn't yet worked to keep her anxiety at bay, maybe this would.

They spent the next two hours discussing each suspect, sharing information, formulating theories, nit-picking every fact, arguing about Jake's possible involvement. Things began to get heated when they discussed Jake, so they agreed to table that conversation until they had more facts. But neither knew how they were going to get more facts.

Plus, despite the fact she was beginning to like Loma quite a bit, something still nagged at her. Maybe sleep would help.

Chapter 13

Though Quinn couldn't sleep, she spent the night in bed running over everything she and Loma had talked about. Loma was so convinced of Jake's innocence that Quinn decided to set aside her feelings about it for now.

She wondered if reading would help her relax. Even though tomorrow was Saturday and Chris and Kristi would handle the diner, another sleepless night would be bad for her health, mental and otherwise. She clicked on her lamp and picked up a magazine from her nightstand. Flipping through the pages, she stopped at a long profile piece about a Silicon Valley wunderkind. It came complete with a full-page photo of him in his office, a mischievous grin pulling the corners of his mouth. If it was a different kind of magazine, she'd expect to read about how much he liked long walks on the beach, candlelight dinners, and smart, playful women who love to travel.

Quinn dropped the magazine. Didn't Jake tell her about some interview he and Emmett had done that caused bad blood between them? She searched their names online and found it exactly like Jake said, more about him than Emmett. No wonder it hadn't come up when Quinn had searched for information about Emmett. Jake was quoted extensively and there were two photos of Jake—one in his chef garb in a kitchen, and one where he was sitting on the arm of a couch, a mischievous grin pulling the corners of his mouth, just like the guy in the other article. It must be the pose du jour for business profiles.

Nothing she read was earth-shattering or gave her any new information, but she read it through again, then took a chance that the reporter might remember any of this. Maybe even give her more information, but of what she wasn't certain.

Quinn clicked on the byline "Patti Rich" and emailed her. She explained that she was curious about the article and linked to it so Patti would know what she was referring to. It had been some years ago, after all.

Just a couple of minutes after Quinn pressed *send* on the email, a reply popped up. *I remember that article and interview. What do you want to know? I'm available to talk now if you want to call.*

Quinn dialed the number she gave. "Hi, Patti. I'm surprised you want to talk since it's so late."

"I'm waiting outside a bar, probably until closing. There's a guy I need to ambush."

"With questions, I hope."

Patti laughed. "Yes, just questions. So what did you want to know about Jake Szabo?"

"I'm not really sure. I work for him and he told me about this interview. And now with Emmett Dubois dead—"

"I heard about that. How terrible! Now I feel bad I didn't highlight him more in the article."

"Why didn't you?"

"Honestly? I found Jake so much more charming and interesting than Emmett. Put them in a room together and see who the crowd gravitates toward. It won't be Emmett." Patti paused. "I guess that can't happen now. Poor Emmett." Patti confirmed everything Quinn had already been told about Emmett and Jake, but then added, "Jake spun out of control after his firing, drinking too much, confronting anyone he thought might be involved in his firing, and he stalked Emmett. No other way to say it. Followed him around town, waiting for him to come out of his apartment."

"And nobody called the cops?"

"Not that I know. I think everyone felt as bad as Jake did, so they just let him rage. Plus, like I said, everybody liked Jake and nobody really understood why Emmett fired him. There were stories about embezzlement and something about an affair, as I recall, but nothing really made sense. All just gossip. Just like some supposed silent partner I could never track down."

They chatted a bit more until Patti interrupted herself. "Gotta go—there's my guy," and disconnected.

Quinn puzzled over why nobody had mentioned Jake's meltdown before this. Was it true or was it the product of a reporter's faulty memory? Surely Patti Rich had written a million words since she'd written that article. She couldn't possibly keep all those facts straight, but she sounded very confident. Maybe it was a reporter's skill.

If it was true, that everyone felt bad about Jake's firing and they all knew he was a better chef than Emmett, Quinn felt even more confident that there was never any reason for Jake to murder Emmett. Jake told her he had received lots of offers from big-deal restaurants over the years, but turned them all down. He liked his diner in Chestnut Station. He could do any menu he wanted, as long as cheeseburgers, BLTs, green chili, and some kind of pie was always on it to satisfy the palate of his regulars. He was able to do a turn at the many hipster pop-up restaurants in Denver whenever he felt like it, and the cost of living was low enough that he didn't have to worry excessively about money. Until now, that is.

The more she thought about it, the more Jake's original assessment of the blackmail notes made sense. If it was Emmett sending the notes, he clearly wanted closure. He was either feeling guilty for treating Jake the way he did, or he truly felt he deserved an apology from Jake.

If Emmett hadn't sent the notes himself, it wasn't a stretch to think that someone close to Emmett who knew about all the bad blood between him and Jake could use that information to pretend to be Emmett and set up Jake for his murder.

At about two in the morning, Quinn decided that Margosha was her main suspect. She had to be involved, probably for the life insurance or some other financial gain. After all, Emmett had owned very high-end restaurants. Surely they hadn't all failed and left him with nothing, despite what Kelli had told her at the Crazy Mule.

Even though it was late, she texted Rico, knowing that he'd answer and that he'd tell her the truth. Are you looking in to Margosha? Is she a suspect?

Don't you ever sleep?

Is she?

She's not a suspect.

Why?

Because she's not. Go to sleep.

Do you know who the silent partner in Emmett's business was?

No. Go to sleep.

Are you sure it's not Margosha?

Go. To. Sleep.

She turned her pillow to the cool side, then settled into it. Was Chief Chestnut tying Rico's hands somehow, or was Rico learning to tell well-placed fibs? If so, did he really have to learn it right now? Everyone knew that to survive this world, both personally and professionally, one had to fib.

When her dad schmoozed clients, he took them out to restaurants that were more expensive than he could truly afford, just to impress them. That was a fib.

When the Retireds complained about the coffee being stale, didn't Jake just take their mugs and refill them with coffee from the same pot? They were none the wiser and everybody ended up happy. That was a fib too.

When Abe the handyman winked at her while telling Georgeanne that it would take him until Friday to paint the kitchen that time, only to finish on Wednesday, he was fibbing. He'd told Quinn so himself. "Just good business," he'd said. "Promise them something they can live with, then deliver sooner. Why do you think I get so many glowing referrals?"

Abe got referrals because he was skilled at his job. Just like Dad and Jake. And Rico.

But maybe, despite the fact Rico was a good cop, maybe he got his head turned by Margosha's extreme beauty. Gorgeous women had that effect on men. "If she's so innocent, why won't she talk to me?" Quinn angrily punched her pillow and turned it over again, knowing that Margosha had absolutely no reason or duty to speak to her about anything.

Quinn flounced on to her back and interlaced her fingers behind her head. Was Margosha Emmett's beneficiary? Quinn picked up her phone and texted that very question to Rico. She couldn't believe she hadn't asked him that already. She stared at her phone: one minute, two minutes. Loma told her that Margosha and Emmett didn't have any children. Five minutes, ten minutes. No answer. He must have turned off his phone for the night.

But if not Margosha, then who?

It seemed all of her theories so far had yielded nothing; been wrong, wrong, wrong.

Quinn sat bolt upright in bed. Wrong. When she was talking to Jake's headhunter he'd said "Wrong" and so had the murder mystery guy. It bothered her both times because it was a weirdly antagonistic thing to say. Narcissistic, perhaps. It couldn't be a coincidence. Jake's headhunter was the murder mystery guy!

She scrambled for her phone and texted Rico again. Jake's headhunter is the guy from the diner who was with Emmett that night. He works for Colorado Premium Employment. I don't have the number here because I called from Jake's call history at the diner.

She hoped Rico would call her back, despite the fact he hadn't answered her earlier text.

Typing *Colorado Premium Employment* into an internet search would show the phone number and she could pass that along to Rico. She stared at her phone. No results. *Did you mean Colorado Prestige Employment?* the internet asked. Quinn was sure it was Premium. She typed it again, slower and more carefully this time. Same thing. How was that possible? She squeezed her eyes tight to better access the memory of Jake's call history. She saw it very clearly in her mind: Colorado Premium Employment. His name was Sam. She thought he had indigestion. He called Chestnut Station a wasteland. It was Premium.

She texted Rico again.

* * * *

Rico had just fallen back to sleep when another text woke him. He groaned, fumbling for his phone, hoping it wasn't Donnie needing him at the station. Quinn again. He read the text, a solid block of disjointed facts he couldn't understand. He stared at his phone but didn't respond to her, suddenly very concerned she was heading directly into an OCD spiral. Maybe she was in it already.

He'd done some internet research about OCD when he found out about her diagnosis, but not much and not in any great depth. It wasn't because he didn't want to know about OCD, but because he was afraid if he knew too much it would color his thinking about her. He wanted their friendship to stay strong. It wasn't until a couple of days after their so-called date that he realized she'd been right. That could have been a complete friendship-ruiner.

But now he wondered if telling her she could help with his investigations wasn't just as potentially dangerous to their friendship as it was to her.

Texting him questions and unfocused notions in the middle of the night couldn't be healthy.

No matter how much he wanted her to pursue a law enforcement career, it wasn't his decision. He shouldn't push her and he shouldn't let her involve herself in his investigations.

A job in law enforcement might not even be possible for her anymore.

Rico placed his phone back on his nightstand without answering her.

* * * *

Quinn must have fallen asleep because she'd forgotten to lower the volume on her phone and the sound of a new text landing in her inbox launched her out of bed. "Serves me right," she grumbled as she hoisted herself up off the rag rug on her floor. She picked up her phone to see what Rico had to say. But it was just a text from her cellphone provider advising her she was now eligible to upgrade to a new phone. No thank you.

She called Rico and he answered with a grunt.

"I know it's early, but you didn't answer my texts last night."

"Because I was sleeping. Like you should have been."

"I was too excited to sleep. Didn't you see what I sent? The guy in the diner is Jake's headhunter! They both said *Wrong* to me in a really weird way."

"So you say. Did you know there's no business called Colorado Premium Employment?"

"Well, there's none listed on the internet. But it exists. I called it from Jake's office phone and talked to the guy the other day. He gave me some snooty attitude, so it's probably one of those word-of-mouth-only places. But it exists, Rico, it exists. You can call him yourself. Go into Jake's office and hit the *call history* button. You'll have to scroll, but it's right there under Colorado Premium Employment. Oh—or maybe look in Jake's Rolodex. Maybe he has a card in there. Then go over there and arrest him."

"Go over where, Quinn? Do you have an address?"

"No, but—"

"Do you know this guy's name?"

"I told you in my text. It's Sam."

"Sam what?"

Rico had steadily dropped his voice and Quinn realized he was trying to placate her.

"Rico, I am not some toddler who missed her nap! I have figured out something important in our case and I'm sharing it with you so you can do your police thing and catch this murderer!"

There was a long pause, then Rico said softly, "It's not *our* case, Quinn. It's my case." After another pause he added, "Why don't you try to get some sleep? We can talk more later."

* * * *

At a more reasonable hour, after she'd had a heart-to-heart with Fang, taken a long shower, and calmed down from her conversation with Rico, Quinn texted Loma for Margosha's address. Just because Rico wasn't going to investigate didn't mean she wouldn't.

Before she headed to Denver, Quinn swung by the jail. She hoped Rico would be there so she could give him a piece of her mind, but he wasn't.

She'd been so stunned by what he'd said it had rendered her speechless. He'd finally simply hung up. She felt like everything she wanted to say to him was going to choke her if she didn't get to speak her mind.

Donnie unlocked the door to the lockup and waved her through. When Jake sat up on the side of the bed, he looked like she'd awakened him. She knew from experience that sleeping too much was a sign of depression. Or was it just a sign of Jake's boredom? Or the fact it probably was the crack of early for people who actually slept normally.

"Tell me about your headhunter, Sam at Colorado Premium Employment." Jake yawned and rubbed his face. "What do you want to know?"

"Where's his office?"

"No idea. Never been there."

"What's he look like?"

"Never met him. Only talked to him on the phone."

"What's his last name?"

Jake cocked his head and stared into space. "I don't think I've ever known it. He always just says, *This is Sam from Colorado Premium Employment.*"

"Did you know his business isn't listed anywhere on the internet?"

"What's all this about, Quinn?"

"I think he's the guy with Emmett the night he was killed."

Jake stood up and walked over to her, gripping the bars of the cell with both hands. "Why?"

Quinn didn't want to get into the whole *Wrong* thing, since in the daylight it was beginning to seem like a very tenuous clue. "Just some things he said to me when I talked to him."

"Did you tell Rico?"

She looked at Jake's hopeful face. How could she tell him that Rico didn't believe her, didn't seem willing to pursue it any further, and didn't really want her involved in the investigation anymore? "Yeah. We're going to talk about it more later. But I wanted to ask you something else. I talked to that reporter last night…Patti Rich. The one who wrote about you and Emmett and the restaurants."

Jake ran his hands through his hair, making it stand up in odd directions. "And?"

"And she said you were a wee bit annoyed when Emmett fired you. *Raged* was the word she used."

"Yeah, so I raged." His voice was monotone. "Said some things I probably shouldn't have. But I got over it. I knew I was the better chef. More creative and more intuitive and had better people skills. After a few days, I realized I'd land on my feet while Emmett would always have to struggle. I didn't want to pile on." At Quinn's skepticism he added, "We had history. We'd been friends for a long time before that."

Quinn asked, "Did you ever clear your name, set the record straight, that you were the better chef?"

"No. Seemed like bad form, sour grapes, taking advantage when he couldn't defend himself. People were mad. Turned against him. What good would it have done? I just moved on."

Quinn stared at him, wanting to believe, but just not sure.

Jake was studying her sundress and sandals. "Are you on your way to the diner?"

"Nope. It's Saturday. My day off. I'm heading to Denver today. Maybe walk around the lake at City Park." But he didn't need to know the rest of her plans.

She left the jail. Still no Rico. It was probably just as well. She was still too angry and, if she was being honest, hurt and embarrassed that he thought of her as a child he needed to pacify. He'd go over to Jake's office and find that phone number, call it, talk to Sam, and figure out she was right about the whole thing.

Quinn debated whether she actually needed to go to Denver, now that it was pretty clear Sam the headhunter was the one who killed Emmett. But she was still curious about Margosha and wanted some answers from her. Plus, it was a glorious day off and she could leave Chestnut Station for an excursion if she wanted.

As she turned her ignition, she had a fleeting thought that maybe Rico *wouldn't* go over to Jake's office and get that phone number. Maybe he wouldn't be able to get away from his desk today. Maybe he wasn't even going to be in Chestnut Station today.

Quinn pulled away from the curb and headed for the diner. It was a bit too early for Chris and Kristi to get there to start prep, so she used her key and hurried to Jake's office. It seemed to be too early for Jethro as well, which saved her the time waiting for him to make his rounds of the diner. Chris could give him his bacon payment.

She checked Jake's Rolodex first, but there was nothing under *Sam* or *Colorado Premium Employment* so she hit the *call history* button until she saw it. It was too early to call and see if she could get the address, so she entered it into her contacts.

Then she texted Rico. In case you can't get over to the diner today, here's the headhunter's #. Jake doesn't know his name or address.

* * * *

"Oh, shoot." Quinn pulled to the side of the road and dialed her phone. "Hey, Chris, I forgot to tell you that the guy never showed up to fix the credit card machine. I told him that Saturday was our busiest day and—"

"Don't matter to me."

"Okay, that's great. I've just been keeping track of the cash, then dropping it in the night drop at the bank. Nobody has complained yet. If you want me to, I can swing by later and do the deposit for you."

"Won't be here."

"What do you mean?"

"I mean, we won't be here so you can come whenever you want."

Quinn felt her jaw tighten. "Where will you be?"

"Me and the missus are on our way to Boise."

"Boise? Idaho? You and Kristi are supposed to be working at the diner today and tomorrow! Why are you going to Boise?"

"We're moving there! Rad, huh? Got a sweet deal on a house and a job with Kristi's dad."

Quinn stared out the window, counted fence posts, and snapped the rubber band on her wrist.

"You still there?"

"Why didn't you tell me this on Thursday when we talked?" Quinn tried to control the volume and tone of her voice. Screechy wouldn't help solve this problem.

"We didn't leave until yesterday. Tell Jake he can just send our paychecks to us at—"

Quinn disconnected. "They can shove their paychecks right up their—" She covered her face with her hands and tried to steady her breathing. The only thing that had kept her going all week was the thought of a glorious weekend away from the diner. Now—poof—gone to Boise.

She snapped the rubber band as she ran through her options. Keep the diner closed until she got back to Chestnut Station. Turn around right now. Dynamite Jake out of jail. Get someone else on the payroll yesterday.

With a sigh, she put the car in gear to go back to Chestnut Station, then immediately put it back into *park*. She picked up her phone. "Mom? Are you and Dad busy today?"

* * * *

"Hurry up, Dan! We have to get to the diner. Quinn's counting on us."
"I'm hurrying." Dan finished lacing up his sneakers. "Nobody wants to see me in my flip-flops when they're eating."

As they sped to the diner, Georgeanne ticked off the instructions Quinn gave her. "Spare keys in the electrical box. Simple is better, nothing fancy. And we don't have to offer Jake's menu. We'll have to make do with whatever is on hand and she's not sure when they'll get the next delivery."

"Is that all?"

"Oh, and the credit card dealybob and the cash register are both broken, so we can only take cash. She said she'll be back as quick as she can. And she'll do a deposit when she gets here."

"Sounds easy enough." Dan squeezed his wife's knee.

"Right? Easy peasy lemon squeezy!" Georgeanne grinned at him and rearranged the canvas bag on her lap.

"What do you have in there, anyway?"

"Nothing much. Just my spices and things from the cupboard I might need." Georgeanne's dimples deepened.

* * * *

Quinn sat on a bench in front of the lake at City Park in Denver. There had been no traffic on the drive so she had plenty of time for a visit with the ducks and geese. When she lived in Denver, this was one of the places she liked to hang out whenever she had the time. Normally, she liked to walk the path around the lake, but today she decided on the bench. The morning sun cast long shadows across the lake and park. Not many people were here yet, but she knew it would be crowded before long with families heading to the zoo and the Museum of Nature & Science, or just enjoying the lake with its swan-shaped paddleboats, picnic spots, and playgrounds. For now, though, it was quiet and peaceful. The only people around were a group of yoga enthusiasts saluting the sun and the occasional jogger or biker.

Quinn took the opportunity to practice what to say to Margosha. Because she couldn't leave her parents to run the diner for too long, she decided a quick conversation with her was the way to go. But now she worried that it would come out bossy and curt.

"Margosha…" Quinn practiced. "Hi there, Margosha, isn't this a lovely…Good morning, Margosha. We've never met, but I'm a friend of Loma's. She told you I wanted to talk to you? I need you to tell me…"

Good grief. She's never going to talk to me. Why would she? She'll just slam the door in my face.

She tried several more openers and segues, but landed on nothing that would be surefire.

Quinn gave up and checked the time. She scrolled her contacts for Colorado Premium Employment and then groaned. It was Saturday. It wouldn't even be open today. She immediately brightened, thinking that if it went to voice mail, maybe there'd be an address or something on their message. She clicked the number and almost instantaneously heard the dreaded three tones that signaled a disconnected number.

She stared at the phone in her hand. She knew she'd input the number correctly. But what did this mean? Was her theory completely off base? Or was Sam the headhunter on the run and covering his trail?

She sat on the bench a while longer, getting more and more depressed as it became increasingly clear they'd never find him. Without another suspect, Chief Chestnut wouldn't let Jake go.

Well, I'll just have to make a pretty compelling case for someone else.

She practiced more opening lines for her meeting with Margosha while she picked her way through the park, trying to avoid the copious quantities of goose poop on the way to her car.

* * * *

She pulled to the curb in front of Margosha's neighbor's house, where a beautiful honey locust shaded the street. She sat for twenty minutes with her windows rolled down to catch a breeze while she tried to screw up the courage to ring Margosha's doorbell.

A noise caught Quinn's attention and she saw Margosha's garage door slowly rise. A pristine BMW backed out. When it got to the end of the driveway, Quinn saw Margosha check for traffic. Quinn ducked down and immediately regretted it. Her posture reeked of deceit and suspicion. If Margosha saw her planted there in front of her neighbor's house, spying on her, she would never in a million years talk to her.

Quinn slowly lifted her head in time to see Margosha drive away. "She must not have seen me." Quinn rolled slowly away from the curb. *Maybe I can think of something to get her to talk to me that won't sound crazy. And if she's in public, she can't slam her door in my face.*

Margosha drove to a hair salon in Cherry Creek and dropped her keys with the valet.

Quinn passed the salon, pulling around the corner where there was an empty metered space. "A dollar for thirty minutes? Jeez." She fed the meter, then slowly made her way back toward the salon. She found herself tiptoeing and counting her mincing steps. She blushed when a woman passed her holding hands with a little girl, who began walking on tiptoes.

Quinn reached the salon and pivoted three times, each time stepping away to reassess her inadequate plan. She couldn't very well barge in there and start talking to Margosha while she was getting shampooed. Too weird. *Or cut, I'd be in the way. Or styled, too loud.* Instead, she got an iced coffee at the place across the street and waited for Margosha to come out, hoping she wasn't taking the time for a full dye job or anything. She was torn about feeding the meter. She didn't want to miss Margosha. Besides, what were the odds she'd get a parking ticket?

All the ice had melted in Quinn's drink by the time Margosha left the salon. She chatted briefly with the valet, then walked away. She looked as stunning on a Saturday morning as she did at the fancy fundraiser at the governor's mansion. Up close, there was no indication of enough makeup to paint a barn, nor did Margosha look—as her mother would say—Botoxicated.

Quinn followed, still hoping for an opportunity to speak with Margosha and praying for the right words to come to her.

Margosha walked a block, then crossed the street before entering a jewelry store. Quinn hurried to catch up with her, deciding to speak with her as she came out. Quinn loitered on the sidewalk near the jewelers, pretending to study the flowers in the landscaping while waiting for Margosha. She finally emerged and Quinn took two steps toward her, but a woman squealed, "Margosha? It's been ages! How are you?"

As they air-kissed, Quinn pretended to tie her shoe. They stood in the shade of the jewelry store's awning while they caught up. Quinn couldn't justify hanging around any longer, and didn't want to be rude and interrupt their reunion, so she sauntered past to study the window of a bookstore. She could see Margosha and her friend through the reflection of the glass. Her attention bounced between them and a poster for an event with two Colorado mystery authors, Charlemagne Russo and Cynthia Kuhn. That's what Quinn needed, an author to write some dialogue for her.

Finally, Margosha and her friend parted, traveling in opposite directions. Quinn waited until Margosha had almost reached the bookstore window before saying, "Excuse me," and stepping forward, gesturing with her empty cup.

Startled, Margosha crossed the wide sidewalk, giving Quinn a wide berth. "I'm not havink any change," she said, hurrying away.

Quinn frowned before it dawned on her that with her empty cup, Margosha mistook her for a panhandler. She looked down at her sundress. It wasn't terrible; no holes, fairly clean. Was this what people wore to beg in this upscale part of town? It seemed offensive somehow, but Quinn didn't have time to question how homeless she actually looked. She maybe should have taken the time to shave her legs, but it had been eons and would have required expertise in weed-whacking.

Margosha had disappeared into one of the stores, so Quinn peered into each as she passed. Quinn finally found her in a boutique. Just as she reached for the door handle, so did a man in uniform.

"Oh, excuse me, Officer."

"After you." He held the door for her.

The air-conditioning felt good and she blinked to get her eyes to adjust to the indoor lighting faster.

"That's her. She follows me all mornink."

"Is that true, ma'am?"

Quinn glanced around the store and was surprised to see Margosha pointing at her. "I'm not following—" Wait. Yes, she was. "Well, I am, but only to talk to her about her husband." Quinn leaned around the police officer, who had moved directly to her side, blocking the distance between her and Margosha. "I didn't mean to scare you—"

"Do you know this woman?" he asked Margosha.

She shook her head and moved closer to the sales clerk.

The police officer took Quinn by the elbow. "Let's go outside and let these women get on with their business." He propelled her toward the door.

"I'm not a stalker or anything." Quinn laughed nervously. "I just want to—"

"Outside, ma'am."

He moved Quinn about three doors down where there were some benches. "Take a seat, please, and tell me what's going on."

Quinn sat while the officer loomed over her. His name badge read *Childers*. He wore mirrored sunglasses and a no-nonsense demeanor. She'd met many like him and knew enough to do what he asked.

"Nothing's actually going on, sir. I just needed to ask her something and she misunderstood."

"Misunderstood how?"

"She thought I was panhandling."

"Were you?"

Quinn shook her empty cup at him. "No. Just couldn't find a trash can."

"The two of you know each other?"

"I know her, but she doesn't know me. I mean, I've seen pictures of her, but she doesn't know that."

The officer lowered his chin just the slightest bit and Quinn realized she sounded exactly like a stalker. She snapped her rubber band. "See, we have this mutual friend, Loma, and I got her address from her— Margosha's—and I drove to her house but before I got there she drove out—Margosha." Words cascaded, unhindered, from Quinn's mouth. "I need to find out some things about her husband because my boss is in jail for his murder—Jake—and I don't think he did it and maybe Margosha, that lady in the store, did."

Without seeming to take his eyes off her, the officer pulled out a tiny notebook from his pocket. "What's your name, ma'am?"

"Quinn Carr."

"Address?"

Quinn rattled off all her information, which he wrote down, then cocked his head.

"Chestnut Station. Is that the town with all those crazy nut statues?"

"Yes, sir."

He snorted. "My mom took us there when we were kids. I swear she made us pose with every single one of them." He smiled briefly at the memory, then returned to cop mode.

"Who did you say was in jail?"

"My boss, Jake Szabo."

"Where is he being held?"

"In Chestnut Station."

"On murder charges?"

Quinn nodded.

Another police officer joined them, carrying two iced drinks. Even though she was a woman, she also loomed over Quinn on the bench, staring at her through government-issued mirrored sunglasses. They must have learned that at the police academy. It was quite effective.

Officer Childers took one of the drinks. "Thanks, Jefferson." He took a long gulp. The two officers stared at Quinn. After an uncomfortably long time, at least for Quinn, he said, "Tell you what I'm going to do." Quinn hoped he was going to say he was going to let her go, but instead he continued, "I'm going to call over and have a chat with someone at the Chestnut Station PD and find out what's going on."

Quinn breathed a sigh of relief. "Yes, call Rico…Officer Lopez. He'll vouch for me. He'll tell you everything is perfectly fine."

Both officers pulled out their phones. Jefferson held hers out so Childers could see. He lifted his glasses to see the number, then dialed his. "This is Officer Childers with the Denver PD. To whom am I speaking?" He stepped into the shade of an awning, but not before Quinn heard him say, "Ah, Chief Chestnut. I have a couple of questions for you."

Quinn thought she groaned silently, but Jefferson said, "Excuse me?"

"Nothing." Quinn snapped her rubber band. "I didn't do anything."

The officer lowered her sunglasses. Quinn saw her staring at her red wrist. "Then you don't have anything to be nervous about, do you?"

Quinn sat on her hands. She didn't know how long she sat on that bench, but she began to wish she'd thought to slather on sunscreen that morning. She was going to get burned by the sun and by Chief Chestnut today. *He'll fill Officer Childers's head with deep-seated hatred for me. These two examples of Denver's finest will haul me off before I can lodge an official protest.* Against what, she wasn't sure, but she was fairly certain she'd need to protest something that Chief Chestnut had told him.

After an excruciatingly long time, Officer Childers returned to the bench, pocketing his phone. Quinn steeled herself for whatever came next.

"Okay, Ms. Carr. You're free to go."

That wasn't what she'd steeled herself against. "What?"

"You're free to go. Chief Chestnut vouched for you."

"Vouched? For me?"

Officer Childers removed his sunglasses. "Is there something else I need to know?"

Quinn scrambled to her feet. "No, sir. Nothing else."

"Head on back to Chestnut Station and your nutty statues and leave Mrs. Dubois alone."

"Yes, sir. On my way." Quinn scooped up her purse and her empty cup. "It's just that…he vouched for me? Chief Chestnut?"

"Did I stutter?"

"No, but…I just didn't think he knew me that well."

"He knows your mom. Seemed a little afraid of her."

"Afraid of my mom? That's hilarious. My mom is the sweetest, most—" Quinn quit talking when she saw Officer Childers's face. Clearly, he was uninterested in pursuing this conversation. "Thank you, Officer. Off I go!" Quinn race-walked back to her car. It might have been her imagination, but she felt the officers' eyes on her back until she turned the corner. She fumbled for her keys and didn't see the parking ticket until she was in the driver's seat.

Chapter 14

While Quinn had been driving to Denver, Georgeanne had made herself at home in the diner's kitchen. It was a good thing she brought along the contents of her spice cabinet. Jake didn't have any cardamom, turmeric, or peppermint flavoring and not nearly enough Jamaican jerk seasoning. After studying the contents of the walk-in refrigerator and the pantry items, she designed the day's menu.

First things first, she started up the huge pot to make her signature oatmeal.

There was a ton of pancake mix and she knew people at the diner loved their pancakes, but she also knew that Quinn had been making pancakes for days now, so she decided to spice them up. She whipped up a big batch, added this and that and, along with two eggs and two slices of bacon, dubbed it Georgeanne's Saturday morning special.

She checked on Dan, who was making coffee and setting tables. "Anybody here yet?"

"Somebody rattled the door a couple minutes ago, but I told them to give us a few more minutes. I didn't want you to feel like you had to rush."

She put a hand on his cheek. "You're a dear, dear. But go ahead and open the door. I think I'm ready."

Dan gave her a peck on the cheek. "You're absolutely glowing, Georgie."

"I've waited a long time for this, Dan. I feel like a junior varsity baseball player called up to the majors." She waved at the sandwich board. "Open the doors and let's get that erased. As soon as the oatmeal is cooking, I'll get the menu written."

She hustled back to the kitchen and Dan unlocked the door. Jethro padded in and Dan stared as he made his rounds. Georgeanne yelped in the kitchen, then came out chasing Jethro with a dish towel. He loped in front of her toward the door. As he passed Dan, Jethro looked up at him with indignation etched on his face and infinite sadness in his droopy eyes. Dan held the door for him. "Sorry, pal. You heard her. Out."

Diners trickled in and Dan pointed out the two offerings for breakfast: *Georgeanne's famous oatmeal…healthy oatmeal that tastes good* and the Saturday morning special.

Abe came in and clapped Dan on the back. "Got yourself a new job, eh?"

"Georgie and I are just helping out Quinn for the day while she takes care of some business."

"Business like getting Jake out of jail?"

"Sure hope so," piped up Wilbur as the Retireds shuffled in. He studied the sandwich board menu. "Oatmeal, eh?" He looked at Dan. "Any good?"

"I eat it every day."

"That's a good enough recommendation for me. Set me up with a bowl."

"Me too," said Bob.

"And me." Silas rubbed his hands together.

"Coffee first," said Larry.

Herman held out his cup for Dan to fill.

Abe sidled up to Dan, who was pouring coffee for the Retireds. "I've heard about your oatmeal. I'll try the pancakes." He laughed.

"Now don't you go hurting Georgie's feelings, Abe. She works real hard on her cooking," Dan said. "There's not enough kindness and empathy in the world today. Why does everyone have to snipe at each other? Why can't everyone get along?"

"Get a long what?" Silas said, to the laughter of all the Retireds, except Herman, who was still cogitating over the joke.

Dan set the coffeepot down and leaned in, getting the attention of all the men. "You lot behave yourselves today. And if you have any complaints, you tell me in private, like in a whisper. I'm an easygoing guy, but I do not like to see my wife cry." He picked up the pot. "Are we understood?"

All the men agreed, some more grudgingly than the others. After all, the Retireds' raison d'être was to complain loudly about the food and the service at the diner. Without that, how would they spend their time?

Georgeanne cooked and Dan took care of the tables for the breakfast rush. He only had to quell a small uprising when a family of tourists passing through complained there was too much peppermint in the pancakes, their bacon was too crisp, and the oatmeal was gross. Dan tore up their check and sent them on their way, making the father happy. He could deal with his hungry teenagers and surly wife himself. Not Dan's problem.

* * * *

Quinn started her car and blasted the air-conditioner, but didn't pull away from the curb. She called her mom. "Hey, how's it going over there?"

"Fine, dear. Your dad and I are really in a groove."

"A groove like good rhythm or a groove like quicksand?"

"Quicksand doesn't come in a groove."

"You know what I mean."

"Everything's fine. Quit obsess—quit worrying."

"Are you sure everything's okay?"

"Absolutely. But I've gotta go. I'm almost out of both breakfasts and I haven't even thought about lunch yet."

"Okay. Oh, Mom, one other thing. Why would Chief Chestnut be afraid of you?"

Georgeanne paused a bit, then laughed. "Afraid of me! I can't think of one reason why." She turned serious. "Why are you asking? Did something happen? Did he say something to you?"

"No. Everything's fine." *Either Mom didn't know why he'd be afraid of her or she didn't want to tell me she had some dirt on him. They went to school together. Surely she knew things about him. Like me and Rico.* "I'll talk to you later. Be back in a while. You're sure everything's under control?"

"Yes, Quinn. But it won't be if I don't get off this phone. Do what you need to do and we'll see you later." She disconnected.

Quinn drummed her fingers on the steering wheel and enjoyed the cool air that was finally wafting from the AC. A blast of a horn made her jump and she saw a car next to her with a driver whose face was contorted with anger. He flapped his hand at her to get her to move out of the parking spot. She waved him around, not ready to drive yet. She still had calls to make. Besides, blasting his horn at her only made her want to stay longer. People should learn to be polite. And patient.

She didn't want to, but knew she had to call Rico. She didn't want him to know she tailed Margosha today and hoped Chief Chestnut wouldn't spill the beans, but she had to tell Rico about the disconnected number. She hoped it wouldn't be awkward. She'd made such a big scene about it and now what would he think? Would he even believe that she had talked to the guy?

"Hi," Rico said.

Pause.

"Hi," Quinn said.

Pause.

It was awkward, all right.

"Quinn—"

"Rico—"

"You go first—"

"Go ahead—"

Pause.

Quinn took a deep breath.

"Ricolcalledthatguy'snumberanditwasdisconnected." *Like ripping off a Band-Aid.*

"I know. I called too."

"You did?"

"I did. What kind of a cop would I be if I didn't follow up leads?"

"But what do you think it means?"

"I think it means if he really was the guy in the diner with Emmett, he's tying up his loose ends so he can erase his trail and disappear."

Quinn pressed the heel of her hand to her forehead. "Rico, it's my fault. I scared him off. I called him, asking about the diner, talking about Chestnut Station."

"You couldn't possibly have made the connection without talking to him. If you didn't call, we'd never have heard of him or Colorado Premium Employment. It's not your fault. But I think that clue is a dead end."

It seemed to Quinn that Rico had softened his attitude since their early-morning call. She decided that meant she was back on the case. And if Sam the headhunter was a dead end, it meant her questions about Margosha were still pertinent.

"Why isn't Margosha a suspect in Emmett's murder?"

"Because she's not! Quit harping on this, Quinn. Let it go."

"Why should I?"

"Because I have more important things to worry about."

"I can explain. I was in Cherry Creek and she got spooked and called the police—"

"Who got spooked?"

"Margosha."

"What have you done?"

"Nothing. I just…nothing." *What* have *I done?* "What are the more important things you need to worry about?" Clearly, he hadn't heard about the fiasco this morning. Not yet, anyway.

"For one, I'm trying to solve Emmett Dubois's murder."

"So am I, Rico!"

"Well, it's not your job. Believe it or not, Quinn, this is serious and some things are none of your beeswax. Like my investigation into Margosha."

Quinn felt like she'd been slapped. "But you said I could help." Her voice came out meek and soft.

"I know what I said. But I didn't think you'd go full Nancy Drew on me." Rico took a breath. "I'm sorry. I didn't mean to hurt your feelings. But I can't talk to you about this right now. I have work to do. You okay?"

Quinn's feelings were still bruised, but Rico was right. *It's not my job. If he's convinced Margosha isn't a suspect, then maybe I should let it go.* "I'm fine."

"Lunch today?"

"My parents are handling the diner for me. I'm not sure when I'll be back."

"Your parents?"

"Long story. I'll try and catch up with you later."

"Okay." He paused. "I'm sorry I snapped at you."

"Talk to you later."

Quinn knew Rico was a diligent, conscientious cop. If he hadn't put Margosha on his suspect list, he must have a good reason. She just hoped it wasn't because Margosha was gorgeous and used some sort of mythical siren charms on him.

But if Margosha wasn't the murderer, it could only be Jake. He was the one with the motive and what about his alibi? Said he didn't know anything about those mushrooms and then when Emmett actually died, claimed to be out in a field in the boonies on a wild-goose chase. And now it came out he had a temper and stalked Emmett?

Quinn just couldn't picture Jake killing Emmett, though. It was entirely possible that someone was setting him up. But who? That cater-waiter who asked Donnie to serve that plate to Emmett? Wouldn't that just implicate Donnie? Quinn rehashed the conversation she'd had with Donnie about that night and remembered that he'd told her a lot of the cater-waiters at the fundraiser were ex-employees of Emmett's, which meant they might know Jake as well.

An SUV pulled up next to Quinn, casting a shadow over her car. She glanced over and the woman in the passenger seat made a please-roll-down-your-window gesture. When Quinn did, the woman said, "Are you leaving soon? We'd love your space if we're not rushing you." She flashed a hopeful grin.

"Absolutely. Back up a little bit so I can get out." Quinn put her car in gear and pulled away from the curb, waving as she did so. The SUV gave a happy toot of its horn and the woman waved back.

"That's how you get me out of a parking space," Quinn said out loud. "Politeness." She followed the route to the Crazy Mule and hoped Kelli was working and willing to chat with her again.

When Quinn got there, Kelli waved her to take any seat, then immediately came over with a menu. "Coffee or iced tea?"

"Tea would be great. It's beastly hot out there."

When Kelli placed a condensation-covered glass in front of her, Quinn said, "Do you have a minute? I wanted to ask you about cater-waitering. Do you know anything about it?"

Kelli glanced around the quiet restaurant, then slid into a chair across from Quinn. "I should. I do it on the side. What do you need to know?"

"How does somebody get hired, exactly?"

"In my case, I work for a couple of different catering companies. It's a pretty lucrative side hustle. Kinda like being a substitute teacher. I only work when I want to. But I almost always say yes when they call me. This place is on its last legs and my tips are practically nonexistent these days. Are you looking for a job? I can get you some contacts."

"That would be…great. Do you know who put on the governor's fundraiser? Is it one of your regular ones?"

"No, that was a new one. Some guy called me because Emmett told them I was a great crew chief." She made a sad face.

"Wait. You actually worked at the fundraiser for the governor?"

"Yeah. Made some fat tips too."

Why hadn't this come up before? Quinn wracked her brain. Surely she would have remembered if Kelli had already mentioned it. It suddenly seemed very suspicious, but just as quickly flitted away. Kelli was answering all her questions without seeming nervous or anything. She had no motive, plus she actually liked both Emmett and Jake.

She reprocessed Kelli's earlier comment. "What's a crew chief?"

"I'm in charge of the other waiters. Like their boss. Which is weird, since I never met any of them before."

"Never?"

"I don't think so." She pulled her phone from her apron, tapped on it, then shook her head. "Nope, don't know any of them."

"That's a list of all the cater-waiters that worked the fundraiser?"

Kelli held out her phone to Quinn, showing five names and phone numbers. "Yep."

"Can I have that list?"

Kelli shrugged. "Sure. They could probably get you on some catering company lists too."

Quinn took a screenshot of Kelli's phone. Maybe Paul Sothern, Ahmed Mehta, Jimmy Kane, Sasha Brown, or Brittany Cohen could give her more information. But not about getting a job.

A customer started snapping his fingers in an attempt to summon Kelli. She rolled her eyes.

"How rude. Reminds me of a guy who wanted my parking place this morning."

"Ooh, did he honk at you?" Kelli stood.

"Yes!"

"When people do that to me I just—"

She and Quinn spoke in unison: "Stay in the space longer!" They laughed.

Kelli said, "Guess I better get back to it. You want anything else?"

"Nah, I've got to get going. Thanks."

"Sure thing."

Quinn slipped a five under the saltshaker.

At the hostess stand, Quinn saw, on top of a pile of newspapers, the catalog for the FUNdamental Restaurant Products that she'd picked up after it fell out of the manager's back pocket. She skidded to a stop. The bottom half of the cover was torn off. She grabbed for it. The blackmail notes swam in front of her face. The black lowercase J. Red capital A. Blue lowercase K and E spelling out *J-A-K-E* on the blackmail note Jethro sniffed out. *I know what you did, Jake.*

Quinn fanned the pages. An entire section in the middle had disappeared, pages 77–102 gone. Only the ragged traces torn at the edge remained.

The hostess walked up. "Party of one or are you waiting for someone?"

"Actually, can you tell me about this?" Quinn waved the catalog at her.

She shrugged. "That's the catalog Mr. Koneckny, the manager here, orders supplies from."

"Does this come in the mail? How often?"

"I don't know. Probably monthly." She squinted at Quinn. "So, no table?"

"No, I'm on my way out." Quinn huddled near the door until the hostess stepped away, then she grabbed the catalog and fled, giddy at the prospect of finding the blackmailer. If it wasn't Emmett, then it had to be Vince Koneckny. Quinn paused and gazed at the Crazy Mule as she unlocked her car door. Koneckny hadn't seemed at all suspicious when she talked to him the other day. Granted, he didn't know she worked for Jake at the diner. But still. Wouldn't a blackmailer be a little nervous when they'd begun chatting about Loma, his blackmailee's ex-wife?

Maybe not. That grease fire didn't faze him a bit.

* * * *

The parking lot was practically empty, so she didn't think anyone would be honking at her for her space. Again, she fired up the engine and blasted the air-conditioner. She'd ask Jake about the catalog later. For now, she dialed the first name on the list of cater-waiters from the screenshot.

"Is this Paul Sothern?"

"Yes."

"I understand you worked at a fundraiser for the governor recently."

"I already told the cops everything I know."

"Just a quick follow-up question. Did you serve, or ask anyone to serve, a special request plate with mushrooms to anyone?"

"No."

"Do you remember Jake Szabo, the guy cooking that night?"

"Yes."

"Did he ask you to do anything with a plate of mushrooms?"

"No."

"Do you know any of the others you worked with that night?"

"Nope. Not that I remember. And that was four questions, exactly what you guys asked me before."

"That was a test. Cops—uh, we—do it all the time to make sure you're telling the truth. You passed with flying colors, by the way. Thanks for your time."

Quinn called the other names on the list, even the two women, despite Donnie's description that it was a man who asked him to deliver the plate to Emmett. They all gave similar statements, including Brittany, who spoke at length about how dreamy Jake was and how it was a shame what had happened to that poor man. Quinn wasn't sure if she meant Jake or Emmett. When Quinn asked if she knew any of the others she worked with, she said, "I've seen the guy with the dimple before, but I don't know him."

She couldn't give any better description than that, so Quinn called the other men back and asked each if they had a dimple. Paul Sothern and Ahmed Mehta claimed they had no dimples but Jimmy Kane told her, "Do you count the one on my butt?"

"No, probably not." Unless he was wearing just a pair of chaps, Brittany probably didn't see his butt-dimple. *How does he even know he has a butt-dimple?* Quinn wondered what was on her butt she'd never know about.

This seemed like another dead end to her. None of the cater-waiters claimed to have touched the plate of mushrooms, but Donnie clearly told her that one of the waiters asked if he'd do a solid and deliver it for him. Maybe Donnie had a better description of the cater-waiter, now that he'd had a chance to mull it over.

Quinn called the Chestnut Station PD. Chief Chestnut answered. She disguised her voice, making it deep and gravelly, and asked to speak with Donnie.

When he got on the line, she forgot to change her voice back. "It's Quinn. I wanted to ask—"

"What's wrong with you? You sound terrible."

Quinn cleared her throat and spoke normally. "Frog in my throat. Can you describe the guy who gave you the plate of mushrooms to deliver to Emmett?"

"Haven't we been over this?"

"Did he have a dimple?"

"A pimple?"

"No, a dimple."

"Do you really think guys notice stuff like that?"

"That sounds a little homophobic, Donnie. Besides, I thought police were trained to notice things. A dimple is a thing."

After a pause, he said, "No dimple," and hung up.

Quinn looked over her dashboard at the Crazy Mule. She turned off her ignition and went back in. When she saw Kelli filling glasses at the drink station, she went over.

"Can I ask you something else?" Without waiting for an answer, Quinn held up the screenshot for Kelli to see. "Do any of these guys have a dimple?"

Kelli glanced at the photo, then quirked an eyebrow at Quinn, reality dawning on her. "You're not looking for a job, are you?"

Quinn shook her head.

Kelli thought for a minute. "I don't remember any dimples."

"Is it possible that one of these cater-waiters has a dimple that nobody saw?"

"Usually you only see someone's dimple if they smile," Kelli said. "Working a fundraiser isn't a laugh-fest."

"I guess not. Thanks again."

Either somebody was lying, or some guy snuck into the fundraiser to poison Emmett. *What about that ex-employee of Jake's who keeps hanging up on me?*

Back in the car with the AC blasting, Quinn called her dad. "How's it going?"

"Like a well-oiled machine."

"I doubt that."

"Why?"

"Because it never ran that way when Jake was there."

"I guess your mother and I will just have to give him some additional training once he gets back." Dan spoke to Georgeanne in the background. When he came back on the line he dropped his voice a bit. "Your mother is having the time of her life today. Thank you for letting her do this."

"Dad, I didn't *let* her do anything. I begged you guys to help me out of a jam. I owe you big-time."

"Potato, potahto. And you don't owe us a thing."

Quinn laughed. "Then I need another favor. In Jake's office are a bunch of old employee files. I need you to pull out the one for Michael Breckenridge and give me his address." After Dan rattled it off to her she said, "Are you sure everything is okay? I still have a couple things I need to do."

"Take your time. Everything is perfectly fine here."

"Okay. Thanks, Dad. I'll be there as soon as I can." Quinn left the Crazy Mule and headed for the address back in Chestnut Station her dad had given her. *If Michael Breckenridge won't talk to me on the phone, I'll have to make him talk to me in person.*

On the drive back to Chestnut Station, Quinn decided to go undercover and had a great cover story all ready, but the woman who opened the door recognized her.

"Quinn Carr! I ran into your mom at the store the other day and she told me you were back in town. How are you? Haven't seen you in ages. Come in, come in! Have some tea."

Undercover work was impossible in a small town.

"Is Michael Breckenridge your son?"

"He sure is. Are you a friend of his? Come inside so we don't let all the cool air out." Quinn followed the woman inside, but declined tea.

"I can just stay for a minute. Actually, I was looking for Michael. I'm having trouble talking to him on the phone."

The woman nodded knowingly. "He doesn't return my calls either. I don't know if it's because he's too busy or too lazy or something else. You just missed him, though. He mowed my lawn this morning. Brought me this lemon pound cake he baked. I was just going to have a slice. Would you like some?" When Quinn declined, she said, "I can't imagine why Michael wouldn't call such a pretty girl back right away."

Quinn blushed and left with Michael's address, on the new side of town. She drove over and parked a few doors down, but with a view of his front door. Quinn was afraid to go ring the bell. Despite how sweet his mother was, he still might be a murderer or something. Moms sometimes had no idea what their kids were up to, whether they were teenagers or adults, like Michael. She considered calling Rico or even Donnie, but what would she say? Some guy who used to work for Jake wouldn't take her calls? And even though he just mowed his mother's lawn and baked her a cake, he might be a dangerous murderer? The idea was ridiculous, but still.

She hadn't decided how to proceed when she saw a man come out of the house with a young girl. Quinn felt safer knowing there was a kid there. She sent a quick text to Rico giving him the address, then sauntered up to where they played in the yard.

"Hi."

The little girl ran over and said, "Hi!"

The man called her back. When she returned to his side, he held her hand.

"Are you Michael Breckenridge?"

"And you are...?"

"My name is Quinn. I work at the Chestnut Diner, where you used to work."

He abruptly picked up the girl and returned to his house. *To get a gun? Probably not to bring me fresh-baked lemon pound cake.* Quinn ran for her car and locked the doors. She stomped on the gas pedal and twisted the key in the ignition, but the engine didn't turn over. A car that didn't start created the same panic as a computer that wouldn't start. She only knew to put the key in and turn it, maybe give it a little gas. At least with a computer she could reboot it, if turning it off and on didn't work. And turning the car off and on was decidedly not working. In her haste, she realized she'd flooded it. She let her car regroup while she repeatedly snapped her rubber band while counting all the trees she could see. She reached fifty-seven before she ran out of plants, realizing there were probably some shrubs included as well. This was not the time to learn botany.

Michael Breckenridge stomped out of his house, down the driveway, heading right toward her.

She frantically turned the key again, willing the engine to roar to life. It took two tries, but it finally did and she stepped on the gas.

Michael Breckenridge stepped in front of her, blocking the street. She had no choice but to stop.

He came to her window, waving cash, and talking. She cracked open her window a bit to hear him.

"I only have fifty-five dollars."

"Okaaaay..."

He pushed the bills through the window. Quinn scootched over as far as she could. The money fell in her lap.

"Now will you quit bothering me?"

"Um…"

He stared at her angrily through the window.

Quinn stared back. What was happening here?

Finally he broke eye contact. "Fine. I'm sorry. It was a crappy thing to do."

Was he confessing to Emmett's murder right here on the street? Quinn didn't want to spook him by calling Rico, but had to know. "What was a crappy thing to do?"

"Stealing that money from Jake."

"When?"

"Back when I worked for him."

Quinn relaxed. Michael Breckenridge was confessing to an entirely different crime. "You stole money from Jake?"

"From the cash register, technically. Fifty-three dollars. Tell him I'm sorry." He turned and walked back to his house.

Quinn collected the bills from her lap, smoothed and counted them. "Two bucks interest? Pretty cheap conscience."

She left Michael Breckenridge's house and headed to the diner. The parking lot wasn't very full even though it was well into what should have been the lunch rush. There was no billowing smoke to be seen or crowds of curious gawkers, so she rolled slowly past, squinting through the car windows into the diner. Everything seemed okay. Jethro was sacked out on the sidewalk in front of the door and almost lifted his head as she passed by. He followed the slow-moving car with his droopy eyes.

"I'll be right back. Gotta go talk to Jake real quick."

* * * *

Quinn went to the jail, where she was met by Rico. Quinn still felt iffy around him because of all the drama between them lately.

Rico watched her snap her rubber band. "Is that helping anything?"

"I'm fine."

"That's not what I asked. Ignoring your problems won't make them go away."

"So I've heard." Quinn shoved her hands in her pockets. "You just worry about yourself and this case. Where have you been, anyway?"

"Chief's got a bug up his butt about re-interviewing some people, so I've been doing that all day."

"Like who?"

"Loma, Margosha, and Michael Breckenridge."

Quinn was beside herself with joy that her crossword plan worked with Chief Chestnut. She was anxious to tell her parents—the only people she could—but it would have to wait until she had some time alone with them. They were the only ones, aside from Vera, who knew she made the crossword puzzles. But would they understand that she was helping with the investigation? Quinn snorted. Of course they would. "You can forget about talking to Michael Breckenridge again, because I just talked to him."

"You were talking to Michael Breckenridge?"

"Didn't you get my text? Fat lot of good it does me to let you know my whereabouts in case I get into trouble if you never even know it."

Rico checked his phone. "Ringer was off." He clicked it back on. "Now what's this about you being in trouble?"

"It was just a precaution. I went to talk to Michael Breckenridge and wanted someone to know where I was."

"What on earth were you talking to him about?"

"I've been trying to talk to him on the phone, but he kept hanging up. There was something weird about him."

"Weird how?" Rico's jaw tightened.

"Weird because he wouldn't talk to me. So I went to his house."

"Quinn..."

"I know, I know. But it was really his mother's house."

"So his mother was there when you talked to him?"

Quinn wrinkled her nose. "Not exactly. But she said I was pretty and gave me Michael's new address, so I went over there."

"You are really starting to annoy me."

"Relax. Everything turned out fine. He didn't attack me and I didn't run over him with my car."

"Was that an option?"

"Kinda seemed like it at the time."

"You're enjoying this, aren't you?"

"Little bit."

"I really wish you would just cut to the chase here. What happened?"

"Fine. Turns out that Michael Breckenridge stole fifty bucks from Jake's cash register back in the day. He wouldn't talk to me on the phone because he thought that's what this was all about. Like I was a collection agency. What would the interest be on fifty bucks over ten years or so?" Quinn saw the impatience on Rico's face, so she continued: "So when I showed up, he threw some money at me and told me he was sorry for stealing it."

"Why did he steal it?"

"I don't know. But it couldn't be anything too important if it was only fifty bucks. The upshot, though, is that now you don't have to talk to him again because it's pretty clear the reason he was acting suspicious was because of the guilt of this petty theft hanging over his head for so long."

Rico had been clenching and unclenching his fists during their conversation.

Quinn finally noticed. "What?"

"You're acting reckless."

The anxious sound of his voice made Quinn's stomach tighten up, so she tried to lighten the mood. "The only reckless thing I've done is stay too long away from the diner."

A horrified look crossed Rico's face. "You haven't been to the diner yet? Jake is gonna freak."

"He's going to freak more when he hears that my mom and dad have been handling it all day. Can I go down and see him?"

* * * *

Rico watched Quinn walk downstairs to the jail. He didn't mind her talking to Jake in the lockup as much as she had been, but wasn't sure the chief would be so amenable. Rico almost told Donnie to keep Quinn's visits quiet, but then he realized Donnie barely cared when and whether she was there. No conversation necessary.

Despite what Quinn said, she *was* being reckless, whether she knew it or not. And he was fairly certain she knew it.

Rico dropped his head back on his neck and rolled it, then hunched his shoulders in a useless attempt to alleviate some stress. He thought he'd moved past it, but he kept coming back to his original assessment that he'd wished he'd never agreed to let her help with this investigation. She was still snapping that ridiculous rubber band and had added in all those other tics. Her compulsions. Maybe other people didn't notice, but he did.

It was interesting that Quinn had spoken with Michael Breckenridge just before I was going to interview him. Did she have some sort of insider knowledge I should know about? I shouldn't be surprised. She had a knack for figuring things out, finding people to talk to and get information from. A sixth sense about investigations, which I should support.

Rico was conflicted. If he wanted her to pursue the police academy again, he felt he should help her more than he had been. Maybe this time instead of being a problem, her OCD would help her. Rico thought about her snapping that silly rubber band on her wrist. If she could learn to live with it, that is. And that was a big *if.*

* * * *

"Back from Denver so soon?" Jake asked.

"Yeah, I didn't want to leave Mom and Dad alone too long." Quinn grimaced, then backed away a bit from the bars of the cell. She decided that ripping off the bandage was the best course of events.

Concern etched Jake's face. "Your parents? Are they okay? What happened?"

"Chris and Kristi happened. They moved to Idaho."

"They *what*?"

Quinn flinched. "Not to worry. My mom and dad are at the diner." She added an extra-chipper nonchalance to her voice. She wanted her words to come out standard Times New Roman, but was pretty sure they ended up being Comic Sans.

"Your mom of the cumin cupcakes? Is that really a good idea?" Jake's voice, on the other hand, was Arial, all caps, 24-point, bold.

Quinn straightened her spine. She took one step toward the bars, but thought better of it and stepped back where she had been. She tried to speak evenly and calmly. "Listen, Jake, I don't know if you realize it or not, but you're in there and I'm out here—"

"Yes, I'm aware."

"—and I'm doing the best I can from that chaos you left at the diner. I'm figuring things out. I established a logical workflow. I implemented easy daily specials I can handle. And when I needed help, I asked for it."

"Did you fix the credit card machine?"

Quinn glared at him. "No."

Jake glared back, then softened, clearly resigned to a reality he couldn't change. He looked down at his government-issued plastic sandals. "You're right. I'm sorry. You stepped into a huge mess and I'm grateful." He raised his eyes. "But really? Your parents?"

"It's perfectly fine. I've been checking in with them all morning and just now drove by and all was well."

"You could tell everything was okay from the street? Did you go in? You should have gone in."

"Everything's fine. Right as rain, as Grandma used to say. And if you'd quit grilling me, I could get back there faster."

"So this isn't a social call."

"First, I just talked to Michael Breckenridge and he gave me this for you." Quinn pulled some wadded-up bills from the pocket of her sundress and held them through the cell bars.

Jake smoothed them. After he counted them, he ejected a one-syllable laugh. "Finally. Mikey came clean."

"You knew he stole from you? Is that why you fired him?"

"I didn't fire him. He quit. He was washing dishes for me in high school, got some girl knocked up, and panicked. I figured he'd think about swiping from the till, so I left a hundred bucks in there. He didn't even take it all. I don't know how he thought fifty-three dollars was going to help, but kids' brains are a mystery to me. I'd heard scuttlebutt around town about the impending bundle of joy and tried to get him to talk about it, but he wouldn't. Not to me, anyway."

"Did you say, 'Hey Mike, heard you're gonna be a daddy. Anything you want to talk about?'"

Jake recoiled as if she'd slapped him. "No! Yuck. Feelings?"

"I swear, men are so infuriating."

"That's rich, coming from Ms. Don't Want To Talk About My OCD."

Quinn had no response, so she snapped her rubber band and changed topics. "At the governor's fundraiser, did you know any of the male servers?"

Jake shook his head.

"Did any of them have a dimple?"

"A dimple? Are you hunting for the world's sexiest man? A dimple. What kind of question is that?" He looked both worried and appalled.

Quinn rolled her eyes at him. "What is it with me running into so much latent homophobia today?"

"I'm not homophobic. But I am on my way to the Denver County jail soon, according to Chief Chestnut. I guess I'm a little ... twitchy."

"Denver? Why?"

"I don't know. Something about jurisdiction and the fact they still have a working guillotine."

Quinn gasped. "They do? They sounds positively barbaric! Does the ACLU—" She saw the look on his face and realized he'd been dealing in a bit of hyperbole.

Jake pushed the fifty-three dollars back through the bars of the cell. "You better keep that. Use it to fix the cash register or something. They'll just take it from me when they check me in."

"Check you in? It's not the Holiday Inn. It's called *intake*." She shot him a stern look. "And don't joke around with those guys. They don't all have a sense of humor."

"Roger that. Now get back to the diner before your mom poisons all my customers."

"She wouldn't—okay, but not on purpose. And nobody ever died from eating too much cumin. Besides, I bet she made her pretzel pancakes today. They're oddly compelling." Quinn started for the stairs but turned back. "Almost forgot the most important thing. Tell me about the affair you had with Margosha Dubois."

"I never had an affair with Margosha."

"I heard you did."

"From who?"

Quinn decided Jake didn't need to know about Kelli, her font of information at the Crazy Mule. "Never you mind that. Just tell me. Was it because she was married to a gay man? Is *she* the homophobe?"

"Nobody is a homophobe."

Quinn raised her eyebrows.

"What I mean is, nobody in my circle is a homophobe."

"So tell me about you and Margosha."

"Nothing to tell. I was helping her with her English."

"Then why did everybody think you were having an affair?"

"Because Loma told everybody we were."

"Why?"

"Because she is a naturally suspicious woman. And it didn't help that when she suggested to Emmett that they have an affair to get back at Margosha and me, he laughed in her face."

"Did she know Emmett was gay?"

"Not when she suggested the affair. She's not a masochist."

Quinn stayed quiet for a moment, thinking. That squared with what Kelli had told her and what Loma had told her about Margosha's English skills. And she'd seen for herself the volatility that Loma possessed. It was perfectly logical that if she'd suspected her husband was having an affair with a gorgeous woman, she would strike back and strike back hard. "So. You were teaching her English. Is it possible she was faking her poor English skills?"

"Why would she do that?"

"I'm not sure. Just working on some theories." Quinn was quiet for another moment. "Is it possible that Loma was Emmett's silent partner in his restaurant businesses?"

"Silent? With that mouth? That's a laugh."

Despite his tacky joke, or maybe because of it, Quinn thought Jake showed guilt. She grabbed the bars of the cell with both hands. "Do you think Emmett was really the one blackmailing you? Could it be that someone was just pretending to be him in order to blackmail you?"

Quinn held up the FUNdamental Restaurant Products catalog. "Those letters were cut from this. I got it from the Crazy Mule."

"What did you tear off?"

"I didn't tear it. Emmett must have." Quinn frowned. "Wait. It couldn't have been Emmett. He was already dead when it fell out of the Crazy Mule's manager's pocket." She squinched her eyes, replaying the scene. "And it wasn't torn when I picked it up." She slumped against the cell. "This proves nothing. Dead end."

Jake held out his hand for the catalog. Quinn handed it through the bars. Jake flipped through it, stopping at the section torn from the middle. He ran his thumb over the jagged remnants. "Every restaurant gets that catalog every month. There's probably one at the diner." Jake cocked his head. "Have you picked up the mail from the post office box?"

"Have you mentioned a PO box to me?" Quinn heard the irritation in her voice.

"No, I didn't mean—I just—it's box three-oh-three." A flush crept up from Jake's neck to his cheeks. "When you get a chance. The key is the little one on the ring I gave you. Didn't you wonder what it was for?"

Quinn gave an exaggerated sigh. "No. Do you think I obsess about *everything*?" She shook her head at him. "But back to the question. Could somebody have pretended to be Emmett to blackmail you?" She pointed at the catalog. "Somebody who gets this?"

"Who would do that? And why?"

Jake looked so sad it stabbed Quinn in the heart. It seemed this was the first time Jake truly grasped that he might have an actual enemy and this was not just some kind of fluke. Not a bad twist of fate. Not a case of being in the wrong place at the wrong time.

"It was wrong of me to hold her back." Jake stared into the distance.

"Who?"

"Loma. And I was wrong to mock her just now for being the silent partner. She sure could have carved a niche for herself if I hadn't insisted she help me so much when I was getting started, but I was so scared I'd fail." He looked at Quinn. "Who else have I hurt without even being aware?"

"I don't know, but it would have to be someone who would benefit from both blackmailing you and from killing Emmett."

"And for making it look like I killed him."

"Yes. Who would fall into those categories?"

Jake simply shook his head. Quinn could see by the conflicting looks that crossed his face that he couldn't imagine knowing anyone who could do such things. Was Loma upset enough to lash out at him this way?

Do we really know everything that people are capable of? Don't we all have those people in our lives who we are fairly certain could hurl a racist insult, or launch into violence, or maybe even kill a person in a pique of fury or passion?

Quinn thought about her parents. She couldn't imagine either of them doing anything of the sort.

What about Rico? As a police officer, he came across situations all the time where he had to make split-second decisions and assessments of people. What if he got it wrong? Nothing much happened in a small, out-of-the-way place like Chestnut Station—if they were lucky—but cops all across the nation, all across the world, were constantly in the news for making an instantaneous decision that got second-guessed by everyone. *We see body cam images and think that we would have done things completely differently. But would we? We weren't there. We didn't know what had happened before someone's cell phone started capturing the altercation.* Quinn wanted to believe that Rico would never be in a situation like that. That he would always choose the right thing to do and say every time. But was that even possible? It was a high standard to hold him to, but Quinn held him and everyone she knew to a higher standard. No different than the standard she held for herself.

Which she couldn't always reach.

Was it possible that she didn't—and couldn't—know the people in her life so well to know how they would react or behave in a given situation?

She looked at Jake looking at her. She'd only known him for a few weeks. Was it possible she didn't know him at all?

"Jake, who lost money when Emmett's restaurants failed? Did you?"

"Yeah, I lost a lot but it wasn't an investment. It was my whole life. I poured blood, sweat, and tears into those restaurants. They were like children to me." His face hardened. "It was my whole life."

The change in Jake's demeanor and voice startled and unnerved Quinn, reaffirming her earlier impression that she didn't know him very well. As she climbed the stairs she wondered, was Jake the silent partner?

* * * *

Quinn went straight from the police station to the post office. When she opened the box to collect the mail for the diner, all she saw was one postcard, an official request to pick up everything at the service counter. She took the postcard, locked the box, and waited impatiently for the lone clerk while he took care of an elderly woman sending a birthday gift to her granddaughter.

"You should see her, Mel," she trilled. "Getting ready to start ninth grade. Plays the tuba in the marching band, on the mathletes team, *and* was voted in as treasurer for the Future Scientists of America chapter at her school."

"That's great. You must be so proud."

Quinn couldn't tell if Mel was being genuine or sarcastic, since he spoke in that dreary monotone that comes with a career in a soul-sucking quasi-governmental organization. Didn't matter. Quinn was impressed with the granddaughter's accomplishments. Tired of waiting in line listening to them, of course, but still impressed. Quinn tapped her index finger in quarter-inch intervals along the edges of the postcard she held.

Mel finished up the transaction and gave Grandma her change. When she turned to leave and saw Quinn, her hand fluttered to her throat. "I'm sorry. I didn't know anyone else was in line and me going on about my granddaughter like that."

Quinn smiled at her. "No worries. I wonder if my grandma bragged about me."

"I'm sure she did." The woman stepped out of the way.

"I never played the tuba."

"I bet you had other charms. Bye now."

Other charms? Not really.

Quinn handed the postcard to Mel. Without speaking to her he took it and left her alone at the service counter. He returned with two bundles of mail, each with fat rubber bands encircling them. As she gathered them up she said, "You guys can put the mail in the box again. I'll pick it up so it won't get so full next time."

Mel said in his monotone, "That's great. You must be so proud."

* * * *

Back at the diner, Jethro was waiting for her, panting in the heat, eyes looking even sadder than normal, if that was possible. Quinn was probably just projecting her own sadness after her encounter with Jake at the jail.

She opened the door and ushered him into the air-conditioning. He padded around the restaurant making his rounds, but Quinn stopped mid-stride, taking in the scene before her. As her eyes adjusted from the bright white sunshine, she grew more and more horrified.

Every table was piled high with dirty dishes. Jethro deviated from his route to hoover up half a piece of toast that had landed jelly-side down on the floor. He lapped up the remaining jelly, then altered his route for any other tidbits. Quinn couldn't see everything that he'd gobbled up, but the fact he'd done so six times made her increasingly frantic. She snapped the rubber band on her wrist.

"Hi, Quinn!"

She looked for the source of the greeting, moving her head in slow-motion. Her vision landed on the group of people clustered in the big corner booth. Her parents grinned and waved at her from the center of the booth, bracketed on both sides by other grinning people.

"Come sit with us," Georgeanne trilled.

Quinn remained rooted to the spot. Out of the corner of her eye she spied an overturned chair. She walked over to it and set it upright, again sweeping her gaze across the restaurant. "What … happened here?" she asked.

"What do you mean, what happened? Breakfast and lunch happened!" Dan said with a laugh. The others laughed too.

Quinn recognized most of the people crowded into the circular booth: Abe the handyman; his daughter Cynthia, who had helped her with the oatmeal disaster; Duke McCaffrey; the ample-bellied O'Shea; a woman she'd never seen before; and her parents beaming in the center of them.

Quinn gave a vague wave behind her with one of the bundles of mail. "But what … happened?"

"Oh, don't worry about the mess. We'll get it cleaned up later. Right now we're taking a breather from our rousing success at the Chestnut Diner," Georgeanne said.

Abe and Cynthia clinked coffee cups. "Here, here."

"You should have seen your mother, Quinn," Dan said.

"And your father." Georgeanne put her arm around his shoulder. "He handled every single customer with aplomb."

"With a plum?"

"Aplomb. Grace, poise, quick thinking. Especially when people were mad."

"Mad about what?" Quinn felt her heart begin to beat a bit faster, now in time with her rubber band.

Georgeanne waved away Quinn's words. "Nothing important. You know how people can get."

Quinn started to speak, but Dan interrupted her. "Nothing to worry about, Quinn." Dan moved to get out of the booth and elbowed Abe, who elbowed Cynthia, who elbowed the woman Quinn didn't recognize.

But the woman stayed right where she was and spoke to Georgeanne. "This was so much fun today." She turned toward Quinn. "I've never had such a delightful experience here. Good company, new friends, laughs galore, and some of the most innovative food I've ever had. Those pretzel pancakes were scrumptious. You should be proud of your employees."

"They're not my employees. They're my parents." She narrowed her eyes at Georgeanne. "Who I expressly requested to follow the instructions I laid out for them."

Georgeanne made a little turtle movement like she was going back into her shell. Dan clasped his hands together in prayer position.

"Aw, honey, don't be like that. Your mom handled the kitchen like a dream and I know it doesn't look like it, but I worked my butt off out here. And if you'll go look, I think you'll see we made some money today. It was a messy day, but I think a pretty successful one."

Quinn felt a stab of remorse. Her parents came through for her in a pinch and here she was chastising them for a little mess.

Dan was jabbing Abe in the ribs again and trying to scoot out of the booth. Quinn waved him to stop.

"You're right, Dad. You guys deserve a break. It's obvious you worked hard today. Let me clean up." She addressed the entire group. "Anyone want anything? Coffee, soda, hazmat suit?" They murmured their orders and Quinn went to the back to drop her purse and the mail. When she saw the state of the kitchen she gasped and swooned like a Civil War bride. She turned her back on it to drop her apron over her head and tie it around front. Drinks for the back booth first.

After serving everyone, Quinn took a look at the envelope stuffed with cash that Dan had left in Jake's office. If she had been able to whistle, she would have given a long, low one here. He was right: They'd made some bank today. Impressive. She felt a bit competitive and would have to check her daily notes to see if this was more than she'd been making. If it was, she already knew that her parents wouldn't take credit. They'd just say it was because they double-teamed it and Quinn was always on her own at the diner.

At any rate, she reminded herself, it wasn't a competition and she should be thankful for their help, even if they did outshine her at her own job.

She grabbed a dishcloth and a plastic bin to bus the tables while her parents laughed and chatted with the others in the booth. She was surprised that no other customers came in to eat. She knew the door was unlocked because she'd just come in it, but glanced at it anyway and saw the *Closed* sign was turned. She gave a tiny snort, debating for longer than she should have before flipping it back to *Open.*

She finished busing the tables and sweeping the floor of the restaurant, hoping this would not be the day of a surprise visit from the health department. As she leaned the broom in the corner, she saw the bundles of mail she'd dropped on Jake's desk. She eyed the catalog, but couldn't bring herself to study it until all the mail was sorted into three piles: important-looking, not important-looking, and oversized.

When she finished, she pounced on the FUNdamental Restaurant Products catalog Jake had received. The multicolored font was the same as the one she swiped from the Crazy Mule, and the display ad on the lower half of the front cover looked the same until she studied it closer. This catalog had an ad for small appliances, not knives. This was the current catalog. The one with the knife sale was last month's issue. It could absolutely have been used for those blackmail notes.

But by Emmett? She didn't know.

Quinn wanted to rehash the events of the day with Loma, since they'd gotten along so well when they'd hung out. A week ago Rico would have been her go-to, but since she'd met Loma, she felt like they were developing a bond. And it was nice to have a friend besides Rico again. It had been a long time.

She especially wanted to tell Loma about Margosha siccing the cops on her. Quinn still hadn't decided if that was suspicious or prudent on Margosha's part. She was leaning toward suspicious. Loma would know which was which. If Margosha was trying to ditch Quinn, that alone was suspicious, since Quinn didn't believe she posed anything close to a threat. If Margosha was trying to permanently get Quinn off her back, that seemed like maybe Margosha had something to hide.

And she wanted to talk about her visit with Jake. The abrupt change in his demeanor when she'd asked about the silent partner and if he'd lost any money worried her. Did Jake really believe that he'd lost everything when Emmett's restaurants failed? What about the diner? Jake told her himself that he loved his diner, even though he sometimes yearned to create fancier fare. Jake seemed to have a great life in Chestnut Station. But maybe it was yet another reminder you couldn't know what was under the surface for other people. Quinn looked down at the rubber band on her wrist. *After all, people might look at me and see someone normal, someone who wasn't fighting depression, someone who didn't have to count chair legs or ceiling tiles*—Quinn drew her hand back from the task she was methodically and very consciously undertaking—*or line up salt and pepper shakers just so.*

With a sigh, Quinn returned to the dining room to see what else needed her attention. She mentally assessed the remaining work.

"Are you sure we can't help, Quinn?" Georgeanne asked. "I'm beginning to feel guilty just sitting here."

Quinn smiled. "You have two choices. You can quit feeling guilty, or you can go home and sit there."

"Maybe I'll have another glass of tea, then. If you're sure."

"I'm absolutely sure." Quinn filled a pitcher of tea and a pitcher of lemonade and brought them both to the booth. "Knock yourselves out."

"Seriously, Quinn, do you need any help?" Dan asked. "I'm happy to—"

"I know you are, Dad, but I've got this. I kinda want to keep busy right now. Plus, I have a … system."

Dan gave a slight nod and Quinn disappeared into the kitchen.

As she loaded dishes into the dishwasher, she heard the tinkle of the doorbell. She peeked out the pass-through, hoping whoever it was only wanted a slice of pie. She grinned when she saw Loma striding toward the kitchen. Quinn dried her hands and met her at the entrance to the kitchen. "Am I happy to see—"

"What do you think you were doing telling Rico to re-interview me for Emmett's murder? He came to my office when I had a client there!" Loma crossed her arms in her power pose.

Quinn took a step backward. "I didn't—"

"Don't lie to me, girl."

"I'm not! I don't know what you're talking about."

Loma glared at Quinn. "You have no idea why Rico came to talk to me again." She said it with a completely flat tone, the one people use when they absolutely cannot believe what you just said.

"No, I—" *Ohmygawd, the crossword puzzle.*

Loma must have seen the guilty look that settled on Quinn's face. "I knew it! What did you tell him?"

Quinn couldn't explain about the crossword, so she simply said, "Nothing. I didn't tell Rico anything." *Not technically a lie.*

"Then why did he want to know about me asking Emmett to have an affair to get back at Jake? That sounds like your doing."

"It's not!" Quinn frowned. She had told Rico that, but that wasn't why he was re-interviewing Loma. That was all Chief Chestnut's doing. "I'm not the only one who knows about that. Don't blame it on me. I don't have that kind of power." *Or did I, now that I knew I could drop clues into the crossword puzzle?* "Loma, you should have told me about that mess between you and Emmett."

"And you should have told me you were one hinge short of a nuthouse door!"

Quinn instinctively covered her ears. She didn't want to hear—or believe—Loma would throw her OCD back in her face, and worse, act like it made her mentally unstable in any way. *That would be like me saying she was crazy for having diabetes.* "That's completely—"

Loma pulled something up on her phone and read from it. "Someone should tie up the cook and force-feed him his own fettuccine Alfredo until he explodes. One less bad chef in the world."

Quinn fought to control her voice. "That was just an old restaurant review I wrote when I was mad. Asking Emmett to have an affair was germane to—"

"Germane?" If Loma could have killed with the daggers she shot out of her eyes, Quinn would have dropped to the floor instantly. "I don't owe you any explanation of anything. Certainly not of what went on—or goes on—in my marriage."

"No, of course you don't, but—"

"Ain't no *but* about it. There's no time, no reason, no way I need to tell you anything. Especially when you're no sweet-smelling petunia in all this either."

"What are you talking about?"

"I thought you were just an outsider trying to help your new boss, but that review you posted about the Crazy Mule, all those threats you made?"

"Threats? Don't be an idiot. I didn't threaten anyone."

"So," Loma glanced at her phone again. "I'm not seeing that you were going to get even with 'the owners and proprietors of the Crazy Mule and everyone associated with them'? And didn't you include a listing of everyone from the servers to the line cooks and the guy who printed their menus and the factory where they got their silverware?"

Quinn deflated. She had said all that. Quietly she said, "I was really angry. They gave me food poisoning and I barfed all over my date's shoes."

"So you say. Did you ever produce medical bills? Dry cleaning bills? Receipt for new men's shoes?"

Quinn shook her head.

"Then there's absolutely no reason to believe you."

"It was a long time ago."

"So what?" Loma snapped. "So was everything between me and Emmett."

"Was it?" Quinn's mouth engaged before her brain did.

Loma looked like she might explode. Before Quinn even realized it, Loma was in her face. "Don't you dare speak one more word to your cop friend about me. It's *you* he should be looking at. I've known it from the get-go. *You're* the one who threatened Emmett. *You're* the one who shows up here out of the blue. *You're* the one begging Jake for a job you can't even handle. And don't forget"—Loma's nose almost touched Quinn's— "you were the only one around when Emmett died." Loma stormed out of the kitchen.

When Quinn heard the door chime, it sounded angry.

Dan came in the kitchen and found Quinn leaning against the sink with her hand to her throat. "I heard shouting." His eyes got wide and he hurried to her. "Did she choke you?"

Quinn quickly lowered her hand. "No, everything's fine."

It was clear he didn't believe her. "What was all this about?"

Quinn waved a hand through the air. "Nothing, Dad. That was Jake's ex-wife and she thought I did something I didn't do." Quinn began loading dirty dishes into the dishwasher. She couldn't look her dad in the eye, but when she caught a glimpse of his face, he was still staring at her. She stopped what she was doing. "Really. It's okay. She'll realize nothing she said made sense and she'll apologize. She'll cool off."

"And you'll be friends again?"

Friends. Is that what they were? Quinn had thought so. *It seemed we'd hit it off, but maybe Loma didn't think so. Was this just a misunderstanding? Will she apologize? Should I?*

"Quinn?"

"Yeah, Dad. We'll be friends again." She smiled wanly at him. "Why don't you and Mom go home now? I'll just finish up in here and be home in a bit."

"Are you sure?"

"Yep. When I get home we can have some ice cream and watch some vintage *Cagney and Lacey.*"

Dan gave her a hug. When he went out to the dining room she heard him say, "Okay, pack it up, everyone. We've worn out our welcome here. Quinn's almost done fixing the damage we did in the kitchen and we don't want her coming out here finding more to do."

Quinn heard them all chatting and laughing and the door chime as they left. She wiped her hands on her apron to go out and lock the door behind them and almost crashed into her mother.

"Oof."

"Sorry, dear."

They spoke simultaneously.

Georgeanne: "I just wanted to remind you to lock the door."

Quinn: "I was just coming out to lock the door."

They shared a laugh, as if everything was okay. Quinn knew it wasn't and by the look on Georgeanne's face, she knew her mother didn't think so either.

* * * *

Quinn found extra things to do in the kitchen to avoid going home. She even found a video about how to fix the ancient cash register. It kept her brain and fingers busy for a while. If her parents went to bed, she could too and try to forget everything that had happened, at least for a couple of hours.

She drove the few blocks home. The July sun set late. The twilight surrounding her was dreamy and surreal, almost with a movie quality to it. Exhaustion made it difficult to keep her OCD at bay. It forced her to count the seconds she stopped at each red light. When the lights turned green, it only let her proceed when she reached an even number. She wished this personal film of hers would end so she could drop her OCD like a torn ticket stub, then step out of the theater into a dazzling summer day into a world where Emmett Dubois had never died. Because if that was true, then Jake wouldn't be in jail, she wouldn't be trying—and failing—to run the diner, and she most likely would never have become friendly with Loma. Sorrow washed over Quinn. And Rico would not have looked at her the way he did when he'd confronted her about the online review. Maybe she could rewind the film so far back that she'd never written that dumb review. At the stop sign on the corner she counted to twenty before making her turn. What if the film could rewind to before she interviewed at the academy?

When she got home she sat in her car in the driveway. She hoped her parents had gone to bed. She suddenly felt depleted, completely drained. Her legs refused to move. She had no energy. She glanced at the rubber band on her wrist and didn't even have the strength to snap it. The familiar feeling of her depression was settling upon her, the x-ray vest pressing hard on her chest. She knew it and knew she needed to fight against it before it held her down and she couldn't get up again. She'd been doing well enough with the medication, but the events of the day—the week—must have ganged up and sapped her energy.

She forced herself out of the car and into the house, one plodding step after another. When she finally stepped into the kitchen, she felt like she'd run a marathon. Not that she knew what running twenty-six miles felt like, but she knew it couldn't feel worse than this. She leaned against the doorjamb.

Georgeanne turned away from the stove and smiled wide at her. "I'm so glad you're here. Your dad couldn't wait up, though. Told me to tell you he was sorry, but that he'd watch *Cagney and Lacey* with you tomorrow."

At that moment Quinn was overwhelmed with love for her mother and so very thankful she'd waited up. She rushed to her. Georgeanne wrapped her in a hug and let her sob for a bit. When the oven timer beeped, Georgeanne steered Quinn to a chair and plucked a tissue for her.

"You just sit a minute while I get these out of the oven."

Quinn blew her nose. "After cooking all day at the diner you came home and...cooked some more?"

"I knew you needed some redneck ravioli."

Quinn wasn't entirely sure that was true, but gave her mother the benefit of the doubt. A plate of mashed potatoes and melty cheese stuffed in piecrust bites worked when she was a kid reeling from an insult that she was a stinky dum-dum head, or when she got frustrated when trying to learn that impossible piano sonata. But now? For this?

Georgeanne slid a few raviolis on a small plate and placed it in front of Quinn. She sat in the chair next to her. "Now tell me what's going on. Your father and I heard that lady yelling at you. He said it was Jake's ex-wife?"

Quinn nodded. The exhaustion roared back. She wanted to tell her mom everything, that there was a high probability Jake was a murderer. That she'd be out of a job and never be able to move out on her own like other people her age. Never be normal.

"Yeah, that was Jake's ex-wife. I thought we might be friends, but I guess I was wrong. I think I've been wrong about everything."

"Like what?"

"Like...everything." She wanted to tell her mom everything about Jake, Loma, Margosha, Rico. How out of control her OCD felt. But what she said was, "I'm completely delusional, thinking I could run the diner. The stress is too much. I can't handle it. I can't do anything, Mom. I'll never have a normal life."

"Oh, pish." Georgeanne plucked a ravioli from the plate and took a wary bite. "They're cool enough." She pushed the plate toward her daughter. "Have one."

Quinn picked one up, not because she wanted it, but because her mother wanted her to. As she brought it close to her mouth, she inhaled the comforting aroma of butter basted over a stuffed pillow of hot piecrust. Quinn knew the potatoes were mixed with Georgeanne's favorite spices:

pepper, a jerk seasoning mix, a little cinnamon, a pinch of allspice—or was it cloves? Quinn couldn't remember. As she bit into it, a new flavor erupted in her mouth. She furrowed her brow.

"Like it? I added just the tiniest bit of chocolate pudding. All the comfort food you could want in three bites." Georgeanne opened one palm as if it was a ravioli and mimed as she spoke. "Piecrust square. Plop of mashies. Pinch of cheese. Then"—here, her face lit up—"teaspoon of pudding. Another piecrust square on top. Pinch it closed. Brush with butter. Bake and voilà!"

Quinn chewed thoughtfully, finishing the entire square. "It's weirdly delicious, Mom."

"I knew it! Comfort food was exactly what you needed."

"But why do you call them redneck ravioli?"

"Why did they call Twinkies Twinkies? It's a mystery for the ages." Georgeanne bit into another one and a shower of buttery pastry flaked to the table. "Maybe I'll change it." She nodded. "Yes. Now they're called comfort squares."

Quinn ate another one and her eyes got wide. "Is this cream cheese and jelly?"

Georgeanne nodded and began pointing. "Peanut butter, cheddar, and chocolate pudding. Hummus and black olives. Cream cheese and green olives. Peanut butter, banana, and bacon bits." Then she pointed to a very unattractive comfort square. "I'm not happy with how the mandarin oranges and chocolate pudding turned out. They're good, but much too messy."

Quinn chose another one, this time with lacy edges of baked cheese that had oozed out, turning them crispy. She bit carefully but still caused another cascade of pastry flakes to flutter to the table. "Cheddar and black olives?"

Georgeanne nodded. "Now. Tell me everything."

The depression steamrolled over Quinn again. She wouldn't burden her mother with that. Georgeanne was too worried about her already, as evidenced by the cookie sheet of comfort squares. "I've told you everything. I'm just really, really tired. Working at the diner was hard before, but now, doing Jake's job too…" Quinn trailed off. But before Georgeanne could speak she said, "I'm just tired. And I really thought Loma and I could be friends."

They each ate another comfort square and Georgeanne replaced the empty plate in front of them with the entire cookie sheet.

Quinn thought about how sweet her mother was and always had been. *What other mother would be content with as little information as I provide her?* Quinn knew she was itching with a million questions, but also knew she'd ask when the timing was better, preferring to allow Quinn time and space. It reminded her of what the cop in Denver said today, that Chief Chestnut seemed scared of her. "Hey, Mom, what's that dirt you have on Chief Chestnut?" If Quinn knew, maybe she could use it to manipulate him out of his job and Rico into it.

"You just leave Myron alone. He and I go way back." Georgeanne took another bite. "Don't tell your dad, but Myron was always sweet on me."

"That's no secret." Quinn and Georgeanne both jumped at the sound of Dan's voice. He reached for a comfort square. As he bit, his pajama top was covered in crumbs. "Whole town knows Myron Chestnut is sweet on you." Dan addressed Quinn. "Didn't you notice him following her all around the festival?" He shoved the rest of the comfort square in his mouth, then brushed the crumbs to the floor.

"Hm. I thought he was following *me*," Quinn said.

"Now why would he do that?" Dan asked.

"I guess he wouldn't," Quinn said quickly.

Dan pulled up a chair and bit into another. "Ah, peanut butter and pickle. Just what the doctor ordered, eh, sunshine?"

The three of them polished off the rest of the snacks, while Dan and Georgeanne regaled Quinn with anecdotes and snippets of what went on at the diner today.

Quinn half-listened with a smile pasted on her lips, hoping she was nodding in the right places. When she'd finished counting the crumbs on the cookie sheet, she counted the tiny cherry clusters woven into the fabric of the tablecloth. She moved the cookie sheet out of the way to count under there.

Her dad placed his hand over hers. "I think it's time for you to get to bed, sunshine. And you too." He kissed Georgeanne's head as he stood. "Let's reconvene this meeting of the Carr Corporation tomorrow."

"Will we be able to entertain motions from the board?" Georgeanne asked as she stood. "I'm wondering why I don't have a new company car, maybe a Cadillac. But I'd settle for a new stand mixer. Saw a Dolce and Gabbana one I think was hand-painted. A steal at fifteen-hundred dollars."

"Did you submit agenda items in triplicate?" Dan said with a grin.

"Sorry, Mom. I have to open the diner in the morning. You won't have me for a tiebreaker."

Dan feigned outrage. "You already know you'd vote with her?"

"She made me comfort squares."

"You got me there."

After saying good night and getting into bed, Quinn thought her exhaustion would send her immediately into a deep sleep, but she was wide awake. Her exhaustion, she decided, wasn't physical.

She couldn't keep this up, not any of it.

After lying awake for an hour, she swung her feet out of bed and to the floor. She sat in the dark, listening to the *tick-tick-tick* of the clock in the kitchen and the soft rhythmic snores coming from her parents' room; for how long, she wasn't sure.

She held up Fang's bowl to the window to show him the stars and moon. After a few minutes, she returned him to the nightstand, wondering if she just blew his tiny mind. She counted out three flakes of food and dropped one in his bowl.

"Midnight snack, dude?"

Fang let it drift to the gravel.

Quinn watched him swim slowly around the bowl, long, fluttery fins and tail moving languidly through the water. She dropped the other two flakes in, one at a time. He ignored them both. Either she really had blown his mind or he wasn't a snacker.

Hypnotized by Fang's calming movements in the moonlight, she became aware again of the ticking clock.

Finally, she padded out to the kitchen. The moonlight streamed in the window so brightly she didn't need to turn on the light to find what she needed.

She stared at the therapist's business card, tacked exactly where her dad had put it when they'd returned from the hospital. Name, address, phone. Such a simple thing to print and hand out to potential clients. *Specializing in Obsessive-Compulsive Disorder*. Quinn aligned the card with the other business cards around it. If she really specialized in OCD, Quinn thought, she wouldn't have left-justified her contact information instead of centering it. But maybe this was a test, a way to get clients to call her, or maybe a way to weed out those who were just persnickety. Quinn shook her head to clear it. "It's just three a.m. talking to me," she whispered to herself. But why did three a.m. have to shout so much of the time?

She reached a shaky hand toward the push pin and pinched it between two fingers. She rubbed them back and forth on the cool molded plastic. She knew she needed to pluck out the pin and make the call, but what she really wanted to do was switch this red pushpin with that yellow one holding Abe the handyman's card. And then the blue one with that white one. The colors were so random, no pattern to them at all.

Before she realized what was happening, her fingers flew over the corkboard. Reds with red, blues with blues, yellows with yellow, whites with white. Business cards marching down the left side in two columns, alphabetized by business name, or last name in the event of none. Flyers and other odd-sized bits arranged with a quarter-inch margin separation from everything.

She stepped back and inspected her work, relieved to have fixed everything, but horrified once again she couldn't control the need. She saw the therapist's card smack-dab in the center of the column. She knew a normal person would just pluck it off, but she chose to take a picture of it with her phone.

Then she dialed the number.

A bored voice answered. "Mary-Louise Lovely's office. What is the nature of your emergency?"

Hearing the therapist's name out loud made Quinn's pleasure center buzz. That hyphen. Those matching syllables. The alliteration, but not too much. *Laura* Louise Lovely would be too much. And Lovely was so… lovely. It all added up to the perfect name.

"I…don't have an emergency. I don't think so anyway." Quinn kept her voice low.

"Then I can have Mary-Louise Lovely return your call. This is Mary-Louise Lovely's after-hours answering service." Quinn heard shuffling of papers and then the voice returned, still bored, but clearly reading from a script. "If you are having an immediate crisis, please call 911 or go to the nearest emergency room. Mary-Louise Lovely will be in touch within four hours at the phone number you leave. If you need help sooner than that, please call 911 or go to the nearest emergency room. Otherwise, leave a message." Quinn heard the papers shuffling again. "Your name and number for Mary-Louise Lovely to contact you?"

Quinn gave all the required information, then wondered what she was going to do for the next four hours while waiting for Mary-Louise Lovely to call. Probably regret calling Mary-Louise Lovely.

She wasn't sleepy, so she set up her laptop on the kitchen table to work on her next crossword puzzle. She was contemplating mental health as a theme when her phone rang. She dived for it so it wouldn't disturb her parents' slumber. That's what she told herself, anyway.

"Is this Quinn Carr?"

"Yes."

"I'm Mary-Louise Lovely."

"I'm Quinn Carr."

"Yes, I know."

Quinn covered her face with her hand. "Of course you do. I called you. And then you asked if it was me and—"

"Quinn, I want you to take a deep breath and then tell me why you called me in the middle of the night."

Quinn filled her lungs, then released the air slowly. When she finished, words gushed out of her, a burst dam of jabber. She explained all about the police academy interview, the end and the beginning of everything. How she felt like she was floating away from the three men and their questions until she anchored herself by counting the decorative holes in the ceiling tiles. When they tried to make her stop, how she floated away again and again until the next thing she knew she was in the emergency room with her father, medicated and confused.

"That's where I met you," Mary-Louise Lovely said.

"We've already met?" Quinn shook her head, as if to return her memories to the appropriate places. "I don't remember."

"You were given something to help you relax. I spoke with your father and gave him my card. I told him you'd call when you were ready. I hope you've been taking your meds?" She asked what Quinn had been taking and Quinn listed them for her. Softly she asked, "Has something happened for you to call me tonight, Quinn?"

Quinn took another deep breath and another torrent of words gushed out. She told Mary-Louise Lovely about having to move back home and take the diner job, how it was really hard learning everything, but she thought she was doing a good job, but didn't really know if Jake thought so or not. "But then this guy came in the diner when I was *alone* one night and *he died* right there in the back booth and at first I thought I *poisoned* him—well, everyone in town probably thought that—but then Jake was *arrested* for it and I've had to run the diner all by myself except for Mom and Dad yesterday and—and—"

"And you're overwhelmed?"

"Yes. Overwhelmed is a good word."

"Even after everything you've told me, I still suspect there's a lot you haven't told me—"

"So much!"

"—it makes sense that you're overwhelmed. I'm a little overwhelmed just hearing about it." She paused a moment, perhaps to catch her breath or let Quinn catch hers, or both. "How have you been coping?"

"I haven't. I thought I made that clear."

Mary-Louise Lovely laughed. "Let me be more precise: How have you been *trying* to cope?"

Quinn glanced at the rubber band she'd been snapping without realizing. She felt like she was in a confessional. The kitchen was dark and quiet. She kept her voice low and Mary-Louise Lovely did too. Must be a three a.m. thing. "A…friend told me to wear rubber bands on my wrists and snap them to remind myself not to do stuff."

"Is that working for you?"

"No."

"How 'bout you take them off your wrists now. Go ahead. I'll wait."

Quinn put the phone down and extracted her hands from the elastic. "Okay."

"How does that feel?"

Quinn held her wrists to the bit of moonlight streaming in the window. It was probably magnified in the low light, but her wrists looked dark and angry, especially the one she'd been snapping tonight. She massaged it. "Better."

"Good. Now I want you to try to keep them off." When Quinn agreed, she continued. "Now, what other things do you do to cope?"

"I organize things, color-code them and line them up. And…and I still count things."

"You make it sound like it's a moral failing."

"Isn't it?"

"No, of course not. There's no reason you can't still count things if you find comfort in it. Counting, organizing, color-coding are all part of you. You needn't remove them any more than you'd need to remove an entire fingernail because it breaks, or extract a tooth that gets a tiny cavity."

"Really?"

"Really. Have you done any research into OCD?"

"No. I've been meaning to, but—I should be more—I'm sorry."

"There's absolutely nothing to be sorry about, Quinn. Just like everything, there's a lot of information out there, some good, some bad. But let me just tell you this to start with: OCD has many forms. It manifests in many different ways and people have varying degrees of trouble with it. There's no one, single way to have OCD. But it's been my experience that it all stems from the same underlying problem, and that's fear."

"But doesn't everyone have something they're afraid of?"

"Absolutely. In people without OCD, fear still leads to stress. If you have OCD, that fear and stress grows into something overwhelming that robs you of joy and can wreck your daily life in many different ways. But OCD is only a problem when you don't take care of it, like that tooth with a cavity, and it begins to hurt you. Which is what it sounds like it's doing now. Do you want to work on some coping skills?"

"Yes, please." Quinn used her red, raw wrist to wipe her suddenly swimming eyes.

Chapter 15

Quinn talked to Mary-Louise Lovely for more than two hours and was so energized when the sun came up, she sang with noisy abandon to her car radio on the way to open the diner. She considered walking—or skipping or dancing—to work, but knew that she'd probably crash by midafternoon due to lack of sleep. But right now, she realized she felt better than she had in months. Happier. Lighter. Peppier.

Jethro was sleeping in front of the door and seemed grateful to see her. Quinn realized she hadn't told her mom and dad about poor Jethro and his recon trips through the diner or about his payment. She reached down and rubbed the side of his blocky head. "Sorry, dude. Let me make it up to you."

When he finished his rounds, Jethro padded over to her to tell her he expected his paycheck. She tipped her head toward the kitchen and he followed. As she reached to fire up the grill, she spied half a dozen slices of crisp bacon on a cookie sheet. Her mom was brilliant! Cook the bacon in the oven in a big batch. Genius. *I would have put the leftovers in the fridge, but whatever.* She broke a piece of bacon in half and carefully offered both pieces to Jethro, who waited with slobbery patience. He gobbled them up and she avoided getting her hand covered in drool. They did the same dance with another piece. Jethro stared at her and finally raised his eyes to the cookie sheet with the remaining strips on it. He couldn't see it, but it was clear he knew it wasn't empty.

"What the heck." Quinn bit into a piece of bacon, relishing the salty, hickory flavor before plating the rest of the bacon and placing it on the floor in front of Jethro.

He snarfed them up almost before she'd let go of the plate.

Quinn filled a bowl with cold water and exchanged it for the empty plate. Jethro lapped up almost all of it, leaving droplets spread in a three-foot fan in front of him. When he finished, he plodded out of the kitchen. After a few seconds, Quinn heard the jingle of the bell as he let himself out and went about the rest of his day.

While she filled the saltshakers, she thought about her therapist advising her that when she began to feel her thoughts ramping out of control, she should stop herself with a verbal clue. Most people chose some affirmation like *success!* or *good enough!* but Quinn chose *baba ghanoush!* It was fun to say and didn't make her feel so New Agey.

As she moved on to the pepper and sugar containers, she found herself whispering *baba ghanoush* over and over. It felt good.

Luckily, the five Retireds came in and distracted her while she fluttered around, catering to their whims.

"Hi, Herman. Coffee?"

He looked at her like he'd never heard of coffee. "No, dear. Get me a big glass of buttermilk."

Quinn felt her gorge rise, but tamped it down. A full glass of buttermilk? She steeled herself against the inevitable onslaught of phlegm, but consoled herself that it was just one old man. Hopefully, buttermilk hadn't been included in the delivery yesterday. "Sure thing. How 'bout the rest of you...ready for coffee?"

"Hm. Buttermilk sounds good. Extra butter," Silas said.

"Me too. And make sure it's fresh." Bob smoothed his movie star hair, even though it was perfect as always.

Quinn wondered how much phlegm this joint could handle, then processed what exactly Bob just said to her. "That's offensive, Bob. Have I ever served you something not fresh?"

"That tuna salad that one time."

"We've been over this before," Quinn scolded. "Just because you don't like dill doesn't mean the tuna was bad."

"Tasted bad." Bob jutted out his lower lip.

"Coffee for me." Larry patted Quinn on the arm.

"Me too." Wilbur turned the mug right side up at his place setting.

Quinn was grateful not everyone would be phlegmy from excess lactose.

"Lots of cream," Wilbur added.

Quinn sighed, then fetched the Retireds' dairy-laden beverages and indulged their cravings as they discovered them.

As she took orders from the customers, she very consciously tried to be less linear. She started some hash browns, she pulled one tray of bacon out of the oven and replaced it with another, she cracked eggs for all different palates—some to fry, some to scramble, some to omeletize—she poured pancakes, she toasted bread. She drew the line at waffles.

She was practically giddy when she delivered two plates with no food in common to the same table. And they thanked her and said it looked delicious! Which wasn't to say there were no more issues at the Chestnut Diner.

Quinn continued to be run ragged, correcting orders of toast that were too light, then too dark; exchanging butter for margarine, margarine for strawberry preserves, strawberry preserves for orange marmalade; eggs that were too runny or too hard. She didn't know whether to be happy or sad the menu was beginning to get back to normal.

Despite her mini-breakthrough, her nerves were frayed by the end of the breakfast rush.

Wilbur was her very last straw when he insisted his omelet had the wrong filling, even after she showed him her order pad and brought him exactly what he ordered.

He pounded a fist on the Formica-topped table, making Quinn jump. "I don't want your fancy red onion in there. Bring me a normal onion like a normal person can buy down the normal street at the normal market. Are you trying to gentrificate Chestnut Station?"

She was so taken aback at his outburst she didn't even correct his word usage. She fled to the kitchen to take four deep breaths and say several *baba ghanoushes* instead of catastrophizing into a downward spiral.

When she finished, she delivered Wilbur's new omelet, really just the old one but now covered in green chili. What he didn't know wouldn't hurt him. Someday they'd catch on to that trick, but today was not that day.

"Here, Wilbur. Sorry about the confusion. I added that green chili you like, no charge."

Wilbur was caught a bit off guard. Normally his complaints didn't warrant upgrades. "Okay…thanks. But see that it doesn't happen again!" So much wind had been taken out of his sails, it was uttered with a mildness Quinn hadn't realized he was capable of.

The Retireds finally ran out of things to complain about and forgot she was there. She took the opportunity to take some deep breaths while she ran dishes through the dishwasher and cleaned up a bit.

Quinn ventured out of the kitchen after a while. She stood in the back and checked on table five. Looked like they were ready to go. She reached in her apron pocket, pulling out her pad. As she totaled and delivered the bill to them, she mulled over her idea about disgruntled customers blackmailing Jake.

Most of the complainers she'd ever served were sitting over there at the Retireds' table. She supposed any of them could have swiped one of the catalogs from Jake, just like she swiped the one from the Crazy Mule. But studying the men, she couldn't picture any of them—not even Wilbur—creating that note, or worse, murdering anyone.

After a small, confused shake of her head, she cleaned the empty tables again before the lunch rush. The Retireds scooted out their chairs, screeching them across the floor. They dropped cash on the table and shuffled out the door.

Wilbur made a move for the door, but veered in her direction. He started to speak, but Quinn held up her hand.

"Don't start with me, Wilbur."

He glanced back at the rest of the Retireds, fighting over the toothpicks and mints at the cash register. He kept his voice low, fingering the brim of his Panama hat so it went in slow circles. "Just wanted to say… thanks for working so hard here, keeping this place open."

Quinn could form no words, so simply nodded, as if this kind of thing happened between them all the time.

Wilbur plopped his hat on his head and turned to join his friends.

Quinn hurried after him and tapped him on the shoulder. When he turned, she hugged him, hard.

After a bit, he pulled away, calling to the Retireds. "See that, boys? I still got it!"

"Well, don't give it to Quinn! She's finally figured out how to make my toast," Silas said.

Wilbur was the last one out the door. He stopped to unwrap a peppermint, saw Quinn watching, and winked at her.

The diner was empty now and Quinn found her mind working over the events of the last couple of days. She found herself whispering *baba ghanoush* repeatedly and had to stop herself for fear this would become an unwelcome habit. She needed to use the phrase to disrupt her obsessive thinking, not replace it.

But still, she thought about the word while she cleared the Retireds' table. She'd never actually eaten baba ghanoush. She dried her hands and Googled it. She thought it was a kind of hummus, but didn't know where it was from. Wikipedia told her it was "a Lebanese appetizer of mashed cooked eggplant mixed with tahini, olive oil, possibly lemon juice and various seasonings." Maybe she should make some for the diner. That might be asking too much of the Chestnut Diner community, though. But maybe not, now that Georgeanne had fed some of them. Aside from the green chili, there wasn't a lot of ethnic food on the menu. And green chili was hardly ethnic.

Not a lot of anything was very ethnic or exotic about Chestnut Station. Certainly not the diner. Not the clothing stores, unless you counted Rick's Western Wear, with his selection of ostrich-skin boots. And Quinn didn't. None of the people in Chestnut Station were very exotic. They were all interesting, charming even, in their own way, but none could be described as exotic. Not like Margosha Dubois.

Quinn went back to cleaning the tables, but now Margosha was on her mind. She didn't think Margosha was Lebanese, but there was a connection between her and baba ghanoush. With Jake helping Margosha with her English skills, and the multitude of recipes for baba ghanoush, it seemed to Quinn that they were both trying to fit into the mainstream, maybe pretend they weren't as foreign as they seemed.

Quinn was woke enough to know that just because someone was foreign didn't make them bad. She was ashamed the idea flitted through her mind. But then she stopped, mid-wipe of the tabletop. She remembered all the reasons she had suspected Margosha for killing Emmett and setting up Jake for the murder. None of it had to do with the fact she was foreign.

Quinn simply couldn't accept that either Jake or Loma were guilty. They were both people she liked and got along with. At least until recently. She couldn't let it be true. She plopped down into one of the chairs. But Margosha could definitely be Emmett's silent partner. Wives and husbands were in business together all the time, and it would make sense that it wasn't public information since she wasn't in the restaurant business. That might make other potential investors nervous. As a partner, she absolutely would have been harmed by the falling-out Emmett and Jake had. She knew Margosha was in a sham marriage to Emmett and was going to get a payday when they got divorced. The restaurants would have been worth a fortune, and if she blamed Jake... well, murders happened for lesser reasons. And the life insurance, now that Emmett was dead, must be worth a pretty penny. Didn't Kelli tell her all the employees at the Crazy Mule got a $500,000 policy if they hung around long enough? Maybe management received even more. With no kids and no second marriage for either of them, she was still the logical beneficiary.

The diner wasn't busy, so Quinn cleared away some things from Jake's desk and unrolled the big butcher paper sheet of clues that she and Loma had worked on the other day. She gasped when she saw blood in the corner, then smiled when she remembered that Loma had made a late-night doughnut run and had dripped jelly doughnut on the paper. She'd said, "Doughnut you dare spill jelly on my homework!" and they both dissolved into giggles. Stress, lack of sleep, and too much sugar had conspired to help them bond.

Quinn rubbed the jelly stain with her finger. It had been nice to have a girlfriend to giggle with again. She dialed Loma's number and was more than a little surprised when she answered right away.

"What do *you* want?" The words sounded harsh, but Loma's voice didn't. Quinn thought maybe it was just wishful thinking on her part.

"Loma, I wanted to apologize. I didn't mean the things I said. You're not an idiot." Quinn held her breath until Loma spoke.

"And you're not a Crappy McCrapface."

"You never called me that."

"I was thinking it."

Quinn heard the smile in Loma's voice and relaxed.

The pause in the conversation cleared the air between them and reset their relationship.

"Crappy McCrapface?" Quinn asked.

"I was a little off my game. So, what's up? Any news about Jake?"

"No. Well, maybe." Quinn switched her phone to her other ear and proceeded to tell Loma her theory about Margosha's probable guilt in killing Emmett and framing Jake. "It makes perfect sense."

"Not really."

Quinn repeated her argument. "What's wrong with it? Tell me why I'm wrong."

Loma hemmed, hawed, and sighed. "I can't."

"I knew it!" Quinn yelled and fist-pumped in the silent office. She tiptoed to the doorway to see if anyone had come into the diner while she wasn't paying attention. Nobody. Quinn slid into the closest booth. "Okay. So, here's my plan."

"You already have a plan?"

"I always have a plan." Quinn winced at the truth of her statement. "You told me the other day that you and Margosha were having trouble planning Emmett's funeral and you were going to meet with his attorney to try and find anything with Emmett's wishes on it."

"Yeah. So?"

"So, have you done it yet?"

"No."

"Can I go with you when you go next week?"

"We're not going next week. We're going today."

"On Sunday? What kind of attorney is open on Sunday?"

"It was the only time he could meet us. He's heading out of town."

"Can I go with you?"

"I guess, but I'm already in Denver. You'll have to meet us there." Loma paused. "Are you going to do anything crazy with Margosha? I don't want to be a party to a catfight or a crazy citizen's arrest or anything."

"Don't worry. Nothing like that's going to happen." But Quinn wasn't completely convinced. Firmly, she said, "Margosha is the murderer and when we see that life insurance policy we'll know for sure."

"Girl, just because someone is the beneficiary of a life insurance policy doesn't mean they're a murderer."

"Except in this case. I'm sure of it. And an attorney will be a fantastic witness when we confront her."

"What's this *we* of which you speak? Got a mouse in your pocket? Besides, why hasn't Rico gotten the will yet?"

"I don't know," Quinn said slowly. "Maybe he has. I can't tell if he's lying to me or not."

"Have you asked him? I thought you said the two of you were working on this together."

"He's—we're—"

"Did you call him an idiot too?"

Quinn changed the subject because a thought popped into her head. "Why do you have to meet the attorney in person? Why couldn't he tell you about Emmett's wishes over the phone?"

"Margosha begged him. She said—"

"Aha! She begged him! She needs her hands on that will for some reason. And you and I are going to find out why."

"Call Rico and tell him to meet us there, or better yet, have him come with you."

"I'm on it. Either way, I'll see you there." Quinn hung up, then walked over to the door of the diner and flipped the sign from *Open* to *Closed*. She dialed her mom. "Hey. Want to handle the diner for me again today?"

"I thought you'd never ask. Be right over." Before Georgeanne disconnected, Quinn heard her yell to Dan, "Honey! Get some pants on. We've got work to do!"

Next, Quinn called Rico. She reiterated everything she'd said to Loma about Margosha, but on the second telling felt much more confident about her conclusions. She ended with asking him to come with her to the attorney's office.

Rico let her talk without interruption, then calmly said, "I can't."

"Well, meet us there, then." Quinn rattled off the name of the law firm and the rough directions.

"I can't come because it's not Margosha, not because I'm too busy."

"Why do you keep insisting it's not her without telling me why? You can't tell a lie! Why are you lying about this?" Quinn shouted in frustration.

"I'm not lying. It's not Margosha."

Quinn took some deep breaths to calm herself. She knew from experience that nothing she could say would sway Rico from what he believed, even though she was fairly certain she had finally taught him how to lie. She tried a different tactic. "Have you seen the will or the life insurance policy yet?"

"No." Rico expelled a breath too. "Listen, Quinn, don't go doing something stupid. It's not Margosha—"

"But—"

"And I can't tell you why."

"I thought you said I could help you with this investigation."

"I know I did," Rico said quietly. "But I'm just not sure how to make that work."

"Maybe it would work if you'd trust me." Quinn hung up on him. *I'll show him*, she thought. *Loma and I will go down there and confront Margosha and with the help of Emmett's attorney, we'll get her arrested and Jake released.*

* * * *

Quinn was halfway through another set of explicit instructions for her parents about handling the diner the rest of the day, when she stopped mid-sentence. "You're not going to do any of that, are you?"

"Honestly? No," Dan said.

"Not a chance," Georgeanne said. "I've already got a recipe for the lunch special. Have you got any bittersweet chocolate?"

"I'm not sure. What did you have in mind?" Quinn asked cautiously.

"Spaghetti mole."

Quinn squinted at her. "Mole, like for Mexican food?" When Georgeanne started to answer, Quinn held up her hand. "Never mind. I don't want to know. I'll be back as soon as I can." She gathered up her bag. "Oh, and I fixed the cash register."

"And the credit card dealy?" Dan asked.

"Nope. Still a cash business. But it's all good." Quinn tipped her head toward her mother, already bustling around the kitchen. "At least on the money front."

"You don't worry about her. Go. Do your errands. We'll be fine." Dan kissed her on the top of her head.

Quinn left the diner with a smile, turning the *Closed* sign to *Open*.

* * * *

Quinn recognized the neighborhood she drove through near the attorney's office. It seemed like she'd seen it on the news recently, but couldn't quite put her finger on it. It was a gentrified neighborhood in Denver called Belcaro, filled with historic cottonwood and spruce trees and big, old renovated houses with wide porches and carefully cultivated flower gardens. Most were turned into law or dental offices, but many were now upscale boutiques and shops selling one thing. Candles. Kebabs. Cakes.

Quinn parallel parked at the curb a few doors down from the attorney's office. When Quinn reached the wooden sign for Patterson Law Offices planted in the lawn, she glanced around for Loma, hoping she'd get there before Margosha did. She didn't quite know how either of them would be without Loma as a buffer.

She spotted Loma getting out of her car at the Donut King next door. Loma checked her watch, started for the door, then saw Quinn waving at her. With a sigh, Loma pivoted and joined her on the sidewalk in front of the attorney's office.

"If I knew there was a doughnut place next door, I would have come earlier and picked up a dozen."

"I thought you weren't supposed to have doughnuts."

"That's why I have doughnut holes." Loma tapped the side of her head. "They're healthier for you."

"Not if you eat a dozen."

"Better than eating a dozen doughnuts. Portion control. It's the name of the game, Quinn."

Quinn raised her eyebrows, choosing not to remind her that she'd bought full-size doughnuts on her doughnut run the other night. "If those are your only two choices. But let's go over the plan again, before Margosha gets here."

"Look at those beautiful old trees," Loma said, ignoring her. "I'd love to renovate one of these old places and have this landscape to work with. The first thing I'd do—"

"You." Margosha turned to Loma. "Why she is here?"

"I told her she could come," Loma said.

Margosha made a little huff noise and brushed past them, her stilettos *tap-tap-tapping* on the brick walkway. Loma bugged out her eyes at Quinn behind Margosha's back and they followed her to the wraparound porch. Quinn hoped Loma wasn't getting cold feet.

Margosha jabbed the buzzer with more force than was necessary. Someone inside buzzed back and the door clicked open. Just as Margosha tried to go inside, a woman came out. They both startled.

"Excuse me. I was just going out to do a couple of quick errands. I'm Katrina. Attorney Patterson is expecting you—go on back."

Katrina held the door for them, then left them alone. They were in the reception area of an office that had once been elegant and stylish, but had turned the corner into slightly shabby. The furniture showed signs of wear, with scuff marks on the legs, perhaps from years of overzealous vacuuming. The carpet was ragged and stained in the high-traffic areas.

The receptionist's desk had a nameplate reading *Katrina O'Toole*. A pale pink cardigan was draped neatly on the back of a chair.

Margosha and Loma headed down the hall. Quinn stayed in the reception area in case Margosha decided to bolt when they confronted her.

Patterson greeted Margosha and Loma by name and they exchanged some pleasantries. Quinn couldn't hear everything but caught snippets of the conversation, especially when Loma spoke. She hoped Loma would remember everything Quinn wanted her to ask.

Loma's voice boomed louder. "Do you have a copy of Emmett's will or life insurance policy?" *Attagirl, Loma.* "We're looking for something that spells out his funeral wishes."

"Emmett...new attorney...something like that...don't have...can't show it to you anyway."

"Why not?" Loma asked.

"... neither of you...beneficiaries...strictly legal..."

Quinn quit listening to his muffled explanation of estate law. Margosha wasn't Emmett's beneficiary? How was that possible? This was all for nothing? Why didn't the attorney just tell them that when they called to make the appointment? And how did he know who the beneficiaries were if he didn't have the document? It sounded like he'd said Emmett had a new attorney, but maybe she just hadn't heard right.

Ideas whirled through her mind until she realized she needed a restroom. There was no reason to worry about Margosha bolting, so this was as good a time as any to avail herself, especially since there was no way she'd make it back to Chestnut Station without a pit stop.

Quinn looked around for a restroom. The law office was a refurbished old house, so the reception area was the living room or parlor area. She walked around the corner to what used to be the kitchen, set up with the makings of a break room: small table and chairs, three-quarter-sized refrigerator, microwave, coffee station.

Quinn passed through an open archway at the back of the kitchen area. As she turned the corner she ran into a rather inconveniently placed table with a lamp on it. When her knee caught the table, it made the ceramic country-style lamp wobble. She grabbed for it and resettled it in the center of the table. She realized why it was there, however, because it was very dim back here, with no windows or other lighting.

She took another step, being very careful to give the table a wide berth, and realized she was at the end of the hallway where Patterson's office was. The restroom door was blessedly open. It would be embarrassing to have to poke her head into their meeting to ask where it was.

She had just soaped up her hands when she received a text. Before she left the restroom she looked at it.

From Loma. **Where are u? Fancy a donut?** She hadn't spelled out the word, though, just posted an emoji of a doughnut. Quinn texted back an emoji of a smiley face with its finger to its lips as if saying "shh."

She smiled, pocketed her phone, and stepped from the restroom. She hadn't even heard them leave. Before meeting up with Loma at the doughnut shop, though, she wanted to ask the attorney if she heard correctly and that Margosha wasn't Emmett's beneficiary, and if he didn't have any of Emmett's documents, how he would know that. She must have missed something in the snippets of conversation she heard. Maybe she could also get the new attorney's information. She hadn't heard Loma ask for that.

Quinn felt close to the truth; just a bit more information to figure out Margosha's scheme. Directly in front of her was his office door, opening halfway into the hallway. She stood awkwardly behind it. As she tried to decide whether to push it closed while coming around in front of it, or simply knock on it while standing behind it, he got a phone call. Quinn waited for him to finish while she loitered in the hallway, hidden behind the door, still not sure how a normal person would make their presence known.

She peeked into his office through the crack in the door. She saw his profile and a suitcase sitting on the floor next to his desk. His desktop was empty except for a wooden in/out tray, his desk phone, something she assumed was his nameplate, and a stapler. Everything was neatly arranged with straight edges and square corners, except for the stapler. It was at a haphazard angle that Quinn desperately wanted to align with the edge of the desk.

As she tried to push this out of her mind, replacing it with figuring out Margosha's plot, the attorney's voice washed over her. There was something familiar about it.

Before she fully processed the voice, she heard him say, "Wrong," and then after a pause, "Wrong again."

The memory slammed into her. He was the murder mystery guy! The same obnoxious phrase he had used in the diner that night with Emmett.

"Mushrooms," she whispered, then clamped a hand over her mouth. That's why this neighborhood felt so familiar. It was on that news video she watched on the Colorado Mycological Society website.

She had to get out of there, but didn't dare pass his office. She turned quietly to go back to the end of the hallway near the restroom, and then through the kitchen, and out past Katrina's desk.

Adrenaline coursed through her body and her hands began to tingle. Her chest felt tight, only allowing her shallow breaths. She grabbed for the table with the lamp, both to steady herself and to make sure she didn't knock it over. The lamp wobbled, but Quinn steadied it. Gripping the table with both hands, she leaned over and said a couple of *baba ghanoushes*. It didn't do anything to calm her, so she released her grip on the table and sidled around it. She hurried from the dim hallway through the archway into the kitchen, sneaking a glance behind her to check for Patterson. It seemed like it had been a lifetime since she'd heard that *wrong again*, but knew it had only been a couple of moments.

While her head was turned she ran into a tall trash can and sent it sprawling and skittering across the kitchen. She didn't wait to see if Patterson heard, because there was no way he hadn't. She scrambled through the kitchen and had almost made it to Katrina's desk when she saw him between her and the front door.

"You," he said. "I know you." His blank look was replaced with one of recognition. "The Chestnut Diner."

Quinn didn't stick around to have a conversation about the diner. She feinted left but ran right.

He dove for Katrina's desk.

Quinn raced for the door. As she reached for the knob, she heard him slam his hand on Katrina's desk, then a *click*. The knob didn't budge under her grip. She turned it the opposite way. Nothing. She rattled it hard and banged it against the jamb.

He had remote locks to the front door.

Patterson came toward her. She ran back into the kitchen. Old houses had kitchen doors leading outside, Quinn knew, and she scanned the area. She almost didn't see it on the opposite side from the archway because it was wallpapered in such a way as to camouflage it. She lunged for it, but not before she heard the *click* of its lock too.

She scrambled through the kitchen and found herself near the restroom, searching for another way out. She never saw the door, but heard the *click*. She turned and found herself face-to-face with Patterson, who gripped her upper arm and steered her back to his office. He pushed her into an armless leather chair in the corner.

"Don't move," he growled.

Quinn knew Patterson's secretary would be back any minute; she'd said she only had a couple of errands to run. Quinn just needed to stall until then. But, as if reading her mind, Patterson stood in the doorway and pulled out his phone. "Katrina? Hey, I've had a change of plans and won't be needing you to pick up groceries for my house sitter." He listened for a bit. "That's okay, just take them home with you. My treat." He smiled. "Everyone loves some Ben and Jerry's. Enjoy! And I'll let you know when I know my plans. No need to come in before Tuesday, for sure."

Quinn had said a thousand *baba ghanoushes* by the time they ended their conversation.

She was locked in here alone with him. Even though she'd had the wrong killer pegged, at least she'd told Rico where she was going and why. But he said he was busy. He wasn't going to miss her any time soon, or even realize she was still here. Loma was waiting for her at the doughnut shop. She'd come look for her if she never showed up. Quinn groaned inwardly. What would she make of the "shh" smiley face she'd texted? Would Loma understand it meant that Quinn wouldn't tell anyone if they had a couple of doughnut holes? Why in the world didn't she just say "I'll meet you in five minutes," like a normal person?

All of this shot through Quinn's brain in a nanosecond.

Patterson stared at her from the doorway of his office. "You're that waitress. What's your name?"

What's my name, what's my name? "Quinn."

"Well, Quinn, it seems like you and I have a bit of a problem." He tilted his head at her. She recognized the mole that looked like a dimple on his right cheek. He was the man wearing the winter cap at the diner on the day of the festival, and the cater-waiter with the dimple who gave Emmett's plate with the poisoned mushrooms to Donnie to serve.

"No, we don't. We don't have any problem at all. It's just been some…
misunderstanding."

"Why were you skulking in my office?"

"I wasn't skulking. I just had to…use your restroom. But you got a call
before I could ask. I was just waiting until you got off the phone."

"How'd you get in here?"

"I came with Loma and Margosha."

"I didn't see you."

"I waited in the reception area."

"Why didn't you leave with them?"

"I didn't know they left. I was in the restroom. I had some questions I
wanted to ask you, but you got a call, so I waited."

"I thought you said you were waiting to ask me to use the restroom?
Which is it?" Patterson leaned against his desk after sliding his nameplate
aside. It read *Samuel Patterson*. Sam the headhunter had used the same
obnoxious phrase. Patterson was Sam the headhunter, the murder mystery
guy, *and* Emmett's ex-attorney.

"What questions did you have?" he asked calmly.

Why did you freakin' kill Emmett Dubois and frame Jake for it? "Oh,
they're not important anymore." Quinn tried to keep from panicking, tried
to match his calmness.

He studied her. "Did I hear you say *mushrooms* earlier? Who were
you talking to?"

"Nobody. Myself." Quinn felt a drip of sweat run straight down her
spine. She could have kicked herself. If ever there was a time for a well-
placed lie, like she was always trying to teach Rico, it was now. "Actually,
that's a lie. I was talking to Rico Lopez of the Chestnut Station Police
Department. He should be here any minute."

Patterson's eyes got wide with fear and Quinn readied herself to be
released. "Let me unlock the door for him." He hovered his hand over a
button on the corner of his desk that looked like a doorbell. Instead of
pressing it, he snapped his fingers instead. "Oh, I just remembered." His
face morphed from mock fear to sneering contempt. "Rico Lopez of the
Chestnut Station Police Department won't be coming for you. You and I
both know that."

Quinn saw her vision dance with tiny blobs, then close in from the
periphery as she began hyperventilating again. She had to put her head
between her knees to keep from fainting. As her vision cleared and the *baba
ghanoushes* faded to whispers in her brain, she saw Patterson's shoes right
in front of her. She slowly raised her head until she looked him in the eye.

If she was going to die, she was going to die with answers. "What did you gain from killing Emmett?"

"That idiot ruined a good thing by feuding with Jake. He ran Jake off and the restaurants were never the same. He lost our rating, he lost every penny I invested. I had to resurrect this practice and chase ambulances just to survive."

That explains why this place looks so shabby, she thought.

"If Emmett did all that, why frame Jake? He must have lost everything too."

A joyless laugh left his mouth. "Aside from the obvious scapegoating, have you ever ruined someone's life?"

"Probably, but not on purpose."

He stared at her. "You're funny," he said, not laughing. "Jake landed on his feet. It was too tempting not to knock him down a peg or two. He loves that awful diner, but when I heard he wanted to get back into gourmet cooking, the plan practically wrote itself."

"The plan where you pretend to be a headhunter and get Jake that job at the fundraiser so you could slip in those poisonous mushrooms? You must be the anonymous tipper too."

"You're pretty smart, for a girl." He laughed when he saw Quinn's face contort. She was now equal parts terror and outrage. "I knew I should have bugged out of town the day you called me. I meant to get rid of that phone number to Colorado Premium Employment. How'd you get it, anyway?"

"Jake's call history."

"Ah. Well, this is all very *Murder, She Wrote*, but—"

"Why the stupid two-hundred-dollar amount in that blackmail note?" Quinn knew she had to keep him talking. She always thought it was a bit over-the-top when crooks spilled all their secrets in TV shows and books, but apparently that was what they really did.

"Stupid? Genius, you mean. It was just a token amount I knew he could pay. Plus, I knew deep down Jake had a soft spot for Emmett and if he thought Emmett was that hard up for cash, he'd want to give it to him."

Exactly what Jake had said.

"You're Emmett's silent partner, not Margosha."

Another one-syllable laugh shot out of Patterson. "Margosha may have an accent, but she's hardly silent."

That was the same thing Jake said about Loma. What was it about men trying to take away women's voices? A funny feeling dredged up from Quinn's toes. She didn't recognize it until it hit her belly.

Fury. She was feeling fury.

It allowed her to leap to her feet and surprise Patterson with a knee to the groin. He doubled over. Much of her physical training for the police academy kicked in. Thank goodness for Rico's help to learn some of the moves before she applied. She used her knee again and clocked him in the forehead, sending him reeling backward where he hit the wall with a thud and a loud "Ooof."

Quinn scrambled for the buzzer on his desk to unlock the door, but Patterson got there first. He hit her chest with his forearm and knocked the wind out of her. She stood gaping, trying to get breath into nonworking lungs. He came around the desk toward her. With wild eyes, she looked for anything to use as a weapon. She saw it, memorized its location, then locked eyes on Patterson.

At the same time he lunged for her, she lunged for the stapler. As she raised it over her head to strike him with it, it flopped open. When it connected with his temple, she heard him yowl and raise his hand to his face.

"Did you just—staple me?" he bellowed before charging at her.

She scurried away from him, but he kept coming, the staple in the side of his face catching glints of light.

Muscle memory kicked in. When he got close enough, she punched him hard, right in the throat. He crumpled to the ground.

Quinn breathed deeply; huge, convulsive gulps of air. As she tried to control her breathing, she glanced around for something to tie him up with. Her eyes landed on the suitcase on the floor next to his desk, wrapped with a canvas strap.

She removed it and then dropped it on the floor next to the armless chair she'd been sitting in earlier. Scooping Patterson under his arms, Quinn tried to lift and carry him over to the chair. When that didn't work, she let go of him and he thudded to the floor again.

Quinn brought the chair and the strap to Patterson. Bracing herself, she heaved and wrangled him into a seated position in the chair. She tightened the strap around his arms and torso, pinning him to the chair. She didn't like that his feet were free. She unzipped his suitcase, rummaging around until she came up with two neckties. She lashed his ankles to the chair legs.

Finally, she slammed her hand on the buzzer to unlock the front door, and raced from the office.

She and Loma crashed into each other in the hallway, both yelling at once. Quinn's words turned to sobs and Loma held her tight, eventually easing her into Katrina's chair.

"I have to call Rico," Quinn said, fumbling for her phone.

"I already did. He's on his way. You just sit." Loma tiptoed to Patterson's office and Quinn heard her squeal, "Giiiiirl? You're like a ninja!"

"How did you know I was here?" Quinn called to her.

"You weren't at the doughnut shop and your car was still there. Where else would you be?"

Quinn hadn't seen Margosha follow Loma in and was surprised when she tenderly knelt next to her and placed a cool palm on Quinn's cheek. "He has hurt you, yes?"

"I'm okay." Quinn stared at Margosha. "You didn't have anything to do with any of this?"

She shook her head.

"Then why wouldn't you talk to me? Why'd you call the cops on me?"

Margosha stood and leaned against the desk, eyes flashing. "Rico promise no tellink! I say no financial claim on Emmett, just want give him nice funeral. But he tell you about green card marriage."

"He never said a word to me about that." *That's why Rico didn't want to talk to me about Margosha. He'd made a promise to her and if he and I talked about her too much, I might have asked a question he'd have to answer.* "But you had a big divorce party. It didn't sound like a secret."

"Secret from ICE and reporters. Not secret from friends."

"You thought I was a reporter? I'm not."

Margosha nodded, clearly relieved. "Plus, you say friend of Jake's, but Jake in jail so I think guilty. Why reporter want talk to me? Easier no talk."

Maybe for you, Quinn thought.

Loma came back out to the reception area, babbling about how Patterson was still out cold. "What did you do to him, Furiosa?"

Before Quinn could tell her, four uniformed officers from Denver PD stepped into the open door of the law office, weapons drawn. "Hands up."

All three women raised their arms immediately. Two officers passed through and headed down the hallway. The other two stayed and frisked them.

"Quinn Carr."

"Yes sir?" Quinn didn't move a muscle.

"So we meet again."

Quinn glanced at the officer's name badge and smiled. "Officer Childers. I'm very happy you're here."

One of the other officers returned to say there was a man tied up in the office, just coming back into consciousness.

"Who was responsible for that?" Officer Childers asked.

"Mad Max–wannabe there." Loma tipped her chin in Quinn's direction.

"You did a good job. You can lower your hands."

The officers holstered their guns.

Officer Childers bounced his glance between Quinn and Margosha. "You two friends now? You want to tell me what happened here?"

Margosha kept quiet, but Quinn started in on the story, stopping and twisting back when none of it made sense. Finally she said, "Remember how my boss was in jail? That man I tied up in there is the real murderer. He killed Emmett Dubois."

Officer Childers had a lot of questions. As the women were filling in details, Rico burst in. He went straight for Quinn and squeezed her tight. When he was sure she was okay, he and Officer Childers went into the office where Patterson was tied up.

Before they got too far, Quinn said, "Rico, I think you'll find Emmett's will or life insurance papers or something in a big envelope in Patterson's suitcase."

When all the police were in Patterson's office and the women were left alone in the reception area, Loma asked. "What did the 'shh' emoji mean? I didn't know if we were getting doughnuts or you were judging me."

"I have never wanted to get doughnuts with someone more than I do right now." Quinn flung one arm around Loma's shoulder and sagged against her, trusting Loma to support her.

She did.

Chapter 16

At the Chestnut Diner the next day, decorated by Quinn and Loma in a welcome-back motif, Georgeanne called from the kitchen, "Can I get a little help back here?"

Jake jumped up, but Quinn waved him back down. "I'll go. You relax. This is your last vacation day. Tomorrow you're back at work and *I'm* going to sit around."

"I wasn't sitting around on purpose, you know."

"Yeah, yeah. Whatever." Quinn disappeared into the kitchen. "What do you need, Mom?"

"Can you take these out there for me?"

"What are they?"

"Those cumin cupcakes everyone liked so much."

Quinn smiled at her. "Of course."

While Georgeanne made more coffee and filled pitchers of iced tea and lemonade, Quinn arranged the red, white, and blue cupcakes on a platter. She started a pattern, then purposely picked up a white one and replaced it with a blue, then a red one next to another red one. When she finished, the platter was as randomized as she could make it. She lifted it, then set it back down immediately. Was this a patterned arrangement too? Was purposely placing cupcakes in random order the same as obsessively marching them in line by staggered color? Or was she beginning to loosen the grip of one of her compulsions? This was unfamiliar territory, but she felt like she had some breathing room. At least for now. Quinn stared at the platter, then shrugged. These were questions for Mary-Louise Lovely next week.

She carried out the tray and Georgeanne followed with the drinks. Loma asked about the flavors after she grabbed a red one and a white one.

Rico declined cupcakes, but accepted a cup of coffee from Georgeanne. Dan licked the frosting off a blue cupcake before breaking it in half and taking a big bite.

"So, Rico," Quinn asked with a playful grin. "Do you still wish I hadn't helped with your investigation?"

"If I ever say that again, you have permission to throttle me."

"And seeing what she did to Patterson, you know she can too!" Loma said.

"I don't doubt it. I remember all the bruises she gave me when we trained together."

Quinn nodded. "I cleaned your clock more than once."

"That you did." Rico tilted his head, assessing her. "People underestimate you, Quinn Carr."

"At their peril," Loma added loudly.

"At their peril," Rico echoed.

Quinn got all squishy at the praise and deflected the compliment. "People undertip me too."

Everyone ate and drank and chatted about the recent events.

Jake finished his cumin cupcake, wiped his mouth with a paper napkin, and stood. Quinn expected him to drop it into the trash. Instead he walked to the front window, took down the *Help Wanted* sign, and threw it away.

ACROSS

1. Simon and Garfunkel's "A ___ Shade of Winter"
5. Spot of tea, to a Brit
10. Michelle, to Barack
14. One of HOMES
15. Islamic devil
16. Word with rain or rock
17. Type of moth
18. Library transactions
19. Greek sandwich
20. Painter of the Sistine Chapel
23. Dahs' counterparts
24. 14-line poem with only two rhymes
28. Trouble for a tooth
32. Addams family cousin
33. Wade's legal opponent
34. With 45-across, one who provides capital only
35. ___ and outs
36. Campaign funding grps
37. Some campaigns win them
38. Hit the jackpot
39. Book parts
40. Ford contemporary
41. Bud holder
42. Where the chips are down?
43. The beginning of time?
44. Chesapeake or Tampa
45. See 34-across
46. Trout's home
48. Samoan coin
49. Colorado ski town
55. "Not only that ..."
58. Longest river in France
59. Genuine
60. Aquatic mammal
61. All you need in a medical crisis, maybe
62. Leather piercing tools
63. ___ Linda, CA
64. Brother of Jack and Bobby
65. Wall Street Journal subj

DOWN

1. Bridge position
2. North African sheep
3. Sunblock ingredient

4. "Absolutely!"
5. Yo-Yo Ma, for one
6. WWII subs
7. Vague reason for not attending a party
8. Pong preceder
9. Proclaims
10. Prairie schooner
11. Frozen
12. Christmas tree, often
13. Former name of Tokyo
21. Utopias
22. Place to park
25. Come home exhausted
26. Dawn of mammals epoch
27. One receiving a security deposit
28. Fancy ties
29. Bunk assignment
30. Mini hamburger
31. Boardroom bigwigs
32. Holiday or Red Roof
35. Charged particle

36. "Whenever I think of the ___, it brings back so many memories." Steven Wright
38. "No ___ !"
39. Kitchen gizmo
41. King Arthur's hood?
42. Steinbeck's novel "___ Row"
44. Soap unit
45. Gazed intently
47. Deadly virus
48. What they did in Breckenridge
50. Ice cream ___
51. Persia today
52. Like grass in the morning
53. Guys' partners at square dances
54. "If all ___ fails"
55. Digital communication? Abbr
56. Author Tolstoy
57. Famous uncle

RECIPES

Georgeanne's Pretzel Pancakes

Makes about 13

3C white whole wheat flour
2T baking powder
1T sugar
1tspn salt
2C water
1/2 C unsweetened applesauce (those lunchbox cups are perfect for this)
3 eggs
maybe a squidge of vanilla if you like
small pretzel twists (buy a big bag, someone will eat whatever you don't use)

Mix the dry ingredients first, then add the wet ingredients. Or do it the other way around. It all gets mixed up eventually.

Heat some oil in a skillet until a drip of water sizzles. Pour a scant 1/3 C of batter for each pancake. Take your pretzel twists and arrange them in the batter of each pancake, as many as you like, hanging over the edges or completely hidden. Or both!

It's time to turn your pancakes when the bubbles disappear. Flip and cook the other side.

Top these with whatever sounds good. I only use caramel sauce on mine. Here's how I make that:

1C sugar
1/2 C whipping cream
2T butter

In a small saucepan, mix sugar with 1/4C water. Stir it real good over medium-high heat, then let it heat without stirring for 10 or 15 minutes. It should be caramel colored by then.

While that's happening, warm your cream a bit on the stove or in the microwave. Whisk it slowly into the caramel for a couple of minutes until it's smooth. Take it off the heat and add the butter to melt in it. So good!

Here are some things Quinn and Dan like on their pretzel pancakes:

- more pretzels held in place with whipped cream
- maple syrup
- sliced strawberries
- 1T chocolate syrup + 1/2T balsamic vinegar
- flavored yogurt
- peanut butter and maple syrup
- honey mixed with a little mustard (it is a pretzel, after all!)

Enjoy! I'd love to know what you put on yours! Send an email and photo to Becky@BeckyClarkBooks.com

Georgeanne's Redneck Ravioli

(aka Comfort Squares)

Makes more than a few, less than a lot

Basically, these are stuffed pillows of comfort foods, which are different for everyone, so adapt to your comfort level ... pun intended.

You'll need a piecrust, store-bought or homemade. Roll it out thin and then cut it into 2-inch squares, or use a cookie cutter about that size. It doesn't need to be square, but then you'll have to call these something different. You might have a small juice glass about 2-inches across. I just checked my cabinet and I do, so you probably do too.

Cut out as many as you can, but you'll need an even number. Press the scraps together and roll out again, as many times as you need to. Your number of squares will depend on how thinly you roll them out.

Cover a cookie sheet with foil or parchment if you don't want to wash the cookie sheet afterward.

Now, you get to decide on your fillings. You can make them all the same or make each one different. Here's where you make this recipe your own. The only mistake you can make with these is to fill them too full, because then it oozes out and makes a mess. A delicious mess, especially if the cheese gets crispy, but a mess nonetheless.

Here at the Carr house, when Quinn is upset she goes for anything cheesy. I like the sweet stuff, and Dan likes everything, so I always make a variety. When Quinn was little, she used to love using a can of squirt cheese to decorate the tops of hers.

These are some combinations we like:
- mashed potatoes, chocolate pudding, and cheddar cheese
- peanut butter, cheddar cheese, and chocolate pudding
- cream cheese and jelly
- hummus and black olives
- mandarin orange slices (canned, drained) and chocolate pudding
- chocolate pudding and cream cheese
- cream cheese and green olives
- cream cheese, cheddar cheese, and hummus
- peanut butter and dill pickle chips
- just cheddar cheese
- peanut butter and jelly
- peanut butter, banana, and bacon bits
- cheddar cheese and black olives

I could go on, but I think one of my piano students is waiting for me. Just know you can't go wrong with your favorite flavors. And remember not to yuck somebody's yum. If we all liked the same thing, you'd be married to Dan too!

So, once you have an even number of piecrust squares, plop a heaping teaspoon or so of filling in the center of one. If you use more, you'll have trouble pinching the edges closed. Cover it with another square, then using a fork, press the edges together, forming your pillow of delight. Place on the cookie sheet. Brush both sides with melted butter if you like, and sprinkle with salt, or cinnamon sugar, or nothing, or something I haven't thought of yet.

Bake at 400° for 10–12 minutes or until they're golden brown. Let them cool if you can, but I won't judge you when you can't help yourself and start popping these in your mouth. Goodness knows that's what Quinn, Dan, and I do!

I'd love to know what filling you created! Send an email and photo to Becky@BeckyClarkBooks.com

Enjoy!

Acknowledgments

I find writing the acknowledgments for a book more difficult than actually writing the book. It's an almost impossible task to single out the people who have helped me get this book into bookstores. Everyone I've ever met in this industry has offered help in ways large and small, whether they knew it or not, going back to the late 1990s, when I dipped a terrified toe in the publishing water. The sheer number of people who saved me from drowning is overwhelming and humbling. Too many people are left out of this official thank you, but I've not forgotten your generosity.

It never fails to amaze me when readers pick up my book, read it, then tell me they liked it. I wouldn't get to do this without readers in my corner, so you, dear readers, keep being awesome.

Jill Marsal, agent extraordinaire, is always right there with a prompt and complete answer to even my dumbest questions. And she's so polite, she never even hints that they're dumb! She knows everyone and everything and I'm thrilled to be in her orbit.

This is my first time working with Norma Perez-Hernandez at Kensington. I liked her from the minute we chatted on the phone and she said nice things about my writing. She truly knows the way to a writer's heart. She also knows the ways to make a book better and I'm grateful for her guidance on *Puzzling Ink*.

My nephew Michael, newly promoted to detective, has finally learned to answer all of my over-the-top what-if questions with what *could* happen in the wild world of fiction instead of what *would* happen in the boring world of police work. I love that he doesn't even flinch anymore when I text him things like, "So…there's someone tied up in the basement…" I'd be lost without his police expertise. Any mistakes are mine alone, usually because I've decided what would really happen is simply too boring so I snazz it up, much to his chagrin.

Huge thanks to Kathy and Cody for sharing with me the realities of living with OCD. No amount of research could take the place of your insights. I'm honored you trusted me.

Once again, my beta readers worked their magic for me. In this case, Leslie Karst, MB Partlow, and Jessica Cornwell offered excellent advice and so fast it made my head spin. Thanks for your discerning and constructive eyeballs on my work. I couldn't do this without you.

Writers often work in a vacuum, staring at our computers, or out the window, or at that hangnail for far too long to be healthy. So I'm eternally grateful to my husband Wes, my kids Jessie, Adam, and Jeff, and friends near and far for figuring out ways to pry me away from my work and into the real world on occasion, even if it's just long enough to text me something goofy. You guys are the best.

My Chicks on the Case cohorts—Ellen Byron, Vickie Fee, Leslie Karst, Cynthia Kuhn, Lisa Q. Mathews, and Kathleen Valenti—excellent writers and storytellers, all. You raise the level of my writing because I study yours. I love that I can always depend on you for a laugh or a dose of perspective, whichever I might need. I adore you women.

I also adore the members of my Facebook group, Becky's Book Buddies. Thank you for playing in my sandbox with me.

Christina Iverson deserves kudos for her calm and gentle suggestions to help me wrangle my crossword grid when it really doesn't want to be wrangled. Who knew a few black squares could render me so bumfuzzled?

I hope I haven't, but I suspect I've missed acknowledging some of my crossword puzzle testers, but it's more a lack of organization on my part than a lack of gratitude. I started teaching myself how to make puzzles over the last few years, when the idea for this series was just a nebulous flicker. The what-if turned into a maybe-I-can and Chris Reese, Kelli Mahan, Jann Barber, Claudia Rouge, Kristin Schadler, Mary Fraser, Tammy Barker, Katherine Munro, Audrey Natale, Vanessa Blair, Robin Nolet, Claire Fishback, Cathy Stratman, and Bob Clark gave me the thumbs-up on the puzzles, reassuring me not only that I could, but that I did. Their help has been invaluable.

If you've read this far, you might be wondering, *Why crosswords, anyway?* Well, that's easy. My dad is why crosswords. He solved crosswords for as long as I can remember, but I came to it a bit later. Dad wasn't one to gush, but I knew he was proud when I hit certain milestones in my life: graduated from college, published my first book, finally quit putting beans in my chili. But I think the thing that delighted him most was when I started solving crosswords in ink. The true measure of a quality person, in his book. I wish he could have seen this. The whole darn thing's in ink!

Meet Becky Clark

A highly functioning chocoholic, **Becky Clark** is the seventh of eight kids, which explains both her insatiable need for attention and her atrocious table manners. She likes to read funny books so it felt natural to write them, too. She published her first novel in 2001, and is a sought-after speaker.

Visit her at www.beckyclarkbooks.com.

Printed in the United States
by Baker & Taylor Publisher Services